That This Nation Might Live

Butterflies of Gettysburg, Book 1

Sandra Saidak

and

Thomas Saidak

Uffington Horse Press

Books by Sandra Saidak

Kalie's Journey Series

Daughter of the Goddess Lands

Shadow of the Horsemen

Keepers of the Ancient Wisdom

Oathbreaker's Daughter

In the Balance (Short story collection; title
story set in Kalie's universe)

Other Books

From the Ashes

The Seal Queen

Mesopotamia: A Bronze Age Adventure

It has been said that something as small as the flutter of a butterfly's wing can ultimately cause a typhoon halfway around the world - Chaos Theory

*Now we are engaged in a great civil war, testing whether that nation, or any nation so conceived and so dedicated, can long endure. We are met on a great battlefield of that war. We have come to dedicate a portion of that field, as a final resting place for those who here gave their lives **that that nation might live.** It is altogether fitting and proper that we should do this.*

From The Gettysburg Address, by Abraham Lincoln

Foreword

Writing this novel has been a fascinating journey for both authors. Our time spent at Ohlone and Miwok gatherings, as well as at lectures and discussions on cultural appropriation and how to be an ally was invaluable. Special thanks go out to Ohlone elder and culture bearer Ann Marie Sayers, and culture bearers Greg Castro, and Kanyon Sayers-Roods, for sharing their knowledge of the First Peoples of the United States. Any errors in presenting their stories are those of the authors. And, as African-Americans play a prominent role in the story, we would also like to thank Jason Stewart, and Justin Gray for their input.

Authors' Note

One of many ghost stories from Gettysburg, Pennsylvania involves three college officials riding an elevator to the library basement. When the doors open, the three find themselves staring out at a battlefield hospital (which the building had, in fact, been in 1863). In this, as in all similar stories, the elevator doors simply closed, and the officials returned safely to their normal lives and time.

Two authors asked each other two questions: what if they had, instead, been three Civil War reenactors? And what might have happened if they had stepped out of that elevator? The novel you now hold is our answer.

Chapter 1

The trio paused as they reached the steps leading to the wide porch and graceful white columns of Pennsylvania Hall, Gettysburg. Visibly gathering his courage, the man dressed as a Union Army sergeant began the climb upward. After a moment, his companions followed.

"Place hasn't changed much in one-hundred-eighty-seven years," said the second man, lagging behind.

Dani sighed. "It's not like you were there when it was built, Anton."

"True," said Anton. "But if this works, we'll actually get to find out."

"I was kind of hoping to change history and save the planet," said Peter, grimly leading the way toward the building. "But whatever works for you."

Trying to keep it light, Anton asked, "Which movie was it? *Battle of the Bulge?* 'Is this trip worth it?'"

Peter turned and asked, "Did you watch the news this morning? We are now at a four-and-a-half feet sea level change at New York City. They are saying that the original forecasts and amounts werelow. We'll be at six feet of sea level rise by the end of the year, which off the top of my head means we lose all three airports in New York City, MacDill AFB in Florida, San Francisco, and Oakland International airports. Not to mention what that will do to storm surges. The whole rest of the glacier is already starting to move! Just losing the one-seventh of the glaciers was bad enough, but now they're no longer there to slow down the rest. Today's news makes it clear our initial projections were way too optimistic. We are gonna get that full sixty-nine feet in years, and not decades."

All three looked around, as if expecting the building and all the activities surrounding it to wash away in a scene out of a bad science fiction movie. Then Peter overhead a nasally voice mutter, "Nero fiddled while Rome burned."

He looked up to find an middle-aged couple on the steps above them, gazing at the rows of white canvas tents in the field beyond, where costumed reenactors moved about as if they were really in the nineteenth century. "Look at them!" the man continued. "Playing dress up as if the world wasn't about die!"

The women next to him held up her phone, taking pictures. "This is the last of the reenactments," she said. "Maybe forever. You know what'll happen once martial law goes into effect: the first thing they'll shut down is large gatherings. Then they'll go after the intellectuals—"

"Like these clowns qualify as intellectuals?" snapped the man as they moved down the steps.

"And you're wrong: the smart guys will be safe no matter what happens."

"She's not wrong," Peter said as the two passed. "And Nero played the lyre."

"Well, duh," said Anton. "The fiddle hadn't been invented in 68 A.D."

The man glared at them, the woman smiled sadly, and Peter, Anton and Dani continued up the steps.

Once inside, all three sighed at the welcome touch of modern air conditioning. The sticky heat of a

Pennsylvania summer was bad enough for the throngs of tourists and students dressed in shorts and sandals. But for the Civil War reenactors, it was insufferable. Dani, who had made all three costumes, had done her best to make their clothes comfortable, which was easier to do when the garments were custom made for each person. But she was also a stickler for accuracy.

So Peter wore the blue wool uniform of Union a soldier, despite the summer heat—and the way it clashed with his red hair. *Not as bad as when I was a kid,* he thought, the memories of a time when he'd looked like Opie Taylor from the Andy Griffith show appearing incongruently from the past. *Well, the past is where we're going. Maybe I'll fit in better there.* He stretched his six-foot frame and tried to appear calm. After all, this venture was his idea.

Anton wore the clothes of a well-to-do farmer, which better suited his shorter, less athletic build. Off-season, he wore his dark brown hair long and wild, but he'd recently shaved his beard and had his hair cut in the most modern style—of 1863. Both men carried a modified soldier's rucksack.

Dani's ensemble included a high-necked, long-sleeved grey blouse with corset underneath, and darker hoop skirt. She carried the same rucksack, but attached to hers were two tubes of different length and diameter. The longer one was made of bamboo, while the other, shorter and thicker, was of lacquered pine. As Dani's ensemble was heavier, the two men knew better than to complain about the heat. They also knew that having a samurai archer around might come in handy. But Peter was more worried about her skin color than her clothing or skills, in the event they really did manage to travel back in time.

Dani was considered a light-skinned African American, not that Peter could wrap his head around why it mattered. But he knew that if this crazy ghost story he was trying to recreate worked, it would matter a great deal. Yet, as always, Dani was the calmest of the three of them.

Halfway to the elevator they saw two tall, young African American men, wearing the uniforms of the Fifty-Fourth Massachusetts. The pair stood in front of a display of that regiment's memorial while a visitor took their picture. Peter, Anton, and Dani paused when they reached the elevator. The fact that no one else wanted to use it seemed ominous. No one touched the call button.

"Shouldn't we be doing this at night?" Dani finally asked. "That's the usual time for ghost stories, right?"

"I talked to the people who did this the first time. We're doing this the same date, same time." Peter looked around the room as though for the last time.

A silence stretched, broken at last by Anton's laughter. "Come on, folks! It's just a game. We're not going anywhere but the basement. Then back to the battle!"

"And if you're wrong?" Dani pressed. "If we really go back in time? We'll never see our families again. And we'll be playing God—which I personally find more daunting."

"That's assuming we're actually able to create any real change, and time doesn't correct itself," Peter said.

"I'd be more worried about making things worse," said Anton. "Which is why I wouldn't be doing this if I believed it could really happen."

Peter took out his phone. "Good, we're ten minutes early. Relax and enjoy the AC."

His two friends looked anything but relaxed, as they contemplated the possibility of never experiencing air-conditioning again—among countless other things.

Anton took out his phone and called out, "Hey, 54th!" When the two men in uniform looked over at Anton, he waved the phone and asked, "Could one of you fine gents take a picture of me and my friends?" The one with Corporal's stripes handed his rifle to his companion and walked over. He took Anton's cell phone, waited for everyone to arrange themselves, and took the photo, with the elevators doors providing the backdrop.

"Thank you kindly," Anton said as the two shook hands.

"My pleasure, sir," replied the corporal.

As their photographer walked away, Dani dug something out of her rucksack. "Just in case this does work, apply this on your upper lips, just under your nose."

She squeezed a tiny blob of something gooey on Peter and Anton's index fingers. It smelled strongly of eucalyptus and menthol.

"What is it?" Anton asked.

"Something we use during autopsies, to keep the smells from making us puke," explained Dani. "Remember, this basement was a hospital one-hundred-sixty-two years ago."

Peter showed no reaction, as he anointed his upper lip with the offering, while Anton swallowed hard and dabbed it on with shaky fingers.

The remaining minutes grew even more strained. Suddenly, Anton laughed. The other two jumped as if they had heard gunfire. Dani, as always, recovered first and asked, "What?"

"I just realized how much this crazy idea actually mirrors the day we all met. That campus reenactment, remember?" For a moment, they all relaxed in the shared memory.

"When you were that little, lost freshman," said Peter. "And I was a senior, and Dani just a few months from being deployed to Afghanistan."

Dani nodded. "You were asking everyone in costume really good questions, Anton. I was about to ask you why you weren't already a reenactor, as much as you obviously loved history."

Anton's face darkened with remembered pain. *Not something foster kids got to do, as one charming 'mom' had told him.*

"And then that drunk came over and asked Dani where the auction was, so he could bid on her" said Peter.

"The sad part is, he wasn't drunk," said Dani. "And you, Peter, running to my rescue in your totally inaccurate captain's uniform—"

"At least I was the same age as the character I was playing!" Peter laughed. "Almost twenty-three!"

"—and Anton getting to me before you did, and calling out, "Moses! I've been wanting to meet you since forever."

"That you called me by my personal heroine's nickname warmed me up to you right off," Dani said.

"I don't think that jerk even knew who Harriet Tubman was," said Peter. "But it looked like his girlfriend was explaining it to him, when the three of us decided to beat a hasty retreat together."

"Things sure went better for me after that," said

Anton. "I finally had a group of people I could fit in with."

"I was just impressed that you knew about her scar, and thought my birthmark was it," Dani said, fingering the mark on her forehead that peeked out from beneath her bonnet.

"Even though it was in the wrong spot," said Anton. "And if this works, you might finally get to meet her."

The elevator door opened.

There was a pause, and then Dani, Peter and Anton all bumped into each other, trying to get inside. With a theatrical sigh, Peter hit the button for the basement.

"Don't forget to show up early for the live mortar fire demo when we get back," Anton said.

"As long as you remember you're playing at the camp dance tonight," Peter responded.

"How'd the sharpshooter contest go this morning?" Dani asked.

"Okay," said Peter. "Anton may learn to hit the broadside of a barn yet."

The elevator stopped, and the doors opened slowly.

Spread out before the twenty first century trio was a scene out of hell—and more real than any film could be.

Wounded men screamed. Medical personnel moved among the chaos with surprising calm, if not efficiency. Light from high windows made the scene more terrifying rather than less. An orderly pushing a wheelbarrow filled with severed limbs bumped into Peter, mumbled an apology and continued past.

Peter and Dani stood still in shock. Anton

turned and tried to run back to the elevator—which had disappeared. In its place stood a rough wooden wall, as one would find in a barn. Anton's body hit the wall with only moderate force. As he slid down to the blood-soaked floorboards he muttered, "I guess I've finally learned to hit the broadside of a barn."

Then he lost consciousness.

Chapter 2

Peter stared, mute with shock. *It really worked*, he said, and then realized no sound was coming out of his mouth.

He'd always loved the supernatural; took it for a promise that the past could be changed and good could prevail. Always the oddball in his family, Peter got away with it simply by being smarter than everyone, earning awards and scholarships, even if he used them to study weird things like History and Climatology. His parents always assumed he'd outgrow it, and come to work in the investment firm which had been in the family for three generations.

Instead, right after graduation, Peter had gone to work for a think tank. While not the only one there to believe that civilization might really collapse within the next two decades, Peter was the only one who believed in time travel. More importantly, that done correctly, time travel could give the human race a better future.

But now, standing in 1863, with the sights and sounds and smells of the bloodiest war in American history surrounding him, pressing against him, threatening to break him like an egg, Peter realized he had no idea what he was doing here.

The sounds of retching made him turn. Anton had regained consciousness and was now doubled over on the filthy floor, throwing up. Peter felt the contents of his stomach rise as well, but kept them down— barely. The stench of blood and loosened bowels was like nothing he had imagined. Dani's ointment was helping, but not enough.

Hey, you!" A loud voice finally broke Peter out of his daze.

He turned to see a burly man unloading a cart full of wounded into what little open space remained in the hospital. "Either help or get out of the way!"

Peter decided to do both by getting Anton to his feet. "We have to find Chamberlain," he whispered, while the man with the wounded went past them.

"Where's Dani?" Anton asked, looking around in less shock than Peter.

Peter looked and saw no sign of the young black woman he had brought into harm's way. Reflexively, he clutched Anton's arm. "I can't have lost one of you already!" he choked out.

Anton removed Peter's hand with difficulty. "Calm down, she's right there." He jerked his head toward where the light was best, and the wounded were thickest.

"What the hell does she think she's doing?" Dani was bending over a wounded Confederate soldier, removing shrapnel from his right leg, just inches below the tourniquet she had already applied. Peter saw that she was using tweezers from the twenty-first century, identical in appearance to those appropriate to this time period.

"You thought you could bring a nurse like Dani to a war zone and *not* see her spring into action?" Anton's voice was dangerously high, but there was a curious sense of delight in his face as he watched his friend save a life.

"We have to find Chamberlain, and she can't practice medicine here!" So far, no one seemed to notice Dani's skin color, but that would change quickly, no matter how chaotic the situation.

"We changed history the moment we stepped out of that elevator," Anton said, clearly not getting it. "What difference more will it make if she saves a few people who would have died?"

An exhausted doctor walked at a near-stagger to the patient Dani was working on. He wore a waistcoat and had not bothered rolling up the white sleeves of his shirt. Both were splattered thickly with blood. A nurse, who appeared to be about sixteen years, old sat beside Dani, sponging the soldier's forehead and watching Dani work.

"Out of my way!" shouted the doctor. "And what do you think you're...?" The man's head nearly swiveled off his shoulders as he did a double take. "What is this Negress doing here?" he roared.

"Well, that's that," sighed Peter, pushing forward, and dragging Dani's manumission papers out of his breast pocket as he went.

Several people stopped what they were doing and stared, just as the doctor did. But to Peter's amazement, most simply went back to the work of saving lives, cleaning up or catching a few moments of sleep. The white nurse across from Dani showed no reaction at all, other than to move her hand from the patient's face to gently pull the skin from his leg wound so Dani could get a better grip on the lead ball she was trying to remove.

"Leave this hospital at once!" yelled the doctor. Despite the way he swayed on his feet, he had considerable volume.

"No!" cried the soldier. "She can save my leg."

"Nothing can save your leg, son" said the doctor, removing a bloody saw from the bag he carried, and seeming willing to use on Dani if she

didn't move quickly enough. For her part, Dani
showed no evidence that she heard anything, so intent
was she on her work.

"She's a root woman," gasped the soldier, who
seemed on the verge of losing consciousness. "'Twas a
gal like her raised me… nursed me through fevers that
shoulda ended me. In God's name, man, let her help
me…"

"Get away from me!" screamed a soldier, three
beds away. The doctor attending him was much
younger than the doctor who was yelling at Dani, and
having trouble keeping his patient calm enough to treat.

"Hold him down!" he called to the young
woman beside him, but when a flailing arm struck her
hard in the face, she screamed and ran away, crying.
"Dr. Henderson!" he yelled.

Reluctantly, Dr. Henderson moved to deal with
the newest emergency, pausing to glare and add, "She
had better be gone when I get back."

Peter, now at a loss as to whom to show Dani's
papers to, simply watched as the two nurses worked on
the now-unconscious soldier. An older woman,
probably the head nurse, spoke up over the pile of clean
(or at least washed) linens she carried. "You heard the
Doctor, missy. They's a hospital cross town that treats
your kind. You best go there." When Dani, now
finished with the shrapnel, began to suture the wound,
giving the woman as little notice as she had the man,
the startled matron turned instead to the other nurse.
"And what you think you're doing, Jenny?"

"Learnin' how to be a healer, ma'am," Jenny
replied in a distinct Appalachian twang. "If she can
teach me how to do what she's doing, I ain't gonna
bother 'bout what color she is."

For the first time in 1863, Dani spoke. "Can you help me loosen this tourniquet, Jenny? I can't stitch the wound close and keep the pressure right by myself."

Jenny looked uncomfortable. "I tied one of them things myself once, though I wern't supposed to. Feller lost his arm."

"That likely was not your fault." Dani carefully turned the stick that kept the tourniquet in place. "Hold it like this." She placed Jenny's hand, showing her how.

"How you make stitches like that?" Jenny asked a few moments later, when it was clear the bleeding was under control. "I want to learn."

"Can you read, Jenny?"

"No. Does it matter?"

"It might —in a good way. I'm guessing it means your memory's better than folks who can read. Just watch what I'm doing. If I get to do it again before they throw me out, you watch again. Next time, you do the stitching and I'll help if you need it."

Jenny nodded. "That's how we do things back home."

An orderly came in and called out that the last of the wounded had arrived—for now, at least. That seemed to bring new energy to the hospital staff, and they moved with efficiency, the end of their shift finally within sight.

Dr. Henderson returned, roughly pushed Dani aside, and muttered curses while he examined the young soldier. Without a word, Dani and Jenny moved to the next patient, working together in a way that would have delighted Peter if he hadn't had so many other things to worry about.

"What's this I hear about a nigger woman in my

hospital?" The new voice drew attention from the people in the hospital as Dr. Henderson's rant had not. Peter saw Dani stiffen, but continue working. Anton turned to greet the man who spoke, Peter an instant behind.

Despite the blood splatter on his white shirt and blue waistcoat, the tall bearded man before them was impressive. He seemed less exhausted than the other doctors, but that might have been a result of sheer will. His brows, meeting in a single line over piercing gray eyes, looked like thunderclouds.

"Sergeant Peter Tormey, sir," Peter said snapping to attention, and saluting the colonel, feeling for the first time in the presence of genuine authority. He held out a small piece of paper, and prayed his hand would remain steady.

Instinctively, the colonel took the paper and scanned it briefly. "You're supposed to escort these two, uh, persons to Colonel Chamberlain on Cemetery Ridge." The commander of the hospital shifted his gaze to include Anton. "What the hell are you doing here?"

"We heard the Colonel would be visiting other hospitals where his men might be. This was on our way."

"No one from the 20th Maine is here," said the doctor, already losing interest as duty called. "You'd best take your people and go. Chamberlain's camp is that way." He jerked his head to the northwest, as he paused beside Dr. Henderson. "Well, Sam?" he asked staring at Dani's first patient.

Henderson shook his head. "This boy's leg is…The artery was severed, the bone crushed. I was going to take it off, but the bleeding has...there's nothing more than a compound fracture—expertly set. And these stitches! I've never seen anything like it."

"The stitches are just a new technique I learned, sir," said Dani, stopping in front of Henderson on her way to rejoin her friends, Jenny like a shadow behind her. "Beyond that, I was just lucky."

The two doctors exchanged glances, both looking like they wanted to argue, but were unsure with what. "We must take our leave," Peter said to his friends.

"Can I come with you?" Jenny asked.

"Jenny!" cried the matron.

"Not today," said Dani. "But I hope we work together again. For now, use what I showed you here, and teach others, if they'll learn."

"What's your name?" Jenny called after Dani as she turned to go.

"Dani."

Jenny chuckled. "Same as my brother."

"It's short for—"

"We've really got to go," Peter whispered. Anton looked ready to pick his friend up and carry her if she didn't hurry.

Dani moved to walk between the two men, and the three left Gettysburg.

Chapter 3

The encampment at Cemetery Ridge was calmer and more orderly than what they'd left behind in Gettysburg. The field hospital was fairly quiet, but Dani was clearly ready to do a repeat of her earlier performance. Anton watched Dani and Peter, expecting one of their usual, passionate arguments to start. He was surprised by Peter's response.

"We need to find a guard. I know Chamberlain is here somewhere close, but not exactly where." As they left the main hospital tent, Anton managed to spot what looked like the classic, bored Private on guard duty.

As they got closer, Anton called out, "Private, you have a reckoning where we might find 20th Maine?"

Startled, the Private turned around, saw Peter, snapped to attention, his rifle grounded, and rendered a salute, left hand flat to the ground, against the stock of his rifle, a careful hands width from the end of the barrel.

"Sergeant!"

Peter came to attention and returned the salute.

"You don't remember your own bivouac?" the private responded tentatively.

"Son, I left last night to find these two people. Welcome to the army. What are the chances the army just let them be?"

"Yes. I do know, or at least I know what direction Colonel Chamberlain went when he left from here." The private pointed to the right of a lone farmhouse.

"Thank you, Private. Last night the 20th was to the left of that artillery target." Peter returned the private's salute and led his companions in the direction of their quarry. As they got closer, they saw a couple of regimental standards to the right of the farmhouse. Meanwhile, the ground became harder to navigate as they reached an area where cannonballs had either impacted the ground and left a crater, or the actual balls still sat above ground. Some distance away, Peter stopped and stared at the two standards. "Anton, would you agree that that one is 20th?" pointing as he asked.

Anton, stopped and stared. "Yeah, a bit far, but it has the right colors and shape."

Peter grunted, and started off again. A few minutes later, Anton commented, "Yup. That's 20th Maine all right."

"Okay, so which one is likely to be Chamberlain's tent? I'm thinking that one —it's a bit away from the other tents, and has the shade attached." Peter turned and looked at Anton.

Anton squinted and looked. "Your guess is as good as mine. He was friendly, but he was a big believer in chain of command. He lectured his brother, Tom, on the subject enough. Think he's still a lieutenant."

Peter turned back and stared for a couple of minutes. "Yeah, okay, this is where we earn our big rewards. Let me start the conversation, join in as needed after that."

The trio made their way towards the tent. Anton noticed that both Peter and Dani were walking as though they were carrying a great weight. Anton realized he was too, his feet feeling like they were hitting the ground harder and harder. He found the air he was breathing seemed to catch at his throat.

As they got closer, both Peter and Anton spotted another lone, bored Private. As they approached, the private called out, "Who goes?"

Peter approached and looked at the regimental patch on the private's hat. "I'm Sergeant Tormey. You one of those boys we added a couple of days ago, ain'tcha?"

The private's face darkened. "Yes, I am."

"Your name, son?" Peter solicited.

"Private Saunders."

Peter stepped forward, reaching out with his right hand. "I am Sergeant Tormey, Private Saunders, and I'd like to shake your hand and personally say thank you. We wouldn't be having this palaver, you and your friends not being there and helping out."

Stunned, the Private stared for a moment, and then recovered himself. "Thank you, Sergeant Tormey," he said.

"I have to conduct these two to Colonel Chamberlain's tent." Peter headed towards what he hoped was Chamberlain's tent, while Private Saunders resumed his guard duty stance—with a noticeable straighter back and more attentive bearing.

When they were more than ten yards away, Anton stage whispered, "What the hell was that about?"

"That private was from the other Maine unit. The ones History remembers as mutineers. His hat patch wasn't 20th. And at the moment, I can't remember their regiment. And I'm wearing a 20th Maine patch. Shit! I should damn well know their unit!"

Anton stopped. "Seriously, you can't remember? This was your idea!"

Peter stopped and sighed. "You totally didn't believe we would be here. I totally hoped we would be, and while I'm a big fan of the paranormal, I do realize most of it is bullshit. And now we're here. Our first big test is Chamberlain. Reading about him isn't the same as knowing him. So yeah, I'm a bit freaked out. Can we give me a break?"

Dani stared into the distance, very quietly chanting what Anton and Peter knew to be a Buddhist prayer, getting her breathing under control.

Anton switched his gaze between his two friends for a moment. "Great, and here I was hoping you guys would be the calm ones."

After collecting themselves, the trio walked to the tent. All of them were sweating in the full heat of a Pennsylvania summer, although Peter, used to the heat, was sweating more than normal. When they reached the tent, another sergeant stepped out.

"May I help you, Sergeant?"

Peter instantly snapped to attention, grounding his rifle, and saluted.

"Color Sergeant Tozier, I presume?"

Color Sergeant Tozier returned the salute. "Yes. And you are?"

"Sergeant Tormey. I was sent to fetch these two," gesturing towards Dani, "This Negress, Dani Davis, is a well-known nurse. Colonel Chamberlain told me to locate and bring her here. This is Anton Pozda, her assistant. They are to help with the wounded here in the bivouac, as we should be moving out soon to chase down the Rebels."

Tozier cocked his head to the side and studied

both Dani and Anton. "You really a nurse?" he asked.

"Yessir. More skilled than some doctors. Oh, and if an Appalachian child by the name of Jenny," Dani indicated Jenny's height, "shows up asking after me, could I impose upon you to direct her to me?"

"Quite a boast. I honestly pray you can match it. If a Jenny shows up, I'll make sure she gets to you. You mind me asking why?"

"Certainly not. I understand you need to know who should be here. I ran into her at the field hospital at Gettysburg. She seemed eager, and able, to learn what I can teach her."

Tozier pointed to a large tent. "Our so-called walking wounded and sick are right over there by the tree."

"Sergeant, one last polite request? Could you please get as much baking soda as you can? At least two pounds?"

"You seriously need that?" Tozier responded, quizzical bordering on suspicious.

"Yessir. I find a light tincture of water and baking soda clears up many malaises."

"Well, I'll send someone to find that for you. Any other requests?" Tozier tilted his head.

Dani curtsied, "I most heartily thank you, Sergeant Tozier." Dani and Anton headed off towards the designated tent.

Chapter 4

Peter stared after his two friends, feeling the full weight of the mission settle on his shoulders. He turned to see Tozier staring at him.

"If the Colonel isn't here, I'll wait for him outside his tent. If he is in, I'll need to report." Peter reached into his pocket and pulled out two papers. He glanced down, selected one, and handed it over to Tozier.

Tozier stared at Peter for a few seconds before responding. "You need to personally report the Negress and her assistant are here?"

"Yes, among other things."

"Very well, Sergeant, carry on." With that, Tozier left Peter in front of Chamberlain's tent.

Peter took out a handkerchief, removed his hat, and wiped his brow and face. He took out his canteen and took several long swallows. He stepped under the tent shade, out of the sun, carefully laid his rifle on the ground, and took off his rucksack—all 70 pounds—and laid it on the ground. Looking around, belatedly, he verified Chamberlain wasn't in his tent. He took off his hat and jacket, then arranged his jacket for a pillow on the ground. Despite his jitters, Peter fell asleep instantly.

An unfamiliar voice combined that of Tozier's woke Peter. He opened his eyes to see the real Colonel Joshua Chamberlain, in color, for the first time in his life. He reached into his pocket, while the two were discussing him, Chamberlain clearly suspicious, and Tozier surprised. As Tozier handed Chamberlain the order directing 'Sergeant Tormey' to find and deliver Dani Davis and Anton Pozda, Peter activated an app, and put the phone back in his shirt pocket, the screen towards Peter's chest.

Peter stood up, grabbing his hat and jacket, putting on the hat first, and then the jacket. Chamberlain, with a look of disdain, waited for Peter to straighten himself, and Tozier looked on in puzzlement. With his last jacket button done, Peter drew himself to attention and saluted. "As the Colonel has directed, I am here for a private report. So glad to see you again, sir. Thursday was a hell of a day."

"Do I know you, sergeant?" Chamberlain asked coolly.

Peter looked Tozier in the eye and responded "You wanted a word in private with me. So you said. How's your leg?"

Chamberlain tilted his head momentarily. He turned to Tozier, "Thank you Color Sergeant. I shall deal with this."

Tozier saluted, and walked away, without once glancing back. Chamberlain limped to his chair and sat down. He stared at Peter for a few moments. Coldly, he stated, "This had better be more than either interesting or entertaining. One shout, and I'll have what remains of my regiment on top of an imposter."

"Yes, Colonel Chamberlain, I entirely understand. You, being a college professor, will want extraordinary proof for any extraordinary claim I make."

"Or more likely a doctor with very hefty orderlies. That rifle and that pistol are loaded?"

"Yes sir. I would like to hand you my rifle first and ask you to look at the underside of the barrel."

Peter handed over his rifle, careful to make sure it never pointed at Chamberlain.

Chamberlain inspected the rifle carefully. Noted that it was loaded, but there was no cap, so set for safe travel. He looked at the underside of the barrel. His expression quickly became puzzled. "These markings do not match anything the Union is currently purchasing."

"No sir, they don't. I would like to hand over my pistol."

Chamberlain reached out his hand. "That would be an excellent idea."

Peter carefully unstrapped the flap on his holster, and pulled out his Remington New Model Army, and handed it over to Chamberlain, the barrel aimed at the ground.

"Under the barrel as well?" asked Chamberlain in a neutral voice.

"If the Colonel pleases."

As Chamberlain read the inscriptions, Peter took off his hat, and then removed his jacket.

Annoyed, Chamberlain stared at Peter. "You have purposely disarmed yourself, and now you are stripping off your uniform. This had better start to make sense, and quickly." Chamberlain glanced behind himself, and obviously to Peter, found where Tozier was standing, talking to other members of the regiment.

Peter picked up his cap, and pulled the velcroed patch off his hat, slowly to demonstrate the sound. Chamberlain tilted his head in puzzlement. Peter handed over first the 20th Maine patch, and then the hat. "Here sir, you try connecting them, and then separating the patch from the hat."

Chamberlain glared at Peter for a moment, and

then did as he suggested. Several times.

      Peter interjected, "It's called velcro. It was tried either now, or very soon in the future. But using natural fabrics, it didn't work well. Er, for the want of a better word, it required development of artificial fabrics to make it work. If I recall correctly, it involved a type of plastic. Gah, I'm fatigued, so I may be using the wrong words."

      "How convenient," Chamberlain said dryly.

      "Not really. But I understand why you said that. So, what would you look for as proof of time travel. Extravagant claim. What extravagant proof would you require?"

      "Sergeant, or whomever you are, I find myself too tired, and awaiting orders to move out soon."

      "Well, here's my first free prognostication. You won't be chasing after Robert E. Lee anytime soon."

      "That sounds rather treasonous to me." Chamberlain sat up in his chair, as though he was about to rise and strike Peter himself.

      "Sorry sir, but Meade will not be providing immediate pursuit of Lee. May I redirect your questions to the inscriptions of my weapons?"

      "As you wish." Chamberlain's response clearly showed his escalating impatience.

      "Use my revolver. Fire two rounds into the ground, and really, really smell the smoke."

      Chamberlain stared for a couple of minutes at Peter, clearly beginning to regard him as insane. Reluctantly, he stood up, and called out, "Sergeant Tozier!"

      Tozier turned around and looked at Chamberlain. Chamberlain continued, "Let people know I am firing a couple of rounds from Sergeant

Tormey's pistol." Chamberlain watched as Tozier made sure everyone was warned. He glanced around for a safe spot to fire. As he pulled back the trigger, Chamberlain saw that only five of the six chambers had been loaded. A quick glance showed the chamber was empty. Chamberlain looked around, found a safe aiming point, and fired two rounds in three seconds. Chamberlain sniffed the smoke from the pistol and recoiled in surprise.

"Doesn't smell the same, does it?"

Chamberlain very carefully lowered the pistol. "You best explain yourself now."

Peter opened his rucksack, and pulled out a black plastic bottle, labelled 'American Pioneer.' Peter handed the bottle to Chamberlain. "Open the bottle and smell. Can you tell me what chemical is missing?"

"I'm a Natural History Professor, not a chemist." Chamberlain sniffed the bottle despite his proclamation. "At a guess, I'm not smelling sulfur."

Peter nodded. "You got it in one. I last loaded my pistol two months ago. When I clean it with hot water and dry it over a fire, there won't be any rust. The powder can sit in the pistol for three plus months without eating the pistol."

"That is an extravagant claim. But how do I know it wasn't loaded this morning?"

"You don't. That was to attract your attention. Here is the next piece. You know what a play is Professor Chamberlain?

Chamberlain arched his left eye and responded "You are taking far too many liberties, suggesting we are familiars."

"My apologies, Colonel. I just want to make sure I have your attention. You do realize you personally won the Battle of Gettysburg? Last Friday on Little Round Top."

Chamberlain responded angrily, "You cannot be serious in that statement. We lost too many to pin victory on any single engagement."

Without hesitation, Peter responded "Actually, with something called a 'movie,' yes we can get across that singular notion. Granted General Buford played a critical role on July 1st. Granted the Devil's Den on July 2nd was important. But your role on Little Round Top? Your destruction of the Alabama 57th won the battle. While for your side, Pickett's charge was threatening. In point of fact it had no chance. No sir, and please allow me to shake your hand. The ultimate victory here was you, the 20th Maine, and nearly 100 so-called mutineers of the 2nd Maine. Your bayonet charge was the right decision, at the right time, and celebrated as such past my birthday."

Chamberlain stared at Peter for several minutes. Reluctantly, he reached out with his hand, and allowed Peter to shake his hand.

"So you know what a play is. A movie is like a play, but it is based on photographs. Following me so far?"

Chamberlain simply nodded.

"You remember the zoetrope? The large cylinder with drawings inside, that when you spin, they form a moving picture."

"Yes. My grandfather had one. Wonderful visual illusion."

"Exactly, sir. So, one way of looking at it is that was the first ever movie. I'm now going to show you a movie, and yes the history is probably incorrect on many factual issues, but overall correct on the fact that you won this battle for the Union." Peter reached into his rucksack and pulled out a 10-inch tablet. Turned it on, and hit a video file labelled "Chamberlain."

The scene started with mythical Sergeant Kilrain informing Chamberlain about the 'mutineers' of 2nd Maine. Eight minutes later, the selected scenes showed Chamberlain's complicated and victorious bayonet charge against the 57th Alabama.

Chamberlain, obviously stunned, took time to stare Peter in the eye, and ask, "You claim you can produce this, but you can't tell the truth of the matter? Not to mention you said visual. This was audial as well."

"Yeah, I hear you. We call it History vs Hollywood. Hollywood makes the movies. History is another matter. But we both know the truth. You held Little Round Top, pretty much destroyed the 57th Alabama, which lead to the Confederate disaster of Pickett's Charge."

"Pickett?" asked an incredulous Chamberlain.

"Yeah, from Longstreet's division."

"I was not informed who lead the charge. We were busy protecting ourselves from the artillery barrage. Getting back to this 'movie.' How is it done? Pictures hand painted for every couple of seconds? That doesn't prove your claim of the future. Except, you did not mention sound."

"True. So to show you a movie, do I have the needed machinery to make one?"

Glaring, Chamberlain responded, "That sir, depends on you taking me for a buffoon!"

"Colonel, the last thing I take you for is a buffoon. Rather, someone intellectually honest enough to discern the truth. But I need an honest answer. Do you see me as having the equipment to make the movie as you described? Is it a set up? You betcha. I'm not a buffoon either. I know the rules of science." In his gut, Peter knew he had reached the make or break point in the discussion. Breathing became difficult.

Chamberlain glared. He ran his hand over his mustache to smooth it down. "If I answer, will you quickly get to the heart of the matter in an honest manner?"

"Yes." Peter found it was suddenly easier to breath.

"No."

Peter's body sagged for a moment. Obviously puzzled, Chamberlain frowned. Peter reached into his shirt pocket and removed his Samsung smart phone. Hitting the side button to wake it back up, he stopped the video recording, and walked over to join Chamberlain on his left side. "I want you to watch me set this up. I also need to make sure you can see it, as the angles can be a bit tricky."

Chamberlain grunted in response.

"I'll be using new words, in a strange way," Peter continued. "I will happily explain them later. First, I am hitting what is called the 'Video App.' You notice this one with a picture of the sky?" Chamberlain nodded. "Now I'm going to hit 'play' like I did to show you the first movie. Remember I had my jacket off, and then put it on, and then off again?"

"Yes." This time, Chamberlain seemed more intrigued than impatient.

Peter hit play. The video showed bright sun, as Peter was on his back when he hit record. It pixelated a bit as he stood up, clearly showing Colonel Chamberlain's disapproving face, and Color Sergeant

Tozier's right arm as Peter put on first his hat, and then his jacket, at which point the video went black. While muffled, the audio continued, replaying the conversation that had happened just over twenty minutes ago. The video showed Chamberlain's head, due to the fact he had sat down prior to Peter taking his jacket off, and stopped at the colonel's clipped response of "No." Peter waited a moment, and then asked, "Do you need to see it again?" Colonel Chamberlain waved him off with his hand.

Chapter 5

Peter stepped back in front of Colonel Chamberlain, cell phone in his left hand, resting on top of his right hand, his left foot forward, and right foot to the rear in classic 'at ease' of the Civil War. He watched as Chamberlain digested what he had just seen. His body indicated that he had reached a decision, but he stopped and reconsidered. Several times he raised his right hand and extended his forefinger as though about to make a point, but then put it down.

At last, he looked at Peter and said, "I think you need a chair, Peter. Pray grab that one and sit down." Chamberlain pointed to a chair in the tent. Startled, Peter obeyed instantly, and sat himself across from the colonel.

"So you can tell me who won this war?" said Chamberlain.

Peter looked off in the distance for a moment, and then focused back on the man seated across from him. "That is both a natural and dangerous question to answer."

Perplexed, Chamberlain responded, "Why? Is not history, well, history?"

"No. There are two complications. First off, if I tell you how the war worked out for you, you will change your behavior. That could lead to you doing something different based on the belief that you either lived or died, but accomplished something in a particular battle or campaign. That change in behavior could change the outcome. To make it even worse, we are talking, and we shook hands. You're aware of both the Greeks and Dalton's theory of 'atoms'?"

"Yes," Chamberlain replied, staring intensely at Peter.

"Well, from my view, it turns out that atoms are comprised of several particles. Those particles are comprised of smaller particles, which we call quarks, and the field of physics is called quantum mechanics. Follow me so far?" Chamberlain nodded. Peter continued, "So to explain the cause and effect of these quarks, a metaphor was derived. And here is the metaphor: A butterfly flaps its wings in Brazil. As a result, a hurricane strikes China. My presence here is quite literally introducing new butterflies."

"And the point is?" asked Colonel Chamberlain.

"My quantum mechanics state is from the year 2025. Yours is 1863. Whatever I thought I knew about your personal future is now in doubt. Whatever you do will have this conversation in mind. We shook hands. Your quantum mechanics state physically touched mine. You may or may not change your behavior. To change that thought, here is another. Just be you. Don't give anymore thought to the future than you have today. You're just as mortal as you have ever been. Behave accordingly."

Chamberlain snorted. "As if that will be easy!"

At that, Peter faltered in the next crucial part of his script. Fortunately, his unplanned laughter put Chamberlain—somewhat—at ease. "I do have favors to ask," he said weakly.

"Why?" the colonel demanded. "From your description, anything you know of me is now fleeting."

"Because what I know tells me you are going to have a great deal of influence, by you just being you. My first favor is that you introduce me to General

Howard, such that he will recognize me in the future."

"Why should I do that?"

"If I'm to change history, I need his help."

"What history do you plan to change? And why should I support it? You already spoke of the dangers of attempting such a thing."

"I'll show you the news that prompted me to attempt so reckless and dangerous a method." Peter pulled out his tablet again, and hit the file labelled "Greenland." He handed it to Chamberlain. "See that triangle pointed to the right?" After the other man nodded, Peter continued, "Just touch it with your forefinger." Chamberlain poked the triangle as directed.

For five minutes, Chamberlain watched the report on the partial loss of Greenland's ice sheet, and the world map showing the impact of a sixty-nine foot rise in sea level. Peter watched as Chamberlain tried to make sense of the change in maps of the United States.

Colonel Chamberlain asked, "Exactly how many states are in your United States.

"Say what?" Peter hadn't expected that--although perhaps he should have. "Uhm, forty-eight contiguous," he responded weakly. Before Chamberlain could follow-up, Peter asked, "Would you like to watch that again?"

Colonel Chamberlain mutely shook his head.

"Just so we're clear," Peter continued, relieved to be back on script, "within two years from my time, at most, all of Manhattan, and most of Florida will be underwater. The effects elsewhere will be as, or more cataclysmic. Man may survive, but the civilization you are fighting to defend will be totally destroyed. Worldwide. You may have noticed most large locomotives use coal?"

Chamberlain, refusing to be knocked voiceless, responded curtly, "Yes."

"Have you heard of finds of 'dinosaur fossils?"

"You're referring to Gibson, no... Gideon Montell, Sir Richard, gah, Owens? Or even Charles Darwin?"

"Yes. So the key words here are fossil and 'greenhouse gases'. You are aware that a glass house can increase heat?"

"Yes, of course."

"Burning coal releases carbon dioxide. It traps heat. Mining coal releases methane. That is twenty-five times worse than carbon dioxide, because of the time it takes to create coal and other fuels. We call these fossil fuels. Where, uh, *when* I come from, we are releasing fossil carbon into the atmosphere, faster than the planet can reabsorb the gases, leading to an increase in global heat. Such that, the weather you know and expect will change And low lying areas will be permanently under the sea. Bottom line, we as a species will survive, but civilization may end up reduced to the Dark Ages."

Peter and Colonel Chamberlain stared at each other intently for a while. Peter, used to the precision of a clock, would never be able to report how long the two of them did so.

Chamberlain finally broke the silence, exclaiming "But why were men of learning not able to bring forth the alarm and righteousness of science?"

Cocking his head, Peter looked at Chamberlain with sympathy, "Really? You haven't noticed that a fair number of people seem allergic to facts? Is not the key issue for this war the fear of the Southern states that slavery will be abolished? And have you never talked to anyone totally opposed to Darwin's notion of evolution?

In obvious shock, Chamberlain stared at Peter. He finally responded, "You are seriously telling me that future Union citizens could not discern the truth?"

"Yessir, I am. That is, in fact, a sad truth. And has been a part of our culture since Plymouth Rock. Keep in mind sir, since our inception, we've had witch trials, with executions, after Catholic Europe gave them up."

Chamberlain first stared at Peter, and then stared into the distance, as if trying to shake off what he had just been told. At least he asked, "So, do you have any hope to offer in this horrendous future?"

Peter felt light-headed. Was one of his many Civil War idols actually saying the words he had dreamed of so often? He took a deep breath and willed strength to his shaky voice. "I would not be here if I did not. My grandfather lived to see eighty-eight years. That was barely considered old in my time. Here and now, with good fortune, I might live to be sixty. I gave up a lot of my years on the crazy notion that I could add a lot more to future generations."

Chamberlain waited, and then realized what Peter was saying. "Do you mean to tell me that you can never return to your own time?"

"That is correct, sir."

"What do you hope to accomplish that is worth sacrificing thirty years of your life? Not to mention your family, your home, and all that you know?"

Peter sat for a moment, feeling as if all his carefully rehearsed words had deserted him. Realizing that Chamberlain would do nothing further without an answer, he discovered he could ad lib. All he needed was the simple, insane, arrogant truth.

"We—my two friends and me—hope to make changes that will save the future. Not just these United States, but the entire planet. We hope to pave the way for a cleaner, healthier, happier world. For everyone."

"There are more of you?" Chamberlain demanded. "Where?"

"Your medical call tent, most likely." Peter suddenly felt like a child who had just been caught misbehaving by his favorite teacher.

"It would have been prudent of you to have told me that at the start, young man!" Chamberlain was suddenly every inch a commander. For the first time, Peter realized he was not the one in charge. He wondered how he had ever been arrogant enough to think he could have been. "Who else from the future is running free through my regimental camp?"

"A dedicated nurse and a gifted musician. Sir, this mad venture was my idea. Their only sin was following me here, and believing they could help save the world—"

Chamberlain stared hard at Peter, but whatever he saw there must have convinced him, for he grew calm and reflective. "And what do you imagine three people can hope to accomplish here, in the middle of a war? Even with all your fine knowledge?"

"We chose to start by meeting, you, sir," Peter said. "That is not idle flattery. In every period of history, there are people who can make a difference, if given the right information, the right tools, the right...nudge."

"And what difference do you hope to make?"

"We have gambled everything on quietly encouraging two things. The first is, to put it simply, clean energy, so the rising tides I showed you will not happen."

"And the second?" Chamberlain asked, and Peter knew it would be impossible to lie to him, despite promising himself not to go there.

"This will sound strange—"

Chamberlain choked back his laughter. "After everything else you have said? Please. Try me."

Peter smiled, and pushed forward. "It is more than machines, sir. It's ideas. Throughout this land are men and women of vision and courage, but whose voices are silenced, because of their skin color, or their beliefs, or their sex. It is these people whom those in power must listen to."

Chamberlain was silent for so long, Peter feared he had lost the battle before it was truly begun. Then the colonel said, "Stand up, son. I want to show you something."

Peter stood, and hoped his shaky knees would not embarrass him. Fortunately, the colonel only led him a short distance from the tent, to where the camp was spread before them. "Take a good look at them," Chamberlain said. "Those men; some still boys."

Peter stared at the same camp he had looked at just hours earlier. That one had been a twenty-first century recreation. This was the very one that he and his group had tried so hard to replicate. For a moment his vision blurred, and then slid into two images which slowly merged back into one.

"They came here for different reasons," Chamberlain continued. "Some perhaps, not entirely pure. But many are here for the same reasons you are. If you are telling me the truth."

"I am," Peter whispered, wishing he could be more convincing.

Once more, Chamberlain stared into his face. "A man does not reach my rank without the skill to read people. I believe you. And since we are both willing to lay down our lives for the same thing, tell me how I may help."

Catching his breath, Peter asked, "Do you have pen, paper and sealing wax?"

"Not quite what I was expecting, but yes."

Peter smiled. "I believe I can trust you not to open the letters before the date I put on them?"

"You have my word," the colonel said solemnly. Peter broke out his notepad and wrote on three separate sheets of paper, and then signed them. Chamberlain walked the short distance to his tent. When Peter finished writing and looked up, the colonel motioned Peter into the tent, and handed Peter three sheets of paper, his personal seal, and wax. Peter quickly folded the paper into envelopes, wrote a date on each of the envelopes inserted a notepad sheet, and used the wax to seal them closed. Peter sighed, and then handed them over to Chamberlain, who stared at the envelopes, and then set them aside.

"So now what?" asked Chamberlain.

"Frankly, sir, I need to find my traveling companions. Considering how long it's been since I've seen them, I am imagining all sorts of mischief."

"Considering how much 'mischief' you have just brought to my life, son, that is cause for considerable alarm. You said they would be in the medical tents?"

Peter followed Chamberlain to two large tents. The tents formed an "L", and in the afternoon sun, one had its south facing side placed on poles to form shade, while the other had the same on its east facing side. The sick and lightly wounded were all gathered in the shade or on their cots, watching Dani and Anton arguing.

Peter's worst fears were realized as he heard Dani speak.

"We need to get to New York as soon as we can!"

Anton responded just as passionately, "We're only three people. We couldn't protect ourselves, much less anyone else!"

Without any thought, Peter interjected just as passionately. "Did you get another letter from your Aunt Harriet? The one who last year read the tea leaves and saw a fire that would burn down all of Brooklyn? And then nothing happened?" Dani, eyes wide at Peter's use of their prearranged signal, just nodded.

"I need to get them out of here," Peter said sotto voce to Chamberlain, who was staring at Dani.

"This would be... the nurse you mentioned?" Chamberlain turned to Peter with a nearly accusatory look.

"Yes." Peter found he had run out of witty replies. "Colonel Joshua Chamberlain, allow me to present Mr. Anton Pozda, and Miss Dani Davis."

"You never said she was... never mind. Follow me, all of you. Now."

Dani and Anton exchanged a sheepish glance, and followed the colonel without a word. Chamberlain stopped when they were far enough away for privacy, and watched the other three form a circle that included him. He watched as Peter glared at his friends for a moment.

"Did I just hear about riots in New York City? And did it occur to you they might have friends and family in New York?" Chamberlain shot Dani a concerned look.

"Yes!" Dani sent the Civil War officer a grateful, but in no way intimidated or deferential look. "If we are here to change history, what better place to start? Especially if we can save some people. At least tell them where to find safety! I'm a nurse for God's sake! I can't just stand here, knowing, and do nothing."

"And exactly how much help do you expect to do swinging from a lamp post? With just three of us, that is more likely than not. We have work to do—situations we can handle. That doesn't include putting down a riot. Especially with a full regiment helping out by just shooting anyone in front of them. We die now, and coming back becomes pointless." Peter paused, looking first Dani in the eye, and then Anton. Anton raised his hands as if to surrender.

Peter turned to Chamberlain. "You just got a freebie." At Chamberlain's confused look he added, "Sorry, let me phrase that properly. You just got a fourth prediction for free. Next Monday, a riot will start in protest of the new draft law that lets rich men buy either their sons or themselves out of the general draft. It then turns into a race riot. And just to make it interesting, a regiment will be deployed from here this weekend. And no, I don't remember which one, although I know it won't be yours."

Peter turned to glare at Dani and Anton. "Because I thought my friends would remember not to discuss the future in front of other people unless we all agreed to the need. Especially as you two have read the likes of Jules Verne and know better."

"So he knows?" asked Dani pointedly.

"Yes."

"I don't recall us discussing that, either," replied

Dani.

Chamberlain inserted himself, agitated. "So how bad was, or will it be?"

Dani answered, "Something like one hundred twenty dead, and two thousand injured when it was finished. Eleven Negroes were lynched."

"But why?" asked Chamberlain.

"The last thought I read on the subject stated that recently freed slaves were competing with longshoreman for jobs," said Dani. "Being poor immigrants, they finally had a target whom they could see as lesser beings. Remember, sir, by the Constitution, I am only three fifths of a woman."

"But that is precisely why we are here," said Chamberlain. "Fighting to end that!"

Anton spoke up. "The problem, Colonel, is this. How do you kill an idea?"

Chamberlain looked Anton in the eye, "We do that by acting to demonstrate what right action is. Through reasonable discourse."

Anton nodded, "Yup. And good luck with that. To hate and fear the other is wired into our brains. To stop it, one has to feel by experience that they are so profoundly wrong, that they will finally see reason. I suggest you don't hold your breath. That blue uniform looks good on you, but your face won't look good that color."

Chamberlain grunted, and then looked away.

Dani noticed Sgt. Tozier looking at her, apparently trying to figure out if it was safe to approach. "Excuse me gentlemen, but I think a friend may have found me." Dani inclined her head slightly, and walked over to Sgt. Tozier.

"Well Colonel, if you would be so kind as to

point where, we should probably pitch our tents. Oh, and I have an explanation for why I am now out of uniform," Peter commented as he handed over a folded paper. Chamberlain opened it up and read what appeared to be a handwritten separation order, signed by General George Sykes himself.

Chamberlain looked at Peter questioningly.

"No, Colonel, it's technology, and I'd just as soon hope General Sykes doesn't see or hear about it. I have another one for my friend here, as well."

"I think you will have nothing to worry about there." Chamberlain walked Peter and Anton back to his tent. Peter collected his weapons, jacket and hat, opened the top of the duffel bag, and put in the clothes. While holstering his pistol, he handed the rifle to Anton, and then picked up his duffel bag, and got his arms into the padded shoulder straps.

"I do not believe I have ever seen shoulder straps like that, much less on a duffel bag."

"Yeah, something Anton and I came up with. We're carrying right about seventy pounds."

Colonel Chamberlain pointed over by the hospital tent, "I imagine Miss Davis would want to be close to the hospital tent. So feel free to encamp there. And supper will likely be at about seven."

"Thank you, Colonel," both men said at once.

Chamberlain left them to set up their tents.

***

Dani walked up to Sgt. Tozier, and as she expected, he informed Dani that her friend had arrived. Dani strode over to the medical tents, noticing that Jenny's clothes were all black and grey.

"Jenny, you're looking a bit somber. Everything all right?"

"Nervous. I hear tell that Miss Dorothea Dix is bringing her Army Nurses here. She don't cotton to bright clothing or young nurses."

"So I've heard. Ready for some more tricks?" Jenny bobbed her head in reply. Dani led Jenny to a table that had been set up as her work station. "First thing, thoroughly wash your hands, including using that brush to clean your fingertips and your fingernails. Remember to always do that between patients, if you touch them or their bedding" Dani then led Jenny through the tent, checking wounds, washing hands between one patient and the next if she touched someone. A young officer, who had lost his left arm caused Dani to pause.

"You seem to be breathing a bit shallow, sir. Does it hurt to breathe?"

"Yes ma'am."

"You were sleeping earlier. When they removed your arm, did they use chloroform?"

"Thankfully, yes."

"Right. So now it hurts to take a normal breath." Dani paused, and the young officer nodded. "I'm Dani, and this is Jenny. And you are?"

"Lieutenant James Wells."

"I have some good news and bad news for you. The good news is that you will get better. The bad is I'm going to have to make you uncomfortable. I need you to take five deep breaths for me."

"Now, Miss?"

Dani nodded.

James started wincing halfway through the first breath. To distract James, Dani explained, "Because of the chloroform, you went into very shallow breathing, and because of the pain, you don't breathe normally. That can cause you to come down with pneumonia. So I need you to breathe deeply as often as possible. As your lungs get used to it, the pain will stop. Also, it's important you get walking as soon as possible. Like today. Are you feeling the melancholy?"

"Yes ma'am, I most certainly am."

"That is because you're not getting enough air. As you work your lungs, you will start to feel better. Walking will also help. And some sunshine." Dani smiled.

"I shall do that, ma'am." James looked puzzled, but more hopeful as well.

Dani and Jenny went off to finish their rounds. Around halfway through, Dani had Jenny take over, and gave her pointers when she missed something. True to Jenny's claim, she never had to be told anything twice. Any errors were Dani's assuming prior knowledge from either training from her nursing degree, or later in her two tours in Afghanistan with the army. As the sun started to drop in the sky, Jenny turned to Dani.

"I fear if I want supper, I needs be getting back. Thank you mightily for your time, Miss Dani. I promise I shan't forget any of this."

"Supper is equally important, as any of these fine men can tell you. How can I contact you at need?"

"Need, Ma'am?"

"Drop the formalities. We are healers who have shared the same blood. Literally. If I write your family, will they pass the message to you?"

"Yes Ma… Miss Davis.." Jenny halted at the

look on Dani's face, and restarted, "Dani. Please address the letter to John Wight's Farm, Woodsville, Richie County. Ma and Pa t'ain't a'mad at me, so they will pass on any mail." Jenny watched anxiously as Dani pulled out a pad of paper and a pencil and carefully wrote down what Jenny said.

"So, it's, uh, it is all right if I put your name as Jenny Wight?" Jenny nodded yes. Dani, without thinking, gathered Jenny in a hug, "Bless you. I will be sending for you when I myself am settled." Jenny froze for a second, and then returned the hug with all her exuberant energy.

Dani watched as Jenny strode away at a fast pace towards a point just north of Gettysburg proper. Dani turned back and walked towards where she saw Peter and Anton completing the finishing touches on their tents and furnishings, which included the most authentic looking Civil War era items that twenty-first century dollars could buy.

When all was in order, the three stood looking at each other.

"I guess it's okay," Anton said. "I mean, they might expect Dani to bunk with the other nurses—"

"Not with my complexion," said Dani. "As the only black woman here…?" They all looked helpless.

"This never came up in the reenactments we did," said Peter. "But I'd feel safer if we all stayed together. Tomorrow, we should be able to head for Philadelphia."

"And a new set of problems," said Anton.

A bugle call sounded. That one, they all recognized. "Gentlemen," said Dani, "I believe dinner has been served. Gah, I meant supper."

The trio went to join the line for the enlisted

being served supper. Not being true members of the regiment, they took care to make sure that anyone in uniform ended up in the line ahead of them. Anton watched as Colonel Chamberlain spoke a brief word in one of the cook's ear. As the approximately one hundred enlisted men went through, and Dani reached the serving line, one cook spoke out.

"I hears tell the Negress tended to our wounded."

"It was my pleasure," said Dani.

The cook smiled. "In that case, it's my pleasure to serve you and your friends. You all enjoy." Dinner was beans with bacon, a fat slice of bread, with a spot of blueberry jam, and an apple. Peter, being last spoke up.

"Thank you all very much for a fine supper." He threw in an impromptu bow.

The cooks beamed their gratitude.

"Next milestone," said Peter. "Food." They settled under a tree on the outskirts of camp.

"Just eat," said Dani. "We haven't eaten since this morning—one hundred sixty-two years in the future. I, for one, am famished."

"Me, too," said Anton. "But what about strange bugs, shocks to our immune systems…?"

"The chance of spontaneously combusting," Peter added.

Dani sighed and tasted the bread. "Better than we ate last night at *our* Gettysburg."

They cleaned their plates without further comment, beyond sighs of contentment. After supper, the three went for a stroll, looking for a private place to talk.

"Well, much to my surprise, we have arrived,"

observed Dani. Anton nodded in agreement.

Peter paced back and forth past his two friends, and assumed his leadership voice. "Okay, so before it makes contact with the enemy, let's review the plan. Philadelphia. Get currency. Go to Saratoga Springs the week the race track opens. Make money. Go to New York City, see if we can find more ways to make money, and set up safekeeping for our money. Then we go find John Ross in Oklahoma, and then to Fort Laramie to find Sitting Bull, all the while keeping our scalps intact. Figure to get to Washington by late February '65, and see if anything has changed. Can we stick to the plan?" Peter glowered at his friends.

Dani glowered right back. "I have a slight change to suggest. I was recalling your concerns about money, so I spent the last few days at home downloading a lot of medical information and technology, like at least two antibiotics that would be easy to make here and now. Along with other things like latex gloves and respiratory therapy. I would need to find someone to work with, and they are going to have to be in the know, like Chamberlain."

Peter rubbed his face. "That's a lot of change you are proposing."

Anton chimed in, "Isn't that why we came back? To change things? That Sten gun you want to introduce is sure as shit going to change things."

"True," Peter admitted. "But that one is for after *this* war. Dani, you are proposing changing things before the war ends."

"Not that much really. Most of what I do will take time to gear up, and it will take time for doctors to start using anything I release. By then, we'll know if the war continues as we learned it. Big war, with lots of people involved. Quite a bit of inertia. Just as long as we don't lose key people like Grant, Sherman, and Howard to name a few, we'll be fine."

"Do you have anyone in mind?" Dani shook her head.

"Not really. A doctor I've read about, but I would have to meet him first. After that, it basically boils down to finding some whites that would be willing to help. Which frankly seems rather daunting at the moment."

"Well, I'm glad we have that all cleared up. Frankly folks, I am dog tired. I suggest hitting the hay." Anton yawned to demonstrate his own point.

There followed another moment of weirdness. "Okay, I'll say it," said Anton. "I'm freaked out by the thought of falling asleep here. I don't know if I'm gonna wake up here, back in the twenty first century, or someplace else entirely.

"All part of the adventure," said Peter. They all made it safely to their tents. And to sleep.

***

The next day, Peter crawled out of his tent and discovered he was still in 1863. His next surprise was noticing that the sun was only a couple of hand spans from directly overhead. The final surprise was to see Dani poking her head out of her tent, obviously having just awoken.

"Ye gods —- when was the last time you missed a dawn wakeup?" Whatever Dani replied, it was unintelligible. Over the next hour, the trio got themselves squared away. Having missed breakfast, they begged some bread and cold coffee from the cooks. Anton broke the silence.

"Did anyone catch the plates on the truck that ran over me?"

Peter just shook his head. Dani shook herself.

"I suspect we just came down with the world's worst case of jet lag," she said. "Years, instead of just hours." Peter noticed that something of an unpleasant thought crossed her mind. "Crap. This is real. My katas are going to get complicated."

Anton, curious, asked, "Your morning kung fu exercises?"

Dani reached over, and ruffled Anton's dark hair. "I keep telling you —tai chi and karate, but yeah. If I get into a confrontation with a white man and win, I will likely end up in jail, or worse."

Peter asked, "Any idea of how to walk away from that?"

Dani replied "Magically figure out how to look and sound like a hysterical woman, and making it look like sheer luck as I take the asshat down? I don't do hysterical, and I have zero belief in luck —"

Nodding, Peter looked past Dani, noticing Sgt. Tozier approaching the group.

"Good afternoon. Glad to see you have something to eat. The Colonel told me to tell you to go to that house over there."

Anton went with Dani to tend the wounded, and Peter went to the lone farmhouse atop Cemetery Hill.

As he approached the house, Peter noticed Colonel Chamberlain talking to a General, who was missing his right arm. Peter stopped within a short distance of the two men, within easy beckoning range—which occurred within a moment or two.

"General Howard, this young man here asked

for an introduction. Peter Tormey, this is General Howard." General Howard nodded affably.

"I have seen you many times. I just got my relief papers discharging me. So I wanted to take this one chance to personally thank you. I wish more generals were like you sir."

Howard nodded. "I thank you for your kind words. Might I inquire what happened to require you to return home?"

"My father passed away. Me and my oldest brother are needed to tend to the farm. We've four sisters and two brothers, all too young to do it. And from what my sisters are writing, my mother may be suffering the dementia as well."

"I am deeply sorry to hear of your loss. I shall keep you and your family in my prayers tonight. Please keep in mind that grief can unhinge anyone for a brief time."

"Thank you for your kindness, sir. General, Colonel." As Peter turned to leave, Chamberlain turned to the General.

"Thank you, General. I best be heading back myself." The two exchanged salutes.

Colonel Chamberlain kept trying to get Peter to talk about the war. Peter kept fending off the questions. As they reached the colonel's tent, Peter made sure no one was within earshot.

"Colonel, if I was in your shoes, I would be asking the same questions. I can never tell you. It would change things, and the problem is I cannot fathom how those changes will impact the War. Or what follows. You have those three letters. If one of those letters turns out to be wrong, it will be a warning that change is occurring. It may be nothing, or it could be disastrous. Like I said yesterday. You just continue being you, and do what you would do with what is in front of you."

Peter made as if to speak, paused, and making up his mind, "Actually, Colonel, there is one piece of research you could help at least one person from the future conduct. It is an answer to an old, hotly debated question."

"And that would be?"

"Whether or not your Union Army supplied caps that could detonate the powder in my revolver," replied Peter.

Obviously amused, Chamberlain, nodded. When they returned to camp, Chamberlain warned Tozier there would be more gun fire. Peter retrieved his holster with the pistol.

When he reached Chamberlain's tent, he noticed that Chamberlain had a small table outside the tent, with a classic Civil War round, yellow, Eley Percussion Cap tin. Peter just stared. He noticed Chamberlain was watching him.

"Sorry," Peter said. "All the original ones of those tins I saw were totally rusted." With that Peter pulled out his pistol, double checked it was sitting on the safety notch, and handed it to Chamberlain. Chamberlain inspected it and saw that the caps had been removed from the three remaining loaded chambers. Chamberlain waived to catch Tozier's attention, and showed him three fingers.

Chamberlain turned to Peter, asking, "I figure you want me to try until I run out of caps, or your cylinder is empty?"

"Huh, to be honest, I hadn't thought it through. How about we stop at ten caps, and go from there. I don't want you running out of caps at the wrong time." Chamberlain went through eight caps, recapping after every three tries. On try number nine, the pistol discharged. Chamberlain paused, and looked at Peter.

Peter thought for a second, "How about another ten and see what happens?" Chamberlain nodded, and resumed. The fourteenth and eighteenth caps lit off the remaining two chambers.

Chamberlain looked at Peter, "So with such a small sample, it seems yes, I could get that powder to touch off, but I would not want to be doing that in a fight."

Peter nodded, "Yessiree. With your caps, you would need all of them in "hot condition." As Chamberlain handed back his pistol, Peter resumed their earlier conversation. "I understand why you are asking, but I just know it is dangerous for me to tell you. I have suspicions about my impact on history as of today, but I have nothing to back it up. So I must err heavily on the side of caution."

Colonel Chamberlain paused, and then blew his cheeks. "Well, I guess I had better finish up writing my reports. Unfortunately, I have a lot of letters to write. Although I am grateful to Miss Davis for her attention to my wounded. She has indubitably lowered the number of letters I will need to write."

Peter gave his thanks, and walked away from his first irrevocable change.

Chapter 6

"That went better than I dared hope!" Peter said as they approached the train station. Dressed now as a civilian, he seemed younger, less certain of himself. Of course, at this moment, certainty seemed like a foreign concept to Anton.

"Next stop, Philadelphia!" Anton said, hoping to hide his fear behind a veneer of excitement.

"We might have a long wait for a train," Peter said, steering the others to an out-of-the-way bench. "Soldiers will have priority."

"I think our focus should be on money for now," Dani said.

Peter looked around. People came and went, paying scant attention to the three of them. If their color mix bothered anyone, no one said anything. Finally, Peter drew out his period wallet, even though they all knew exactly what it contained.

"I could have sold this for more than a thousand dollars before we left." Inside were two tattered ten dollar bills, a five dollar gold piece and several silver coins, adding up to $34.27 in local currency.

"Fortunately, that much goes a lot farther now than when we're from," said Dani. "It will buy us time to rest, and take as much time as we need to sell the jewelry." She grew silent, staring into space again, and Anton knew she was still thinking of the draft riots— and the lynchings —just days away. For his part, Anton worried that three train fares, food and a night's lodging would dangerously deplete those precious antique coins and bills.

As it turned out, the train ride cost them nothing. A large number of wounded were being sent to a Philadelphia hospital on the next train. At Dani's urging, Peter offered their services caring for the men in exchange for passage. It probably wouldn't have worked without Chamberlain's letter, and Anton wished it had not.

"Let's just wait for the next train," Anton whispered, hoping it didn't come out as a whine. But he was exhausted and shaken. The thought of further horrors on top of what they'd just witnessed was too much.

Fortunately, the patients needed little in the way of further treatment; most were asleep or unconscious from laudanum, morphine or their injuries. They were clean, bandaged, stitched and dressed. Yet the flies that hovered and bit, as they never would in a modern train, and the smells fighting to overcome the carbolic acid made Anton want to curl up in fetal position for the space of the ride.

"Just try to keep them comfortable," Dani told the two men. "Use pillows or your own bodies to brace them when the train jostles them. Hold their hands and talk to them, or listen to those who can talk. I'll handle any medical care that's needed, and even that won't be much."

Peter went straight to work, while Anton leaned out the nearest window, breathed slowly and tried to control his anxiety. Philadelphia would be three hours away in 2025. Here? Six hours? Twelve? He couldn't remember. That wasn't part of his Anthropology/Music major, or his recent course of study when Peter suggested this crazy live action role play.

A soft groan, directly behind him, caused Anton

to turn. The last of the row of patients was a boy of about sixteen. Whatever kept him out was clearly wearing off, because he began to thrash about, speaking words Anton couldn't understand. A bump in the train caused Anton to lurch closer, but threw the young soldier against the side of the train. "Mama!" he yelled.

"I'm not Mama, but I'll do what I can," Anton said, gingerly moving blankets and pillows to protect the boy, while trying not to jostle him. The boy settled down, but now he was calling out for Billy. Friend? Brother?

"I'm right here, Toby," Anton said, reading the slip of paper pinned to the young man's collar. Anton took his hand, and Toby gripped back with surprising strength.

"I got hurt, Billy," Toby said. "You told me not to go. I should have listened."

"You did what was right," Anton said. "You were braver than me."

"No one's braver than my big brother, even with only one arm."

That would explain why Billy hadn't enlisted, thought Anton. He squeezed Toby's hand, and tried to think of what to say next. He was spared the need when Toby called out weakly, "Sing to me, Billy, like when I was little. After Pa died."

With something between a sob and a spout of hysterical laughter, Anton muttered a prayer of thanks that he had found the one patient who wanted something he could give. He only hoped his repertoire of period songs, not to mention his shaky voice, was up to the task.

Anton began singing "The Battle Hymn of the Republic" almost without thinking. It was beloved well before 1863, and it was as comforting in its familiarity to him as to all the men on the train. It seemed to help at first, for as Toby slid in and out of consciousness, he smiled, and held Anton's hand tighter. But as he began "The Battle Cry of Freedom," Toby whispered, "Not camp songs. What you used to sing."

Great, thought Anton. *Hymns? Lullabies*? He was having trouble remembering which ones would have been popular when Toby was a child, and had no way of knowing which ones Billy had sung. He tried "Rock of Ages" and was relieved to see Toby smile and lean his head against Anton's leg. Anton began his favorite lullaby, "All the Pretty Little Horses," then foundered when he realized that, while popular at the time, it was actually the story of a slave woman singing to her master's child, while her baby was alone and crying for her.

"Don't stop!" cried a hoarse voice which didn't belong to Toby. Anton looked up to see several pairs of pain-rimmed eyes, waiting expectantly for him to continue.

"Keep singing," Dani said. "It's helping them."

"But this song—?"

"It doesn't matter. It's helping. Sing *Karma Chameleon* if you want to!"

"The music video would at least be period, even if the song's not," Peter said with his characteristic deadpan humor.

"The music video isn't exactly historically accurate," Anton muttered, but continued singing every song that came to him. He kept singing until his voice threatened to give out. Kept singing after a man he didn't know brought him water. Kept singing until every wounded soldier on the train was asleep. Then, finally, still holding Toby's hand, Anton slept.

He woke abruptly when the strain stopped moving in Cheltenham Station. Toby's hand, still clutched in Anton's, was cold. The boy had died on the journey, but his face looked like that of a sleeping child.

Chapter 7

The boarding house was run by a Quaker family. Even so, the middle-aged, plainly dressed woman who showed them to their rooms was not friendly. "Supper will be served in the common room at seven," she said.

"Thank you kindly," said Peter, but the woman waited until Dani closed the door to her own room before walking back down the dimly lit hall to the staircase. Anton collapsed onto the large feather bed that nearly filled the room, while Peter waited for what he hoped would be the right amount of time to discreetly knock on Dani's door.

Before he could even lift the latch, the door opened, and Dani slipped into the room. She eyed Anton critically. "You don't look too good," she said.

"Is that your expert medical opinion?" Anton asked.

"I'm not sure my medical opinion is worth much on the subject of time travel," she said.

Peter sighed. "Let's continue to assume that time lag is like a bad case of jet lag," he said. "Stories about time travel show people adjusting without their bodies disintegrating, imploding or failing in any way. The fact that we're here lends credence to those stories."

After a moment, Dani nodded. "All right, time lag it is. We've been here about thirty hours with severe oversleeping, food we're not used to and lots of harsh shocks to our systems. The simplest remedy would be more sleep. We'll need food, and especially water, but—"

"We could end up with dysentery, or other fun things, because our bodies aren't used to what's in them," Anton finished for her. "Damn. Why didn't we pay a little extra and get the package that included the adjustable immune system?"

Peter smiled at the joke, pleased to see Anton more like his old self. "At least, being living history types, we didn't need to buy the universal translator."

"There is that," said Anton. He began to undress. "I'm for sleeping until supper."

"Good idea." Dani got up and returned to her room.

Peter went to the single window in the room and opened it as far as it would go. There would be noise from the street below, and the smell of horse manure, but fresh air would be preferable to the close confines of the small room on a hot day. He undressed, and lay down on the deliciously soft bed where he found Anton already asleep.

***

Noise brought Peter awake suddenly. After a few moments of groggy confusion, he realized it was the sound of people on their way downstairs: laughter, conversation and footfalls. Had it not been for the rush of hungry people and the luck of having a room by the stairs, they might well have missed supper. And if Peter's grumbling stomach told him anything, it was that he needed food.

They were among the last to arrive in the busy common room. For a moment, the delicious aromas of food and pipe smoke, the sheer realism of a scene that was usually confined to movies and the reenactors' imagination, made them pause and take it all in.

"Over there," said the woman who had shown them to their rooms. She nodded toward a table in the back of the room, set with three places. There were three chairs as well, with a fourth, clearly broken, leaning against the wall.

Peter cast a longing gaze at the center table which ran the length of the room, its twenty seats already filled, and followed Anton and Dani to their table.

"I was hoping we'd be at the main table," he muttered. "We need to find people, learn things—"

"I think it's a little soon to start mixing with the natives," said Dani.

A boy not quite into his teens came to their table with a plate of biscuits in one hand, and a platter of chicken in the other. He deposited them both without a word, and then hurried back to the kitchen, followed by shouts for his attention from various patrons.

"Certainly helps us that there's no menu choices," said Anton. "If this keeps up, we might not have to worry about local speech or strange accents until Lincoln gets—" He was silenced by two pairs of glaring eyes. "Sorry." Anton busied himself with his food.

"These biscuits are amazing," Peter said a few moments later. Dani and Anton were busy applying honey and some kind of berry preserves to what were possibly the lightest and tastiest baked goods they had ever eaten. Why? He wondered. Lack of preservatives? Cleaner air? Something about cooking being a lost art? Peter shrugged and gave up analysis in favor of enjoyment.

The chicken, cold and dressed with some kind

of nutty gravy was likely left over from the larger noontime meal of dinner. But the cold was welcome in the hot, crowded room, and the chicken, while not as tasty as the biscuits, was quite palatable.

As interest in their food waned, the trio resumed their study of the room. "I think Dani is the only African-American here," said Anton. "Strange. It'd have thought in Philly, among Quakers—"

"Anton!" hissed Dani. "Please remember when we are. The polite term in these parts is 'Negro'. Or 'colored'. And I'm a Negress. And if anyone uses courser terms, you can't get upset. Are we clear?"

Chastened, Anton nodded. "You're right. And African-American wasn't in use until the 1980's."

"You could say Afro-American. It was first used in 1853. But only in Canada," Dani added, her lips twitching into a smile.

"I think that man over there is one," said Peter, nodding toward a small table where two well-dressed middle-aged men were dining, engaged in quiet conversation.

Dani gazed critically at the pair, and then nodded. "A quadroon, maybe. Or passing. It's hard to tell."

Their young waiter returned to refill their pewter flagons with water, and then brought them dishes of some kind of apple and berry cobbler laced with heavy cream.

"OMG," murmured Anton. "Even if we don't save the world, the trip was worth it for the food."

After supper, they walked through the Philadelphia twilight, feeling the magic of actually being in the place they had so often imagined. People just like them strolled in the cool evening air, others hurried home from whatever business filled their days. Everyone was in costume, yet no one was. The smells of factory smoke and horse manure couldn't quite overpower the smell of air as it was over a century before any of them were born.

"I used to live just a few blocks that way," Peter said, pointing to what was currently a row of tenements. Twilight deepened into night. A few stars peeked through the clouds—or was it smoke? The streets were soon empty of people.

"We should go back," Dani said. "People don't wander around at night in these times. And we need more sleep if we want our bodies to adjust to the change."

"I'm more worried about our minds," said Anton, but he followed the others.

***

All three slept late into the morning. Dani was the first to tell the others they had missed breakfast.

"Small price to pay," Peter said, half smiling at his pun as he poured water from a nightstand pitcher into a porcelain washbowl. "I feel better! Like I'm me again. A walk through the city looking for breakfast is just what we need."

"What we need is a jewelry store or high-end pawn shop," said Anton, as he tried to figure out how to use the tooth powder they had bought from a shop near the train station.

"I'm sure we'll find both," said Peter. "And God knows what else along the way."

Downstairs, they found an old man —father or father-in-law to the landlady, Peter guessed—sweeping the floor of the deserted common room. "You missed breakfast," he said gruffly.

"Yes," Peter said. "Could you perchance direct us to a bakery or similar establishment?"

"German bakery down the street," said the man, jerking his gray head in a way that suggested they turn right when they left the boarding house.

"Thank you kindly," said Dani. The man nodded and continued sweeping.

"Not the friendliest group of Friends," Anton said, as they joined the foot traffic of the cobbled street. "I was hoping we'd find allies among the Quakers."

"Not with our color mix," said Dani.

Peter shook his head in frustration. "But they run the underground railroad! They're leading the fight for abolition—"

"Hating slavery doesn't mean loving black people," said Dani. "Some do, some don't. I've attended Quaker meetings in the past, uh, future, and felt perfectly welcomed. My grandfather had a very different experience. He told me that even in the mid-twentieth century, many weren't very welcoming of our kind at their meetings, and that up until the forties and fifties, many opposed mixing the races. But they risked a lot for our freedom, so no hard feelings from me."

The mouthwatering scent of baking bread, cinnamon and other fine smells told them they'd reached the bakery. It was a pretty brick building with an open door and a long wooden counter just inside. All three received a warm welcome from a buxom, blonde girl of about eighteen who stood behind the counter. She sold them a loaf of bread, fresh from the oven for three cents, and some delicious sugary confections for an extra dime, all the while flirting outrageously with both Peter and Anton.

Peter was thanking her in every language he knew, which made her laugh, when an angry male voice shouted, "Hilda!" The girl disappeared into the back of the shop, replaced by a large man wearing a flour covered apron and an angry scowl. The group left without asking the location of a jewelry store.

"We don't need directions," Peter said around a mouthful of pastry. "We need to learn our way around. Besides, seeking out the right store will give us an excuse to talk with a lot of people, and sharpen our speech."

"I don't mind that," said Anton. "I just wish we could have asked for butter."

"This bread doesn't need any!" said Dani, handing Anton his share. "Taste it and see! Anyway, there may be more to our hostess's attitude than race." They scurried out of the path of a heavily loaded wagon while continuing with their food and conversation. "I overheard her and a few others last night on my way to the privy. Her husband enlisted, and their congregation is arguing over whether or not to disown the family."

"A Quaker enlisted?" Anton nearly choked on his bread. His friends sighed.

"Lots of them did!" said Peter. "Anton, don't you remember that guy in our regiment? The one playing the Quaker soldier? He and that tourist almost got into a drunken brawl over the accuracy of his character."

"I remember the drunken brawl part," said Anton. "I didn't stay for the whole conversation. What I *do* remember, from both U.S. History class and

Comparative Religions, is that the most basic principle of the Quaker faith was non-violence."

"Except for the ones who thought the sin of slavery was worse," said Dani. They reached a main thoroughfare, and for the next few minutes were too busy dodging wagons, carriages and horse droppings to talk. They were successful at two out of three. Once they had scraped as much manure from their shoes as they could, they began gawking like the tourists they truly were, for they had reached one of Philadelphia's main shopping districts.

Now it was only fine carriages they had to dodge, although, as Peter commented, they'd be just as dead either way if they failed. They peeked into milliners and clothing stores, stopped to inhale some very fine tobacco even though none of them smoked, and lingered outside a fancy restaurant with hopes of returning.

At last they came to an upscale jewelry store. Sunlight poured through nearly perfect glass windows, causing the jewelry in the small display case to sparkle. When the door closed behind them, the noise of the busy street fell away. The trio made their way to an inviting waiting area and took in the scene around them.

"There's more furniture than jewelry here," Anton said. The plush brown carpets and richly patterned wallpaper seemed to muffle their voices as they watched a portly middle-aged man in a burgundy waistcoat and jacket sitting across from a stout matron and her pale blonde daughter, whose pink and white dress matched the rest of her. They were discussing the design of the jewelry to be worn at the girl's wedding.

"More jewelry was custom-made at this time," said Peter. "Plus, security was more difficult. There are probably plenty of pieces in a safe in the back."

The shop owner, still focused on his customers, cleared his throat. A much younger man, though still expensively dressed in a white waistcoat and black cravat, hurried from the back of the store and strode toward Anton and Peter, his hand extended.

"What can I do for you gentlemen today?" he asked.

"We have jewelry to sell," said Peter.

The clerk winced slightly, but after exchanging a glance with his boss, quickly nodded toward a table behind the sofa they where they had been sitting. "Please be seated. Your maid will need to wait outside."

"Of course," Peter said, while Anton tried not to react. Dani merely nodded and walked through the door to the street.

Recovering their composure, both men joined the jeweler at the table, as he spread a black velvet cloth across it, and drew a jeweler's loupe from his waistcoat pocket. Peter took a heavy packet from his own coat, set it on the table and slowly unwrapped it. He tried to gage the young man's reaction to the diamond bracelet, sapphire pendant, gold pocket watch and three gold rings set with various gemstones.

The clerk showed little reaction until he had examined each piece with a professional manner that belied his youth. When he met Peter's gaze, the man was clearly trying to hide his eagerness—and curiosity. "I've never seen pieces like these," he said at last. "Are they of foreign make?"

"You could say that," Peter. "I was told I could

rely on discretion in this establishment?"

"Of course!" The young man looked scandalized.

At that point, the owner, who had just ushered out his wealthy customers, came over. He ran an experienced eye over each piece, and then, without the use of a loupe said, "Four hundred dollars for the lot of it."

Peter cocked his head, "That was rather fast." Haggling ensued, finishing at seven hundred fifty.

The assistant wrote out a receipt while the owner took the jewelry to the back of his store and returned with thirty-eight gold coins. Peter and Anton unbuttoned their coats, and took off their money belts, loading nineteen coins apiece, with Peter ending up with the one Liberty Head ten dollar Gold Eagle coin.. The owner nodded approvingly.

Peter was more excited at the feel of genuine Civil War era dollars than sad over the loss of a significant part of his life savings from the twenty first century. Not to mention the family heirlooms Anton and Dani had agreed to part with.

They observed the pleasantries of the time as they made their way out of the shop, where they found Dani across the street, deep in conversation with liveried carriage driver, waiting outside a bank for his employer, while Dani pretended to do the same.

"I agree that healing the sick is a noble calling, ma'am," the man was saying in a voice so deep it made Peter think of bass drums and black velvet. "But surely a fine looking, God-fearing woman such as yourself is more interested in the state of holy matrimony—" He stopped abruptly as Peter and Anton came over.

"And I am certain that one day I shall be," Dani

said smoothly. "Thank you for your company Mr. Granger, but I must be leaving now."

Peter and Anton followed Dani's lead and began to walk down the street.

"We need a bank," said Anton. "I was hoping for that one."

"Sorry," Dani said tartly. "But I didn't feel like fending off another marriage proposal this morning."

"Another?" Anton and Peter asked in unison.

"Let's just say that free black men with good jobs don't have quite the dating pool now that they will when and where we're from. Especially church-going men." She sighed. "I did NOT come all this way just to learn that my gender would be more limiting than my skin color!"

"Let's go find another bank," said Peter. "Then back to that fancy restaurant you both liked, and celebrate. Two more jewelry stores and we'll have enough for a trip to Saratoga Springs and the New York stock exchange."

Anton brightened at the thought of a historically perfect lunch, but then deflated.

"Don't worry," said Dani, reading his expression. "I saw mixed race patrons being served there."

"We haven't even left Pennsylvania," muttered Anton. "And I'm already sick of the racial bullshit!"

"Funny, so am I," said Dani.

Upon seeing her side-eye, Anton raised his hands in surrender. "Dani, I get that I probably missed ninety percent of the crap you dealt with even before we got into that elevator."

"And that back here, it can turn deadly a lot faster," Peter added.

"I guess my head is just stuck in the hope that we might change it," said Anton.

"That is why we came here," said Dani. "And while we're on the subject, don't forget, you guys aren't much safer than me if we get sloppy. Always listen for the phrase, 'nigger lover' and be ready to back off then and there. Not to mention that you're Jewish and Catholic." She nodded first at Peter, then at Anton. "You guys need to keep quiet about that. Between us, we're the perfect trifecta for the future Ku Klux Klan."

"Only my birth mother was Catholic--" Anton began, but had to check an urge to cross himself. Fortunately, he was able to fight off the dark thoughts that crowded inside him when he felt Peter's hand on his shoulder.

Dani slapped Anton on the other shoulder. "We *will* change it. Now let's go eat, guys."

Chapter 8

Their last day in Philadelphia should have been wonderful. The trio were hale and healthy, had learned things about the past that ranged from interesting to useful to just plain quirky, and the city had been a reenactor wonderland. Most importantly, they felt ready to tackle the insane jobs they had agreed to do.

"One last sale, and we are ready to go," Peter said happily. They were near the train station, tickets already purchased for the train that would take them to Saratoga Springs the day before the opening of the famous racetrack. Dani, wilting in the summer heat, privately thought they had enough money, and was quite ready to go this minute. But Peter was enjoying himself, and she was in no hurry to play the role of maid 24/7 on a crowded train.

The shop Peter and Anton headed to was more of a pawn shop than a jewelry store, as they were in a poorer part of town, but that made sense; they had already sold all the good pieces. Likewise, the street and many of the buildings on it were noticeably in ill-repair, but they were getting used to that—along with an impressive list of things that they hadn't even realized they had taken for granted up-time. And then there were the things they thought they were prepared for but...

Dani didn't see the two men until they were nearly on her. Somehow, her finely honed awareness of the space around her had been filled with the multi-hued crowd of people, horses, dogs, the grinding of factory gears, hammers, and cart wheels, and the end of the day shouting of merchants and tradesmen.

"What have we here?" drawled a menacing voice.

As she had practiced, Dani backed away from the voice, keeping her head down, eyes barely registering the well-dressed young man. Senses on high alert, she tracked the second one behind her, as she tried to get close enough to the shop her friends had entered, to call for help if necessary.

"All by your lonesome, gal?" the second man purred, while his friend circled her. She could smell the alcohol emanating from both.

"I's just waitin' for my employers," Dani said, putting as much submission as she could into her voice.

"Oh, *employers*," called the first. "How d'ya like that, Jethro? We got ourselves a fancy-talking nigger bitch!"

College students, Dani guessed. And from the drawl, Southern bred, but Northern born. Families who had moved back North? Or just sent the boys to school here for safety? No matter; it was Dani's own safety she was worried about now. She risked looking around, hoping help might be available from the busy street. All she saw were people hurrying by, except for a few loitering in front of the bar that Jethro and his friend had likely just left. If they chose to join in, this encounter could become deadly. And Dani didn't know yet for whom.

"How about Travis and me keep you company until your employers come back?" said Jethro, reaching for her.

Dani evaded his grip easily enough, but Travis had moved behind, and they nearly collided as he pulled Dani's hat from her head. Now people were stopping. Dani heard laughter.

Stay calm, she told herself. *Self-defense where you're from can get you lynched here. Let's mix what they expect with what they don't expect, just like you've practiced.*

"Don't be so shy," said Jethro. "That ain't like your kind—"

"Oh, please, massa!" Dani cried, as she raised both arms, waving her hands, and cowering.

Travis used her arms to pull her to him. Dani turned suddenly, trying to look afraid, as she twisted her left arm free, placed her hand against her left shoulder, and cold-cocked Travis with both her full weight as she spun to her right, and her elbow, which caught him squarely on his nose, all the while screaming "Please massah —doan you hur'me!"

"Bitch!" yelled Travis clutching his bleeding nose in both hands, as gasps and laughter poured from the crowd. "Jethro, did you see... I think she broke my nose."

"I's so sorry," Dani said, backing closer to the pawn shop. Jethro, clearly the better fighter of the two, advanced on her. As the crowd got louder, Dani kept screaming as though terrified, careful to keep her hands near her head, just above her ears.

An enraged Jethro threw a right-handed roundhouse, intending to take Dani out of the fight immediately. Dani, still screaming, "Massa' no!", stepped back with her left foot, bringing her right elbow forward. As she slapped her head, her elbow landed on his fist. Dani knew from the way Jethro just dropped his hand, that she had hurt him. But, like the veteran fighter Jethro was, he didn't stop coming at her.

He tried to end the fight with a well-executed, left handed uppercut. Dani didn't register what the threat was; her daily practice took over. She stepped back with her right foot, and her left hand slapped her head, while simultaneously leaning over, planting her elbow squarely on his middle finger's first knuckle as it came up with her weight adding to the impact.

Jethro cried out in pain, clutched his left hand and tried to throw a kick with his booted right foot. Dani, still screaming, balanced heavily on her right foot, and traced an arch with her hard-heeled left foot. At the top of her arch, the heel caught Jethro's shin, just above his boot. Jethro howled in pain. His kick was hard enough to cause Dani to fight to regain balance. She chose to fall to her left. This caused her to throw her full weight into Jethro's chest, and allowed her to regain her balance. Jethro, his right foot trapped painfully under Dani's right, went down with a surprised grunt.

And the crowd went wild.

"Get the coppers!" someone shouted.

"Stay back!" yelled someone else. "She's either drunk or insane!"

"If ya'll'd just leave her alone, she'd simmer down," a woman was saying. "She weren't bothering no one before you goosecaps tried to manhandle her!"

"Quiet, you old rib!" said the man next to her.

"What is the meaning of this?" demanded a commanding voice, and to Dani's surprise, it belonged to Peter. Anton was a step behind, but then walked quickly over, to put himself between her and the crowd, which was blessedly not quite a mob yet.

And then he turned on Dani and snapped, "Your next match ain't for another week, and not even in this city! What do you think you're doing, gal?"

Dani hung her head, trying to keep the smile from her voice. "Jes what ye taught me—"

"Hey!" Travis shouted, voice nasally. "That bitch broke my nose! She's a menace and needs to be locked up!"

"She works for me," Peter said. "And if you touched her, you are in serious trouble!"

"Don't overplay your hand," Dani whispered, as a man from the crowd called, "Works for you how?" Others were calling out similar questions.

"She fights," Peter said simply. He surveyed the crowd, and then raised his voice as if he were back at college, giving a presentation on climate change. "You have all heard of dog fights, am I right? And cock fights? I now present the newest in gentlemen's entertainment: tabby fighting!"

The crowd—mostly men now, as nearly all the women made disgusted noises and hurried away, many dragging children behind them—called out questions and suggestions, and more than a few bets.

"Then you owe me for damages, sir!" said Travis.

Peter laughed. "Really? Make a fist with your right hand. I bet you five dollars that one or most of your fingers are bruised."

"I will take that bet—" a man from the crowd began. His friend beside him placed a hand over his mouth, angrily shaking his head, while Peter moved to clumsily approximate Dani's left elbow block.

Peter turned to Jethro, who was still on the ground, cradling his left hand. "Let me guess. You threw a right hand, roundhouse, and when she blocked it, bruising some fingers, you followed up with a left-handed uppercut. I will bet another five dollars she used her right elbow on your right hand, and actually bent over a bit to plant her left elbow on your left fist." Peter then demonstrated where he thought Dani might have caught his fist. "Since you are on your ass, you tried to kick her. She blocked it with her heel. I'm a betting you got both a bruise and a cut out of that. Last, you have a bruise on the right foot." Jethro just stared in shock.

After a moment, Jethro mustered some anger to respond with, "How you reckon' you do not owe damages to Travis'n me, seeing as you have a dangerous, crazed nigger bitch that you just let run loose?"

Anton joined in with a menacing laugh. "Son, I have seen horses with more horse sense. Let me use small words for you. The only ones to throw punches were you and your friend Travis. Since you tried to punch a woman, that makes you two cowards in my book. You owe my boss, because she bruised her elbow on your upper cut. I suggest you two yaller dogs flicker off away from here. Now."

Anton moved to face Jethro, with a smile Dani had seen on infantry faces before. It meant, "Please make my day".

Before Jethro could make up his mind, Travis spoke up, "I dunno about you Jethro, but I could sure use a doctor right now." Travis helped Jethro up, and the two left. The crowd thinned out.

A large, ruddy-faced man with thinning black hair approached. Two men followed him, acting somewhat like Anton had —except they weren't acting.

"Evening gents, missy," he said, with a nod toward Dani. He walked with an air of authority —just not the legal kind.

Peter tipped his hat. "I fear we have disturbed the peace of your... territory?"

The man laughed, while his henchmen remained impassive. "You may be from out of town, but you ain't fools. I be Sam Malloy, and this is, indeed, my territory. Which means no fights happen without my say-so."

"I do apologize," said Peter, taking his wallet from inside his waistcoat. Dani hoped she and Anton were the only ones who saw how his hands shook. He pulled out a five dollar note. "I hope this will be enough to clear up any... misunderstanding?"

"Of course." The bill disappeared into Malloy's hand as if it had never existed. "But I would like very much to have one such as her fight for me."

Peter nodded, "Understandable. Only problem is, I did not train her, so if I sold her to you, I would not be able to replace her. And with that in mind, there is no reasonable fee I could ask of you."

"I was afraid you would say that. Bound to say, but I have never seen anyone inflict damage like that. Those two college dandies will likely never figure out how close they came to a'dyin'. How about her trainer? Any idea where I could find him?" asked Sam.

Peter nodded his head. "Well, he was a former British Army sergeant, that I ran into in Norfolk, where this young woman and I had a different arrangement, if you take my meaning." Peter paused until Sam nodded. "His story was he spent ten or so years bouncing between China and the Japans. Learned two different fighting techniques. In return, I paid him half of my earning for her first twenty fights, which he helped set up. Seemed to be some kind of vendetta. After that we went our separate ways. He headed west, maybe

Tennessee. Heard from a friend that he died at Shiloh, and his grave is in the Confederate Cemetery."

"Watcha think of having her train one of mine?" asked Sam.

Peter nodded, "Now there is a thought. She is good, but she ain't a getting any younger. I will most certainly keep your offer in my coat pocket. Your career and mine will go for a long time, but any fighter, no matter how skilled, will always have a much shorter and harsher career." A sharp whistle blew across the street, followed by the ageless cry of "All aboard!"

"That be our train," Peter said. "A pleasure meeting you, Mr. Malloy." With that the two men shook hands, and the parties went their separate ways.

"Is that even our train?" Anton asked as they arrived, sweating and panting, at the station.

"I don't know, and I don't care!" said Peter.

It wasn't, but the right train arrived soon after. Despite the luxury of their first-class cabin, no one spoke or relaxed for several minutes. Then Peter and Anton began talking at once.

"We never should have left you there—" said Anton.

"I was an idiot—" said Peter.

"Are you all right?"

"It seemed safe enough—"

"Both of you, just stop!" said Dani. "We all knew something like this would happen." She took a deep breath, held it and released, repeating until her shaking slowed, and finally stopped. "And I'm okay. Partly due to your quick thinking, Peter."

"Although I'm surprised you said 'tabby-fight,' " said Anton. "Why not cat?"

"Tabby means old maid, or difficult woman,"

Peter said absently. "I couldn't remember if cat was in use for women at this time. But we all have to remember how vulnerable Dani is. Not physically," as she began to protest. "You're the best fighter among us. But here and now, you could get lynched, just for defending yourself."

"Not only lynched," said Dani. "A judge could sentence me to hang, nice and legally, for doing not much more than I did to those boys."

"This whole time, since we walked out of that elevator," said Peter, "we've been lucky. But I was arrogant enough to think instead that we had it all under control."

"Does anyone besides me need a drink?" asked Anton.

At his friends combined nod, he left the car, and returned, followed by a porter who carried a tray which held a beautiful cut glass decanter of ruby red liquor and three glasses.

"Just leave it here," said Anton, indicating the polished walnut table between the two plush chairs Peter and Dani occupied. If Dani's seated presence or the extra glass surprised the porter, his dark, calm face never betrayed it.

"Next stop, New York City," Dani said, pouring them each a glass.

Chapter 9

New York City sweltered in the August heat, smelling even worse than it would a century and a half from now. At the corner of 44th Street and Fifth Avenue, Dani stood alone. She would never have thought of New York City as a place to go for peace and quiet, yet it was. They had arrived two days earlier, from Saratoga Springs, flush with real money for the first time since their arrival in 1863.

Dani had to admit it had been exciting, being there for the opening of the famous racetrack. After the fourth race, even Peter had calmed down and gotten into the spirit of the day. Whatever changes their presence had wrought, none involved the outcome of the races. All were as they had been reported in the New York newspapers of August, 1863. The same papers that the three of them had read in the Musselman Library the day before they left 2025. The sheer scope of the crowds and the betting made a pair of lucky young men barely noticeable. Especially since they were careful to lose a few times. While Peter and Anton were busy at the races, Dani found a spot in the nearby woods to keep up on her archery practice.

The end result had been nearly ten thousand dollars. And now Peter and Anton were busy uptown, working on stocks and bonds —and she stood here, before the burnt out remains of the Colored Orphan Asylum, thinking she might just stand here all day.

Or at least until the heat drove her away.

The smoke and ash from the Draft Riots nearly a month before should have been gone by now. Perhaps they were. Perhaps it was only the malevolence; the lingering anger and despair that Dani felt permeating the very air. Maybe it was her own sense of guilt.

"Are you all right, Miss?"

Startled out of her trance, Dani turned to see a grey-haired, mixed race man of about fifty looking at her with concern.

"I came by to pay my respects—" Dani began. And then, realization hit. Of course he would have come to say goodbye before moving to Brooklyn. "Dr. James McCune Smith?" she whispered.

The man sketched a graceful bow. "At your service. Do I know you, Miss?"

Dani shook her head. "Excuse me, I just can't believe I'm speaking with the first Negro doctor in the United States! And the man who managed the only colored orphan asylum, well, anywhere. I had hoped to work here someday."

At that, all sense of concern over Dani's strange behavior vanished from the doctor's face, replaced by sorrow. His mustache drooped, but his back remained straight. "It was a magnificent undertaking, and my great honor to have been a part of it." He turned back to Dani. "You have me at a disadvantage, Miss—?"

"Dani Davis." She extended her gloved hand. "I'm a battlefield nurse, lately of Gettysburg." Smith's eyebrows rose in surprise. "But I have family here and when I heard about the riots…" Her eyes took in the burned building, and other signs of destruction around them. "I had to come."

"Of course you did." He paused apprehensively. "Was your family unharmed?"

"Yes, thank the Good Lord. But so many others…" To her complete surprise, yet strangely, relief, Dani began to cry. She'd have never let Peter or Anton see her like this, and they were her best friends. But somehow, in the presence of one of her childhood heroes, it was all right.

"There, there, Miss Davis." James McCune Smith handed her a handkerchief, and Dani's shaking fingers nearly dropped it when she saw it was monogramed. She tried to dab her eyes without ruining the precious thing. "War brings out the worst in everyone. But even in the worst of it, there are heroes. Did you know that it was Union Soldiers, and volunteers—like yourself—who led the children here to safety?"

Dani nodded. "I had heard. And I am grateful. But I wish I had been here! I could have done something!" She covered a gasp at her reckless behavior with a sob and stopped speaking.

But the doctor she had long admired proved to be a true healer, as well as wise. "There was nothing you could have done, my dear, but time and again, I hear such sentiments from those with compassionate souls. I sometimes think the human heart was designed to bear the weight of guilt easier than helplessness."

Dani stared wordlessly, and then remembered to give him back his handkerchief. "Thank you," she said. "Will you be moving to Brooklyn?"

Dr. Smith looked surprised, and then smiled. "I suppose every Negro family with a pushcart is heading there now. I've already settled my wife and children in our new home. I only came back for one more look at the place. Like you, I suppose."

"I'll not keep you any longer, sir."

The doctor hesitated. "I was on my way to dine with some friends who are already working to rebuild the asylum in another part of the city. Would you care to join me?"

Dani gaped. "I, uh, I would not dream of imposing, sir—"

"There will be a young Quaker lady in attendance who wishes to become a nurse. She is too young as yet, and I am sure her parents hope this wretched war will end before she is old enough, but I think she would like to meet you. And you could learn about what you might do to help, instead of grieving for what is too late to change."

Dani could only wonder if she was meant to bring the famous doctor into the secret, but she did not refuse the invitation a second time. Instead she looked around for a street urchin. There were several to choose from, but Dani approached a boy who looked like he might have lived in the burned out orphanage, and was only waiting here for the people who had cared for him to return.

"Can you carry a message for me?" Dani asked, pulling a scrap of paper from her reticule.

"'O course I kin," said the boy. He was so light skinned, he might have passed for Italian or Greek until his accent gave him away. His young eyes appraised her dress and manner eagerly, perhaps hoping for a dime, rather than a nickel.

Dani gave him a quarter. The boy's eyes grew wide, but the coin disappeared before she could blink.

"What is your name?" she asked.

"Joey." He met her gaze steadily as she gave him the address, and the note telling Anton and Peter where she was going. After describing her two housemates, Dani told the boy they would pay him another quarter, and perhaps give him food if he asked.

Joey sped down the street just as Dr. Smith caught up with her.

He offered her his arm. Dani felt herself blush.

***

An hour later, she sat in a well-appointed dining room, surrounded by some of the greatest minds, hearts, and souls of the nineteenth century—although few of them would be remembered in any history books.

The combination of diversity, ideas and stimulating conversation, like the wonderful meal spread before her, was full of flavor and texture. Dani was grateful that alcohol was not present. She was drunk enough just from the words of Mary Murray— one of the three founders of the now destroyed orphanage—who debated with a Negro minister over the speed with which it could be rebuilt. Not to mention the medical discussion Dr. Smith was having with a white doctor on new ideas for treating infection.

Correction: old ideas. But some of them were fascinating, especially since most hadn't made it to twenty first century practices, even though Dani believed many had merit.

If her hostess, one Susan Jenkins, had not asked Dani if the food was not to her taste, she might have forgotten to eat the lovely slice of roast beef and creamed potatoes on the china plate in front of her— which would have been a shame. She was fairly sure nothing could have gotten between her and the apple pie, but the discussion of what to do about integrating the soon to be freed slaves into American society came close.

While Dani self-consciously watched her table manners, spoke little and tried to make sure she addressed everyone by their first names—as the only surname acceptable in a Quaker house was "friend"—it wasn't easy. For one thing, there were four men named James, two women named Mary, two Susans, and the rest of the women were all named Elizabeth. For another, the oldest of the three children present (yet another Susan) was a bright girl of fourteen, determined to become a nurse. She only stopped peppering Dani with questions when her mother intervened.

"I know healing to be my true calling," Susan said. "I only fear the War will be over before I may begin my work."

"Pray that it is!" said Elizabeth (but not the Elizabeth who was the girl's mother.) "Too many have already died, and others will carry the suffering they have endured for the rest of their lives."

"True," said Dani. "And it is they who will need your help for many years to come, Friend Susan."

The pretty brunette turned wide green eyes to Dani. "But how does a nurse help with that? Is it not a vocation of stopping bleeding, mixing herbs and cooling fevers—?"

"Not a discussion for the dinner table," said their host. "Our guest is barely eating as it is."

Dani quickly took a bite of lovely wheat bread, but was able to speak before the opportunity was lost. "Nursing is a vocation of the spirit as well. It is by listening to what patients confide in you that you will learn the causes of suffering that the doctors may have missed." Dani felt herself blush as she looked toward the two doctors at the table. "Oh, forgive me, gentlemen. I—" She had no idea what to say next but was spared the need to answer by the white doctor.

"You are quite right, madam," he said. "But few are aware of it. Like so many things discussed at this table." The elderly gentlemen nodded to his host and hostess. "Which is why I find myself drawn to these fine people, although I, myself, am not a member of the Society of Friends."

"No one is perfect," said a lanky grinning boy of about thirteen.

"Ned!" said his father (the only man at the table not named James.) Dani smothered a laugh. Susan tried to bring the subject back to medicine, but Dani gave into a life-long dream and asked, "What do you good people think of Mr. Lincoln's Proclamation on the first day of this year? I'm sure after eight months it has been talked to death, but—"

They were happy to comply. "Useless piece of statecraft," said Ned's father. "It frees no one!"

"Not yet," said the reverend. "But as a symbol; a beacon of hope, it was a great gift."

"Your pardon, good reverend," said their hostess. "But Mr. Lincoln has never allied himself with the abolitionist cause."

"Sending your people to Liberia seems far more likely, should his Union soldiers carry the day," said a man who, until now, had not spoken.

"I know what many say about our president. Much with good reason," said the minister with a nod toward Susan and James. "Yet I also sense a great goodness in him; a depth of humanity and compassion that will someday heal this nation. When this tragic war is over, I believe he will make good on his promise."

"I pray so," said Mary Murray. "'T'will be the only thing that can possibly give meaning to this tragedy that has rent our country apart."

"Were you born a slave, Friend Dani?" asked the youngest boy.

"Robert!" said the other Mary. She cast an embarrassed look at both Dani and their hostess. "I do apologize for my son."

"Please do not," said Dani. "There is no need." She caught a look of approval from the hostess. To Robert, Dani said, "I was born free, the child of free parents." Then she nearly giggled at the simple truth of that statement. "And, if I may be so bold: those many who still languish in that state will need more from you, and our president, than just their freedom. They will need your help in learning how to live free."

"Should that not be the easy part?" asked Ned, genuinely puzzled, but still with a mischievous glint in his eye. "They'll be free. They can do whatever they wish."

"'Tis not quite that simple, young man," said the minister, in a voice like velvet and a nod in Dani's direction. "Slavery is a disease that harms the mind and soul, as well as the body. Emancipation is only the beginning of what will be a long process of healing."

"Nightmares," Dani murmured, realizing for the first time, she had let down her guard.

"I beg your pardon?" said one of the men named James.

Dani sat rigidly upright and took a deep breath. "I was remembering the nightmares which plagued so many of the soldiers I have nursed. I would imagine it will be the same for many of the slaves once they are free. After the horrors have gone from their waking lives, I fear they will visit folk in their dreams."

There were many nods of agreement, followed

by a discussion that made Dani see that people didn't need courses in psychology or knowledge of the words Post Traumatic Stress Disorder to know what they meant. The suggestions which followed, ranging from helping to bring the former slaves north to live with free blacks, to sending missions to the south to set up schools and help them locate family members made Dani truly happy that she had traveled back here.

The party broke up soon after, with Dani receiving several more invitations. While she did not commit to any of them, she allowed her address to be known, and hoped she would not have to watch Peter's and Anton's heads explode. Maybe if she could secure them invitations as well?

Dr. James McCune Smith insisted on escorting her home. To her relief, he made no comment about the clearly white, middle class neighborhood to which she directed him. Many of the houses were large enough for servants' quarters. Hopefully, he surmised the family she claimed to be visiting worked here.

After a polite farewell, Dani hurried inside, to find Anton on the floor of the parlor, shooting marbles with the little boy who'd brought her message, while Peter went over their account ledgers. Anton missed his shot when he saw Dani, and Joey—now much cleaner, grinning in a face less pinched by want—sent up a cry of victory.

"Looks like you won, Joey," Anton said.

"All 'em?"

"Not my lucky marble!" Anton sounded panicked. "But all the rest." He smiled as Joey gathered up colorful orbs that Anton had bought from an antique store when they'd all been in college together.

"You best get that chalk circle cleaned off my

nice floor if you want supper, young man," Dani said in her best Southern drawl.

"Yes, ma'am," Anton said meekly, to the shocked delight of the boy.

"Now that you're both here, I was thinking..." Anton glanced around uncomfortably. "Any chance we can let him stay tonight?"

"Would you let us sleep if I said no?" Peter responded. "You know, Anton, we can't save everyone."

"You don't need to tell me that," he sighed. "We can't even buy this one new clothes! The others would fall on him like a pack of wolves. But we can give him a safe place to rest for a time."

Peter nodded. "But just tonight."

"Let Joey sleep in here, on the rug with a blanket," Dani said "He'd probably run away if we offered him a bed, since the house only has three." Anton's face darkened, as it often did when memories of his time in the foster care system threatened to surface.

Anton came back to himself with visible effort. "Maybe we can find work for him, or some excuse to keep him safe," he said.

Dani thought about her day and smiled. "I might have met someone today I could talk to about that."

Joey sat by the fireplace, eyes that were too old for his face taking in everything.

***

Before everyone split up to go to bed, Dani made an announcement.

"As there is no longer any need to whitewash

my resume, I am reclaiming my real name. My name here and now is Miss Danaxe Davis. While it is spelled "D-A-N-A-X-E, it is pronounced "Dan-ah-jay." And yes, it's a thing. Good night." With that, Danaxe went up the stairs to her bedroom. Her best friends' startled discussion followed her.

"Danaxe?" said Peter. "I thought it was Danielle."

"I was betting on Danica," said Anton.

"What's a resume?" asked Joey.

Chapter 10

Over the next few weeks, Danaxe met with Dr. Smith several times, and attended another dinner with one of the Marys. Her talks with the good doctor centered on the medical practices of the day. Danaxe found the discussions challenging, as she had to work to not bring up notions and practices of the future. Smith's declining health made this necessity especially challenging.

Danaxe tried to discreetly suggest treatments for his various ailments, always careful to credit some anonymous doctor she met in the War, or family lore from a long line of root women. She was quite pleased to discover that Dr. Smith was a proponent of Louis Pasteur and Robert Koch's disease theory, as this made it easier to convince him to try some of her more unusual suggestions.

The discussion at the end of a third visit with Dr. Smith became awkward, as Danaxe found herself becoming increasingly agitated.

"Miss Davis, I apologize if anything I said was unsettling or disturbed you," Smith said as he walked her home.

Without thinking, Danaxe reached out with her gloved hand and grabbed Dr. Smith's arm. "You have done nothing wrong, but I have a difficult decision to make, and I cannot make it on my own. There are important things I feel the need to share, but I must consult my friends." As they reached the door, Danaxe came to a decision. She turned back to him. "Would you please come inside? This may take enough time to require that we feed you supper."

Cocking his head to the side, Dr. Smith regarded Danaxe for a full minute. "Normally, such words would cause me to suspect that I am about to be approached by a confidence man. I fully expect that my confidence will remain unsullied."

"I truly hope that will be the case, but I must confer with my companions. If you would not mind, I will escort you to the parlor." Dr. Smith nodded his assent as he offered Danaxe his arm, preceding her through the door as a polite guest.

As expected, Danaxe found Peter and Anton looking through several newspapers and comparing them with the tablets, looking for changes —and ideas for what to buy, and what to sell. Danaxe interrupted.

"We've company, and an important decision to make right now." Peter and Anton put their tablets into a drawer. Danaxe grabbed a newspaper and covered the hand-cranked generator sitting next to the bread box.

"What's up?" whispered Anton.

"I need to bring Dr. Smith into the fold."

A visibly stunned Peter hissed, "What, now? Why?"

"Because I need a known and trusted doctor to start changing how medicine is conducted. Most importantly, we need to get reproductive help going, which means safe abortions, and preventing unwanted pregnancies to begin with. Remember, medicine without birth control is what led to the population explosion that was the main cause for climate change. As a woman, I need a male partner to act on my behalf, and he'll need to know where I got my information."

"You couldn't have waited until he was gone? You want a decision right now?" Peter looked angry.

"You seriously think you can sell modern medical concepts or discuss the tools?" retorted Danaxe.

Anton sat down. "I say do it. So you have my vote."

"How far in?" Peter sat down, looking and sounding resigned.

Danaxe thought hard for a few moments. "In general terms, why we are here. Nothing on the political side, and certainly nothing about Lincoln. Just the medical stuff. So he can help me with patents, and then start up the manufacturing. It will end up making us all rich enough to pay for all our harebrained schemes. It will also take time to really gear stuff up, and teach people. And just so I don't sandbag you, I want to bring Jenny into this as well. But that's a discussion for later."

Peter nodded. "I understand. We've discussed it before coming, but frankly hadn't thought about how to do that or with whom. You have some real ambitious plans. Any chance of giving our methods away to people not in the know?"

"Possibly, but that will be years down the line. We'll get the important stuff done."

"Okay. You sold me. You want to do this, or should I?"

"You start it. I'll take over on the medical side." Grinning, she turned to Anton, "Good thing you made your usual size batch of chili. We'll have enough to feed the good doctor."

Anton nodded. "And the cornbread is set to go.

Meanwhile, I'll check to see what needs recharging. You can include that in the show if needed."

Peter grabbed his tablet and followed Danaxe, who paused to pick up hers, and continued on to the parlor.

Dr. Smith turned from the window he had been gazing through when he heard Danaxe and Peter leave the kitchen. "Well, that was a quick verdict. Usually not good for the defendant."

Peter responded with a wry grin. "Too true. Fortunately, we are not a jury. I am more concerned about involving a doctor in this. I don't want to spend time in an asylum."

"I will certainly do my best not to let that happen." As the two were talking, Danaxe set two chairs next to each other with a small stand within easy elbow reach.

Peter gestured to the chair on the left, saying by way of explanation, "I'm left handed." Dr. Smith startled a bit at the admission.

The two sat down. Peter watched Dr. Smith stare at the tablet in Peter's lap. "I've done this with only one other man so far. Have you ever heard of a zoetrope?"

Dr. Smith nodded.

"Good. So a zoetrope is done using pictures. I am going to show you a video. It's like the zoetrope, but it uses thirty-two pictures a second. Though, this one is mostly showing still pictures." Dr. Smith watched curiously as Peter woke up the tablet, sitting forward as the opening screen was displayed. Where Dr. Smith could see what Peter was doing, he forefinger typed "documentary 1863 draft riots orphanage burning." Peter frowned when the screen displayed "no results." "Danaxe, you have the orphanage video on your tablet?" She nodded and handed her tablet to Peter. She noted the arching of Dr. Smith's eyebrow.

Peter repeated the start up for Danaxe's tablet. This time, when the search came up, Part 9 of 10 *New York: A Documentary Film —Episode Two: Order and Disorder* (1825-1865). Peter brought up the video and handed the tablet to Dr. Smith. "Please do not drop that. That screen, where the picture is, is just plain glass." Responding to Dr. Smith's puzzled look, Peter answered his question. "At the bottom left, see the sideways triangle?" Dr. Smith nodded. "Touch it with your forefinger." The doctor followed the directions.

Peter watched Dr. Smith's face going from surprise, to puzzlement, to consternation. Danaxe, unbeknownst to Dr. Smith, sat in her chair videoing him and Peter.

"Having lived through all of this, I am rather versed on this subject," the doctor said stiffly. "So why show me what I already know?"

Peter blinked. "You seem rather unimpressed. You've seen a video before?"

"Of course not, but you explained the technique. You must have gone through a lot of effort to make this, but why show me?"

Unprepared for this reaction, the three time-travelers stared at each other. Smith, Danaxe saw, was the calmest person in the room, waiting patiently, his face unreadable, but in no way hostile.

She decided to take the plunge. "Because I am going to say something that will sound insane. All three of us were born in the future. We are here because something horrible happened, er, ah, will happen." She took a deep breath and glanced over at the doctor, fearing what she would see.

To her complete amazement, Dr. James McCune Smith smiled. "I was wondering when you were going to tell me," he said mildly, and then sat back in his chair, looking from one to the next of the shocked faces across from him. From the kitchen came a loud crash, as Anton dropped an armload of plates.

Chapter 11

Standing in the doorway of the kitchen, Anton was the first to recover. "Well, I'd say supper just became a whole lot more interesting," he said. He could read his friends expressions easily enough. *Were there other time-travelers here? Was Smith somehow one of them?*

"How did you know?" Danaxe asked, before they could all fall into full conspiracy theory mode.

"Small things, really." The doctor inclined his head toward Danaxe. "You are superb actress, Miss Davis, and in no way do I mean that as an insult. In our every meeting, you have worked to behave as a modest, deferential, well-educated Negro woman. But from the first, I could see that you must *work* to create the illusion. In this time and place, every woman of our race, including my wife, who as a college degree, moves and speaks in a way that..." For the first time, Smith seemed as lost as his hosts. "I really cannot explain it. It is simply... there."

"And that was enough for a man educated in science to decide we were time-travelers?" Peter demanded.

"Of course not," Smith said patiently. "There were other clues. And I was not convinced until this afternoon." He turned back to Danaxe. "During our discussion of vaccinations against smallpox, you compared it to one for measles. I fear that one does not yet exist, although from what little you said, I saw at once how it would work. Quite brilliant. I should like to begin work on it at once, if doing so is... permitted?"

"Not so discreet or careful after all," Danaxe muttered.

Anton patted her shoulder. "Don't feel bad. It was bound to happen. And it looks like we got lucky."

"I regret causing you any distress, Miss Davis," Smith continued, and now his creased and dignified face showed concern.

Danaxe shook her head, striving for her usual calm. "Just embarrassed. Anything else?"

"Well, you did compliment me rather lavishly on my writing of the Revolution in Haiti and the life of Toussaint L'Ouverture. I was so flattered that I thought it would be rude to point out that you quoted a passage that has never been published. It will be published posthumously, if my will is executed as written, but for now, no one but I myself, knows of its existence. Except for those who read it after my death," emphasizing the past tense of "read."

At that point, the three friends did the only thing they could: they burst out laughing. Smith did not join them, although he did smile. Anton recovered enough to ask, "Okay, we get that Danaxe made some mistakes, but how did that get you to time travel? Why not just assume she's an obsessed fan girl who broke into your house and rifled through your desk?"

For the first time, Smith looked baffled. Anton felt better.

"Please excuse the vernacular," Peter said, glaring at Anton. "What he means is, why assume we are from the future? Time travel is barely even thought of in fiction at this time. In fact the only novel written in English, involving traveling backward in time, is—"

"*Memoirs of the Twentieth Century*, by Samuel Madden," Smith finished smoothly. "And, perhaps, *A*

Christmas Carol, by Charles Dickens."

"I told you he was well-read," said Danaxe.

"Not the half of it, you didn't," Anton muttered.

"The first is a story of angels and the second of ghosts!" said Peter, now in full argument mode. "You, sir, are a scientist!"

"To paraphrase Dr. Darwin, sir, religion and science are in no way incompatible," said Smith, graying eyebrows snapping together. "Although I am gratified that you did not assume my race makes me prone to gullibility."

"We did come here with her, if you remember," Anton said mildly, with a nod toward Danaxe.

Dr. Smith took a deep breath. "I apologize. That last remark was uncalled for. I have many concerns about your presence, and am perhaps not so calm as I thought I was."

"That makes four of us," said Anton. "Now, if you will all be seated, I will attend to supper. Let us hope it is still edible."

***

Later, seated around the dining room table, the four easily discussed subjects that had required repeated use of twenty-first century technology to convince Chamberlain to even consider believing. "I am gratified to know that the Union prevailed, and that slavery will be abolished," Smith said. "And of course I will say nothing. You need not threaten me with the nightmare of a Confederate victory if I betray your secret. Furthermore, I am not the least bit surprised to learn that such changes did not end my people's plight."

"More chili?" Anton offered.

"No, thank you, Mr. Pozda," said the doctor. "It was excellent, but I must be careful of my weight and diet."

Anton, who knew that Smith would die in just two years, had been equally careful with the spices.

"Ah," said Smith. "Something else you should be aware of, should you choose to invite anyone else into your home. The lack of servants, and an educated white man doing the cooking—"

"Yes," said Peter, shooting a stern look at Danaxe. "Until today, no one has been inside past the parlor, where Danaxe usually plays the role of maid."

"I thought as much," said Smith. With a sudden change in manner, he continued. "You three have been excellent hosts, and I do not refer only to the cuisine. You have been generous in satisfying an old man's curiosity about the future, though I sense there is much you will not tell me. Perhaps we should now come to the matter of how you hope to prevent these calamities, and why you chose to include me in this dangerous secret."

"The answers are one and the same," Danaxe said. "You and a few other key people, at least. One reason we need you, Dr. Smith, is to introduce what we consider modern medicine. Aside from the fossil fuel issue, the second problem is population. The population worldwide when we left to come back to 1863 was over eight billion. The world population here and now we believe to be about 1.2 billion. We need to keep it below three billion. And that is where you come in. Through you, I can introduce even more lifesaving technologies. I could patent some things, if you would be my representative to make that happen?"

"Pardon my interruption, but would that not cause the very problem you are trying to solve?" asked Dr. Smith.

"Yes, actually, that is indeed what happened. Therefor I also intend to introduce methods for birth control." Danaxe stopped talking and raised her hand to prevent Dr. Smith interrupting with a look of outrage, and a noticeable flush of embarrassment. "There is more to birth control than abortion or abstinence. There are ways to prevent pregnancy from happening. I intend to introduce them, here and now, and get them overseas as soon as possible. Failure to do that? We've come back for nothing, and we have given up way too much coming here to sit back and let that happen."

"While I find such matters offensive, my greater concern is why you chose to come here? To a divided nation. Would not such changes as you propose be better served by an empire, such as Great Britain? They possess the might to impose such restrictions throughout the world. Especially in those parts of the world where population and poverty are the most extreme."

"We have seen what happens when an autocratic government imposes its will, Doctor," said Peter. "We cannot risk such a devil's bargain. It has to start here, in America, where so much is still possible."

"In the *land of the free*?" Smith asked sadly.

"In the land that best represents the world as it is," said Danaxe. "And as it could be. Consider this: every race and most nations are already represented here. From the Gold Rush—the largest voluntary migration in history—to the slave trade—the largest involuntary migration."

"Also, the home of a race of people who lived

here for thousands of years before the Europeans arrived, and have no wish to live anywhere else," Peter said, continuing the thread.

"And despite its shabby treatment," said Anton, "the Bill of Rights promises free speech. We intend to let that promise loose across the land. In the end, I believe most of our answers can be found there."

"Amazing," the doctor whispered, but it sounded like a prayer.

"What is?" asked Anton.

"That you are here. That I believe you."

"Actually, I find that last part rather amazing myself," said Peter.

The conversation returned to Danaxe's plans for patents.

"The sulfides are great for combat wounds in stopping infections. Chloramphenicol is comparatively easy to make. The only problem is it will kill 1 in 24,000 plus people. Latex gloves, a good first to prevent infections, surgical gowns, incentive spirometer, and anyway, what I need is a patent attorney who would be willing to work with me." Danaxe paused.

"If you can show me medicines which I can understand and verify myself," Smith said, "and especially those gloves, I shall assist you with the patents. But since I shall be putting my reputation on the line the moment we enter a law office, I shall do nothing until I am convinced." He pinned Danaxe with his gaze. "I do not need to tell you, of all people, how much I shall be risking."

"No," she whispered. "You most certainly do not."

"Then I shall inquire about the attorney." Dr.

Smith stood, formally thanked his hosts, and took his leave. Anton and Peter, still dazed, cleaned the kitchen, while Danaxe wrote two letters. One to Gettysburg, and another addressed to the British Consulate in New York City.

Chapter 12

When more than a week passed without word from Dr. Smith, the three time-travelers feared they had seen the last of him. More frightening was the possibility that they had shared dangerous information with someone who was not a friend. Then a letter arrived, addressed to Miss Danaxe Davis, containing the name of a patent attorney who would be willing to work with a Negress. Cautious hope turned to excited grins when inquiries led to the discovery that Mr. William L. Barnwell, Esq was himself a Negro.

Danaxe agreed to Dr. Smith as her escort, while Peter and Anton sulked at home, wondering how they had missed this bit of history.

A young Negro clerk greeted them as they entered the building, and led them to Mr. Barnwell's office. Danaxe noticed that there were a fair number of photographs on the walls, a diploma, a large oak desk, and a *tete a tete* set for three people. Mr. Barnwell, rose and greeted his guests.

"Good morning. Dr. Smith I know, so you must be the Miss Davis he spoke of. Pleased to make your acquaintance. If you would be so kind as to sit over here," pointing at the *tete a tete*.

Danaxe appraised Mr. Barnwell as he walked over, noticing that he appeared to have a slight tightness in his back, and that when he sat, he was very careful about how he leaned back. He was much lighter skinned than she was, and Danaxe wondered if one of his parents was white.

Danaxe broke the silence. "Were you born free? Please forgive me for being so forward as to ask."

Mr. Barnwell grimaced lightly. "No. I managed to escape when I was thirteen years old. With a lot of help from the Underground Railroad. Others have helped me greatly over the years, so that now I am here in this office, able to return the favor to many others. How may I help you, Miss Davis?"

"I would like to start patenting some equipment and medicines to help physicians, as well as treatments for some issues regarding women's health. After that, I would need help finding people who could make the items."

"Are you a doctor?" asked Mr. Barnwell, his face a mask of civility.

"Not at this time. I expect that to change, but it will likely be some years in the future." Danaxe reached into the briefcase that Dr. Smith had insisted on carrying for her, and retrieved a large sheaf of papers. Everything was written or drawn in ink, covering over a dozen items, from compounding latex, sulfides, chloramphenicol, and ending with an incentive spirometer. "I expect these to be very helpful. How long will it take, do you think? For both the patents and the, uh, craftsmen?"

Barnwell spent the next fifteen minutes rifling through drawings, and reading the descriptions of chemical processes. "Possibly as long as a year. This is not an inexpensive endeavor. I will likely need to charge roughly twenty-five dollars per patent. As most, if not all of this can be deemed to help with the war, I may be able to get expedited treatment. I am estimating that as much as fifteen dollars will be needed to produce a model for each patent. That includes samples as needed from apothecaries."

"That will be acceptable," she said. To his credit, Mr. Barnwell did not so much as bat an eye.

"I believe I can have the initial papers drawn up no later than Wednesday next," he said. "After that, it is up to the patent office. May I ask what name I should place on the papers?"

"My full name is Danaxe Rosa Davis. Among friends and professionals I use Dani Davis, single 'n', single 'i.' It reads like a white person's name on papers. But it also marks me as a woman. I was thinking of going by either D.R. Davis, or Dan R. Davis."

"Commendable thoughts. I would suggest 'Dan.' It avoids any possibility that you are trying to imply that you are a doctor when you are not, and discovery of your true name will protect you from accusations of any chicanery. And yes, it would be better not to let the Patent Office know you are a woman. It is an unfortunate fact of life. Among other things."

"I am very pleased you are willing to work with a woman. May I ask why?"

"I am pleased to put forward anything that shows what our race is capable of. Anything that advances acknowledgement of our abilities as a group, I believe, will lead to greater acceptance by the Caucasians."

"Thank you. Should I return Wednesday next?"

"I will have a note sent to the both of you. And I may send notes with questions if I find I need assistance."

Briefly, Danaxe and Mr. Barnwell worked out payment, finishing with Danaxe and Dr. Smith taking their leave of Mr. Barnwell.

As Dr. Smith walked Danaxe back to her home, Danaxe exclaimed "Yes!" as she spied Jenny energetically pacing to and fro in front of her brownstone.

"Jenny!" called Danaxe, and the two hugged. Dr. Smith stood back and watched.

Jenny, with very little breathing, caught Danaxe up on her adventures getting to New York City, and when she finally wound down, Danaxe finally got a word in edgewise.

"Please allow me to introduce you two. Jenny Wight this is Dr. James McCune Smith. Dr. Smith, allow me to introduce Miss Jenny Wight."

"Pleased to make your acquaintance, Miss Wight," replied Smith with a slight bow.

"I am delighted to meet you, Dr. Smith," Jenny responded with a curtsey.

Danaxe looked on, obviously thinking. "Dr. Smith, may I impose upon you yet again, and invite you inside to discuss what my plans are for Miss Wight?"

"I have, perhaps, had enough excitement for one day," Dr. Smith replied dryly, and with a straight face. "But I am beginning to find this house and its many surprises quite impossible to resist." Danaxe smiled, and for once, Jenny only shrugged.

The trio entered the brownstone and took over the parlor. Danaxe disappeared into the kitchen, and returned with a tray which held a pitcher of minted water and three glasses.

"I have not discussed this with either of you," she began, "but it has been much on my mind. Dr. Smith, I have plans for Miss Wight, and towards that, I need to find an appropriate situation for her wherein she can train as an apothecary, nurse, or even doctor. She will also need to learn to read and write, in both English and Hindi." Dr. Smith rolled his eyes, but then sat back and studied Jenny for a couple of moments. *Good*, thought Danaxe. *He's learning to just go with my weirdness.*

"Out of curiosity, for someone who is illiterate, how fast do you think this great transformation can occur?" Dr. Smith kept his tone light.

"In all honesty, I think she could possibly do it in three years, although if you decide to take her farther then you may need to allow five years. I also think piano lessons will be in order." At that, both of them rolled their eyes. Danaxe decided not to explain the ways that learning the piano could help Jenny's memory and, more importantly, social skills.

"I know from experience how fast she can learn. If you would be so kind as to allow me a few minutes, I can show you her abilities."

Dr. Smith smiled as he nodded.

Danaxe went into the kitchen and returned after a few moments of bustling about, with a leather pouch, and a whole pickled pigs foot. "For this kind of practice, a raw pig's foot is better, but I was not sure when or where this conversation might happen."

Danaxe handed the pouch to Jenny, and placed the platter on the table. Dr. Smith watched with great interest as Jenny laid out the scalpels and stitching needles and pliers in a quick and concise manner.

"Miss Wight, please carefully hand the scalpel to Dr. Smith, Dr. Smith would you be so kind as to simulate a single knife wound to the foot?" Dr. Smith stepped up, smiling slightly as he accepted the properly handled scalpel from Jenny.

"May I intrude to ask why you do not look happy, Miss Wight?"

"I's supposed to fully practice what I would do," she replied slowly, taking care with her speech. "I was not given a chance to properly wash my hands."

Dr. Smith nodded in agreement, responding "I think this once we can save the time." As he spoke, he made a three-inch incision, and put the scalpel back in its place. Jenny immediately picked up the pliers, grabbed the correct needle, and expertly threaded the needle. She then quickly and expertly stitched the "cut." Dr. Smith nodded in appreciation of a procedure well done.

"Now Jenny, pay attention. I am going to show you a new way to stitch." Danaxe gave a quick lecture on what was needed for deep muscle cuts. She demonstrated the procedure, including the use of retractors to hold the skin back to expose the muscle. Danaxe slowed down to make sure Jenny had the time to see what motions she made. After ten minutes, she was done. "Your turn." Danaxe told Jenny. Danaxe made a second three-inch incision on the pig's foot, and Jenny immediately, and properly duplicated what she had just witnessed. She looked first to Danaxe, and then to Dr. Smith, both of whom were smiling in approval. As the three returned to their seats, Danaxe spoke first.

"As you can see, she has the old memory, from before the printing press. Show her once, she practices once, and then she can do it on a real patient, and teach it to someone else. If you verbally explain it to her, she can recite everything you say. She may not be literate, but that does not seem to hold her back." Turning to Jenny, she added, "Although, eventually, you will need to read and write."

Dr. Smith studied Jenny for a couple of moments. "I do not wish to be rude, but may I ask to shake your hand?" Jenny's initial reaction was to pull her head backwards. She then energetically rose and walked over to Dr. Smith and proffered her hand to him. Dr. Smith shook her hand, taking his time about it, watching Jenny's face.

"That was rather heartening to see, Miss Wight. In order to teach you, I am going to have to touch you. Positioning is very important in our line of work. As I have, up until now, instructed only members of my own race, and all of them men, I had some concerns. You seem to have no trouble with my touching you. Pardon me, but that makes you part of a select few."

Jenny tilted her head and thought for a moment. "I reckon it this way. If God saw fit to give different peoples different colors, then He must have a reason. Nothing in the Bible says that any one color is better than another. Iffen you be willen' to teach, I be willen' to learn good, and fast."

Danaxe sat back, feeling strangely happy. Well, perhaps not strangely, but happy nonetheless. There was still so much to do, with so much chance of failure, but for this one moment, it was enough for former Surgical and Trauma Nurse, Lieutenant Danaxe Rosa Davis to sit in her parlor, and enjoy the company of a great man who had been little more than a footnote in history, and an amazing young woman who had been forgotten by history altogether. Because, just maybe, the new future she was building would honor them both.

Chapter 13

The autumn weather was almost pleasant in New York City when the train left the station. Peter and Anton, dressed more for comfort than style, still looked at home in their first-class seats. With luck, they would be able to join Danaxe in second class when they crossed into Ohio. She could take care of herself in any case, as they well knew.

"Still brooding?" Anton asked. "It's been three months! As far as we can tell, nothing has changed. You can't still be worrying about the Butterfly Effect!"

"I'm not," said Peter. "I'm worrying in the other direction now. What if history can't be changed at all?"

Then we'll have come all this way for nothing, thought Anton. But he didn't say that to Peter. He just muttered, "Talk about zero to sixty in under ten seconds."

"I know. I pull off the impossible, and then I worry like some kid who's afraid of the dark. But this…" he stared out the window of the west-moving train. "This is pretty daunting. I don't want to go into America's last First People's territories and come out as nothing but a witness of a soon-to-be extinct way of life. There's plenty of those already."

"If that were the case we wouldn't be here," said Anton, and for the first time, he felt it. "We're here for a reason. Even if we don't know what it is." Peter shook his head. *That's the difference between us,* thought Anton. *Peter has planned everything down to the smallest detail. He's certain about why we're here and what has to happen. Not me. Never me. And if I sometimes wish I'd never stepped into that elevator; if I go to sleep every night whispering the names of all the people I'll never see again, what of it? All that matters, is that Peter and Danaxe don't know about it.*

"It's going to be rough," said Peter. "At least two of the Five Civilized Tribes in Indian Territory have allied with the Confederacy, while the Cherokee are busy with their own civil war over which side to join. Listening to two white guys who show up out of nowhere isn't gonna be on their agenda."

Anton nodded. "Showing them what awaits is our best bet. We do have some advantages, though. Just three years ago, most of the Five Tribes were working together. We've a copy of the 1905 Sequoyah Statehood Convention's proposed Constitution."

At that Peter brightened as Anton knew he would. "Sequoyah. For once, we get to sell a group on their own idea, not something we pull out of our magic-slash-technology."

"I was going to say our asses."

"To everyone we've met so far, it's the same thing."

The journey was long, and grew rougher as they moved west. In Ohio, the consist changed, and the luxury car was removed, as three passengers were not enough to justify the expense. Anton missed the luxury of velvet covered seats, good food, and ready service, but the people back here were certainly much more fun. Many were immigrants looking for a better life in the west. Others simply wanted to be away from the fighting. And nearly all were delighted to be sharing a car with Danaxe.

As always throughout the trip, Danaxe provided medical advice, a listening ear or stimulating conversation—whatever was called for at the moment. Anton was both content and amused to play the role of her sidekick. Peter practiced his German on an immigrant family who had the bad luck to arrive in the land of opportunity just months before it went to war with itself. He grew thoughtful as he came to see that this family, along with a few others, were also heading to Indian country—in the hopes of grabbing land for themselves, and the belief that the First Peoples could do nothing to stop them.

"Learn what you can," sighed Anton when Peter told him. "This, too, is part of history. Maybe we're here for something as simple as preventing a fight, or brokering a deal that leads to peaceful coexistence."

"Somehow, I don't think that's going to be very simple," said Peter.

In southern Missouri they ran out of railroad. After that, it was stagecoach and rented horses through towns that made all three feel like they were in a Western movie. They had planned to buy a team of horses and a wagon, but decided on a horse and packs for each of them in the hope that when they crossed into Indian territory they wouldn't look like the land grabbers they'd met earlier.

It was late October when the three time - travelers left the official United States—but it was hardly noticeable. Farms grew cotton or fruits and vegetables. Christian churches were prominent in many communities. Some more traditional ceremonial lodges were recognizable, but Anton found the place disturbingly... white.

"Why weren't they granted statehood?" Anton suddenly demanded as they reached a small Cherokee town controlled by Stand Watie, who would be the last

Confederate general to surrender. "I know I'm from a different time, but this looks like any place on the frontier. People working farms, attending Christian churches, and most looking pretty damned white! Half the people we've seen even dress like white farmers. Richard Pratt would love this place!"

"Maybe this is where he got the idea for his schools," said Danaxe.

"Maybe he should have put these folks in charge," Peter said moodily.

They rode through land flatter than any Anton had seen. Sometimes it felt surreal. Danaxe showed impressive calm as they passed black slaves held by the Cherokee. Anton wished they could have chosen one of the other tribes, but the fact was, most of them were slave-owning as well. "I just wish after all the time we've spent here, we had more than just a letter of introduction to John Ross and a copy of the Cherokee Phoenix newspaper," Danaxe said. "And we don't even know where to find John Ross!"

"Hey, we know exactly where to find Stand Watie," said Anton. "If you think we'll have better luck with him—"

"Knock it off, you two!" said Peter. "We've discussed this a million—"

"You folks lost?"

All three looked down from horseback at a woman standing in a seedy cornfield that met the track they were riding down—it wouldn't be right to call it a road. She looked to be about thirty, as faded and frayed as the red gingham dress she wore, and clearly mixed blood.

"Well, yes," Anton replied, while Peter looked annoyed and Danaxe just looked cautious.

"What you lookin' for?"

"John Ross," said Peter. "And yes, we know we're in the wrong place. We were about to flip a coin to decide between Texas and Kansas."

The woman shook her head as if she didn't have time for games, but her hazel eyes kept straying to the worn black leather medical bag tied securely behind Danaxe's saddlebag. "You with some kind of medicine show?" she asked suspiciously.

At that, Peter and Anton laughed. Danaxe managed a smile. "Not us," said Anton.

"Folks sick at your place?" Danaxe asked gently.

The woman's face grew hard, and then sagged as though in defeat—or exhaustion. "Everyone. Except for me. So far."

"Danaxe here is a trained nurse. And a root woman," Peter added. "If you need help, she's the best you will find. At least coming down this road today," he amended quickly.

"Come on, then." She turned without another word and led them around the cornfield to a run-down cabin beside a narrow stream. A trickle of smoke rose from the chimney, but the place looked as worn and shabby as the woman who lived there. "If you're lookin' for work, I could sure use some help. I can't pay much, but I can cook, and there's room for three bedrolls by the fire—" she kept her back straight, but her head turned away, as if afraid they'd find her offer ludicrous. Or perhaps she was afraid of worse. Anton noted the tooled leather belt that hugged her waist— complete with knife and pistol. This damsel might be in distress, but she wasn't helpless.

They tied the horses to a post near the cabin

with grass for grazing well within reach. The men removed their packs; Danaxe took only her medical bag. They followed their hostess into the cabin and found a large single room that had not been cleaned in many days. Dirty dishes were piled in one bucket, dirty rags in another, while a plank table near the fireplace was heaped with all manner of herbs, food, bowls and packets. The smell of sickness and a pervading fecal odor dominated. In a dimly lit corner opposite the fireplace were two beds. A man moaned and writhed on one of them. On the other lay a listless boy of about eight.

Danaxe went straight to the man. "I need light!" she called over her shoulder.

The woman lit a hurricane lamp with a bit of kindling from the fire and brought it over.

"My name is Peter. My friends are Anton and Danaxe—a free woman. What may we call you?" Peter asked the woman.

She looked startled, as if seeing them all for the first time. Impressed by their good manners, or wondering at Peter's strange speech? That was one of the problems with time travel.

"Tayana," she answered. Anton smothered a laugh. If he remembered correctly, the name meant *beaver.* And he wasn't about to risk getting it wrong. Or commenting at all.

The man on the bed began to shout words in Cherokee while Danaxe tried to examine him. Anton was fairly sure he heard "jigaboo," as well as words that meant "dirty" and a few colorful terms for white people.

Tayana hissed something that probably meant "shut up", and then turned to her visitors. "My brother,

Toantuh." Anton was surprised that Tayana looked very embarrassed. When he glanced at the boy, he too, managed to look embarrassed despite his listlessness.

"Please ask your brother Toantuh if it hurts anywhere besides his stomach," Danaxe said.

There was a rapid exchange. "He says his body is on fire," Tayana translated.

"I'm well aware of his fever." Danaxe turned to the others. "It's dysentery. The boy, too, I presume." She moved to the other bed. The child mumbled at her gentle ministrations, but nothing else. "Your son?" she asked.

Tayana nodded and caught her breath. Embarrassment was replaced by fear. "Yes. Little Frog."

"Have you changed the place you get water from recently?" Danaxe asked.

Again Tayana looked startled. "Yes. About ten days ago we had to start using the creek. We shared a well with a neighbor, but she and I quarreled. My husband went to fight for the Union, hers for the Rebs and—"

"Now, where else have I heard that story?" Anton interrupted. "Oh, yes. Every goddamned place we've been since—" Peter coughed loudly. "Sorry ma'am," Anton said quickly. "Please forgive my language."

Suddenly, Tayana laughed. "I could probably out-cuss you in three languages, laddie," a true Scottish brogue appearing in her voice.

"You probably could," Anton began, but Danaxe cut him off.

"The sickness came from the water." Danaxe finished.

"Can you help them?" The laughter was gone from her voice as though it had never been.

"Yes. Your brother should be fine in a few days once we get his fever down, and make sure he drinks safe water. And keep him clean," she added, as the smell of loosened bowels came their way. Danaxe showed no reaction, but Anton gagged and moved toward the open door.

"And... the boy?"

"He's lost a lot of flesh. He needs food that he can keep down. I have some things that will help, but first…" Danaxe looked at the three others who were standing and did what Anton knew she would: played a more believable drill sergeant than either he or Peter could ever do. "Fill the biggest pots you have with water," Danaxe ordered Tayana, while she built up the fire. "No one drinks any water from that stream that hasn't been boiled, understood?" Everyone nodded mutely, and Tayana hurried outside with a battered tin kettle and a large copper pot.

"This place and those two boys need to be cleaned up." Danaxe discreetly gave Peter and Anton each a pair of kitchen latex gloves, identical to the ones she now wore. "Get to it. Any clean rags left?" she asked Tayana as she returned with the water.

Tayana, now moving in a daze, went to a shelf above the boy's bed and pulled a blanket from it. Drawing the knife from her belt, she began cutting it into rough squares. With six or seven thrown onto the table, she began ripping the blanket with just her hands. Danaxe watched for a few moments, then gently took the remains of the blanket from her. "Enough," she said firmly. "You be needin' the rest of this cloth come winter." Tayana, now swaying on her feet, looked at

Danaxe blankly.

"How long since you slept?" Danaxe asked. When no response was forthcoming, she shook her head. "Never mind, I don't want to know." She guided Tayana to the bedrolls that Peter had set up by the now much cleaner and more organized hearth. "Rest here until I get your bed clean enough to be safe." If Tayana understood, she gave no sign, but she curled up on Danaxe's blankets and was soon snoring.

By nightfall, Toantah's fever had broken, and both he and Little Frog had been able to drink—and more importantly, keep down—the broth and tea Danaxe had fed them. The place was clean and organized, Tayana was awake and enjoying a good meal with her uninvited, but useful, guests.

"What did you put in this chicken?" Tayana asked Danaxe. "I couldn't even sell those scrawny things after they stopped laying last month."

"Just some herbs I had with me, plus an onion I found in your root cellar."

"Like those herbs you used to cure my menfolk?" There was no longer suspicion or even wonder in their hostess's voice as she stripped meat from bone with slightly crooked teeth. Only interest and gratitude.

"Common things, really," said Danaxe. "Willow bark for fever. Kapok bark and seeds for the dysentery. Sage for the chicken." She smiled and picked up an ear of roasted corn, eating while Tayana spoke.

"Willow I know of. I tried to give some to both my brother and my son. Toantah just threw it back up. Little Frog took some, but it didn't help much. That other thing? Kapok? What is that?"

"A tree that grows south of here," Danaxe answered cautiously.

Anton knew she didn't want to have to explain where her medicines came from. "Are there others who might be drinking from that creek?" he asked, setting down a cob that he'd completely stripped of kernels. "If so, we should check in on them. This sickness can be... well, you already know, ma'am."

Tayana's gaze traveled to each of them. "One or two, maybe. I'll not argue with your good works, but I'd thank you mightily if you could stay a bit longer. Just until the boys are well, and the corn crib is full."

Anton, who had been about to take another ear of corn, dropped his hand. For the second time that day, Tayana laughed. "Oh, take it! You picked it. Besides, if you work, you eat." She shrugged as if to say it was simple logic. Peter and Danaxe laughed softly, while Tayana gazed at them all again with too-perceptive eyes. "You ain't farm folk, are you?"

Anton had enjoyed his afternoon outdoors, pulling the last of the withered corn and beans from the field, and filling Tayana's corn crib—although not as high as he would have liked. He liked being useful where he could enjoy the wide blue sky and red clay earth, away from the smell of sickness and the monotony of hauling water and firewood and washing linens and clothes in a bucket. "No, ma'am" he said at last. "We ain't farmers."

"You work as hard as any," Tayana said. "And you don't ask for any pay but food and a place to sleep. And you cooked most of the food yourselves. Missionaries?" Her black eyebrows snapped together, and the suspicion returned.

At that they all laughed. "Not missionaries,"

said Peter. "At least, not the religious kind. We're with a different group, hoping to make some changes after the war."

"What kind of changes?" Not suspicious now; just curious. With her long black hair hanging loose and the fear and exhaustion gone from her face, Anton found Tayana very attractive. *You're tired*, he told himself.

"For one, we hope to see Indian Territory join the Union as a state."

"Sequoyah?" Tayana asked.

"Yes!" said Anton. He never got tired of hearing the sound of the name, and all it might represent.

"Best be careful, speakin' of the Union as the winners," Tayana cautioned. "Most folk round here be cheerin' for the other side. But I admit, if my man comes home in one piece, Sequoyah's the place I'd like to live in."

"We're also hoping for a nation without slavery," said Danaxe. "And if you don't mind my asking, how do you folks justify it? I can see taking up with the Rebs. They've promised you your own land, and the folks in Washington done nothing but lie to you and break deals. But the Trail of Tears wasn't that long ago. Why do to others what hurt you so much?"

Tayana looked surprised, but then seemed at a loss for words.

"Maybe now isn't the time, Danaxe," Peter said.

"No, it is all right," said Tayana. "But... 'Trail of Tears'? I never met anyone who wasn't Cherokee call it that. Not even my pa." Her gaze grew distant.

"Scottish?" Anton asked.

Tayana nodded. "He lived with my mother's

clan as a youngster. One of them adventurous boys who ran off to play Indian. But unlike most, he didn't leave us when things got tough. I was just a baby when John Ross went to the Supreme Court and won our case. Them powerful men actually said we had the right to keep our land."

"And then President Jackson said, 'now let the court enforce their ruling,' " Peter intoned sadly.

"I guess they weren't so powerful," Tayana said with the same note of sadness. "It weren't a good time to be an Indian, or friends with one. But my pa left his smithy and his white family and came with us."

Anton didn't want to ask, but no one else was speaking up. "Did he die on the Trail?"

"No. My older sister did, and my ma almost. It was my pa's strength that kept us alive. Ma always said he used himself up, getting us here, startin' this farm." Tayana looked around her one-room home, lip curled as though not impressed with the trade. "He died when I was eight. Same age Little Frog is now. Ma married Toantah's pa soon after. Said he was a good man once. A spiritual leader who studied with Sequoyah. But on the Trail, something inside him broke."

The three visitors sat in silence. It was a story they all knew well.

"Sickness," called a voice from the bed across the room.

Danaxe was on her feet an instant before Tayana. They both went to Toantah, Danaxe grabbing her bag along the way. They hurried to Toantah, but it quickly found it wasn't dysentery he was speaking of.

"Get away from me, Jigaboo," he told Danaxe as he sat up in bed. "I am well enough! I need no meddlesome woman around me."

"That meddlesome woman saved your life!" snapped Tayana, her cheeks red with embarrassment. "And her name is Danaxe." With one hand she pushed her younger brother back against the pillows. He flushed angrily when he found he was too weak to get back up. "She saved Little Frog, too, in case that matters to you!"

Toantah flushed again, but his lowered eyes and tug at his blankets suggested embarrassment this time. "Of course it matters! And I am glad you are well, sister." With a quick glance at Danaxe he muttered, "Thank you."

"You're welcome," Danaxe said pleasantly. She brought more broth and tea to Toantah, while Tayana did the same for her son.

"Real food, woman!" Toantah demanded.

"If your fever stays down and you get through the night without needing help to the outhouse," Danaxe said, "you can start on solids tomorrow."

Toantah looked like he was about to argue—or possibly throw his bowl at Danaxe—but he took the food and medicine without further comment.

"So," said Anton, when Little Frog was resting comfortably in his bed, watching the strangers with wide, intelligent eyes, "about the question of slavery?"

Peter shot him an angry look, but looked interested despite himself.

"My family has none," Tayana said. "We couldn't afford them and I wouldn't own people even if I could. But from what I hear, Cherokee treat their slaves better than the whites do."

"I'm not sure that's saying much," said Danaxe.

"They treat them better than whites treat us," said Toantah. "How's that?"

"Better, I suppose," said Danaxe. "Of course, it couldn't be much worse."

"Our people did not practice slavery until the whites came," Toantah said, sneering over his cup of tea. "My father always said it was just one more way of trying to fit into white culture, like adopting your religion and notions of owning land. You certainly enjoy owning things. So why not people?"

Danaxe smiled. "Strange that you're looking at the only black face in the room while saying that. Still, everyone who's been hurt gets to decide how to react. Hurting others in the same manner is one option. I just hope I never choose it."

Toantah opened his mouth, but no words came out. He turned to glare at the two men. "They are probably Union spies," he told his sister. "Or land grabbers. Or worse."

"If they wanted to take advantage of me, or rob the house or scalp Little Frog," Tayana said, "they had plenty of time while you were too weak to stop them."

Anton stifled a gasp, but his head whipped around to look at the boy, who was listening intently to every word. Little Frog seemed untroubled by his mother's assessment of the situation, but that didn't make Anton less angry.

"Hate us if you want," he snapped. "But don't traumatize the kid!"

At their blank looks, Anton realized he'd forgotten his local speech. Then again, maybe it wasn't "traumatize" that confused them, but rather the notion of protecting a child from a common reality.

Toantah shot Anton a hate-filled glare. "So should we lie to him? Tell him to believe every white man who claims to be his friend?" He looked again at

Tayana. "If they are spies, and the Great Chief in Washington wins this war, they will kill us, just for being Cherokee, since Stand Watie is leading the soldiers of Lincoln's enemies."

"And what if we can change Great Chief Lincoln's views on the First Peoples of this land?" asked Peter. "If we could convince him and the other leaders to make this territory into the state of Sequoyah? Would you turn all that energy and intelligence you're using to hate your enemies into helping your people, Toantah?"

Toantah stared at Peter a moment, and then laughed. "To be his dogs in a pet Indian state? It would be just another treaty with white men. And we all know what happens to treaties." He lay back on the bed and closed his eyes.

"He needs rest," said Danaxe. "We all do. Although I wouldn't mind locking him and Lincoln in a room together for a few hours when this war is over."

"You'd just start another one," said Tayana. "And do you always speak of your president with such disrespect?"

"We prefer to think of it as familiarity," said Anton. "And humor. None of us would have survived this long without humor."

"You are very strange," said Tayana, yawning. "And I am glad you are here."

"Let's all get some sleep," said Peter.

Chapter 14

Three days later, Peter, Anton and Danaxe packed their belongings and prepared to leave Tayana's home. Toantah and Little Frog were well enough to recover without Danaxe's care, the last of the harvest had been brought in and Tayana was feeling rested and strong. The one other family in the area who had been struck with dysentery was on the mend, with many more hands and an experienced healer to oversee their recovery.

"John Ross is in Coldwater, Kansas," Tayana whispered to Peter as they made their farewells. "At the house of a friend named Sykes."

Peter froze, his practiced smile and ready wit completely deserting him. "How do you —?"

"He is a distant cousin of mine," Tayana said with a self-deprecating shrug. "Many here know his location; we just keep quiet. There is a price on his head, after all."

"So why tell us?" Peter asked.

"My way of saying thank you for all you've done." Tayana's gesture took in the clean and repaired cabin, the nearly full corn crib and her recovering family. "And because I believe the crazy stories you have told me. At least enough to think that if we're to become part of the United States, I want John Ross for our first governor." She laughed out loud at the strangeness of that last part.

"You are welcomed to live in the state of Sequoyah, sister," said Toantah, joining them. Seen at his full height, nearly at his full strength, the young man was not someone most would want to fight with. "But everything these crazy strangers have told us only opened my eyes—and what I behold is the opposite of what you see."

"If joining those who keep with our older traditions will make you happy—or at least help you find peace—then I wish you well," Tayana told her brother.

"As do I," said Anton. "Because this country is going to need those ways, and the elders who can teach them—especially the whites."

Toantah shook his head, but much of his anger was gone. "If you could only promise I would live to see such a thing."

"We can hope," said Danaxe. "And we do. For now, that's all we can offer."

***

Danaxe quietly led her horse to the nearby cabin. As she lead the trio towards her goal, Danaxe reviewed what she knew of the Cherokee. No public displays of anger, and don't go directly to the point of her conversation. Too soon for her comfort, she spotted a it, slightly larger than Tayana's, with a classic covered well, a bucket hanging from a rope attached to an axle with a crank handle. Danaxe thought she saw movement at a window.

Silently, she rode up to the fence around the cabin proper, noting that like Tayana's, it was in poor repair. Danaxe dismounted, and looped her mount's reins around the top rail. She reached into the saddlebag, and pulled out a bundle of tobacco, tied in a red cloth. While Peter and Anton stayed in their saddles, Danaxe stepped through the gate, careful not to look directly at the house.

As she was wearing her split riding skirt, she knelt in the front yard on the parched grass. She placed the cloth bundle before her. In front of her was a corral containing a handful of horses and a water trough. Danaxe silently recited one of her daily meditations. When she finished that, noting that whoever was in the house did not appear to be interested in coming out, Danaxe began to speak.

"I have come by to let you know that the stream that Tayana and her other neighbor are using is tainted. Any water taken from that stream needs to be boiled before using. Additionally, I wanted to let you know that Tontuah and Little Frog will survive. I was lucky in coming across them when I did. Tayana did not sicken." Danaxe made sure her voice carried through the shuttered window, although she did not look in that direction.

"Across the United States and the Confederacy, there are neighbors whose menfolk are fighting on different sides, making neighbors angry and afraid of each other. Others are willing to let the soldiers settle their differences on battlefields, and keep the peace at home. I think of my neighbors whose menfolk fight for the Confederacy. I, for obvious reasons, do not care for the Confederacy, but I do not take my anger over slavery, and use it to harm my neighbors. I used to think that the saddest thing that could happen would be for neighbors to die in the same battle, on opposite sides. How sad it would be for their families.

"But I have learned a greater fear. For our menfolk to return, and to find one family had so taken out their anger on the other, that they would find their loved ones dead, at their neighbor's hand. I can only imagine the outcome of that with sheer dread of what harm it would bring about. Family feuds are ugly monsters, and never ending. I hope and pray all your men return to find their families in good health, and trusting that their people worked to take care of each other during these troubled times. I must continue my journey. I hope yours improves."

Danaxe quickly and quietly recovered her mount's reins, mounted, and rode off in silence, behind her companions. As she made her last turn to catch up, she thought she saw a woman at the window, her hand over her mouth, and tears silently spilling down her cheeks and hand.

"Okay. I'm curious,"Anton asked as they rode off, "What is in that cloth bag you left behind?"

"Tobacco. As I came to ask her to do something, I came bearing a gift. I have read that the Lakota tie such bundles to the horns of buffalo using red cloth, that adorns a sweat lodge," replied Danaxe

"Huh," said Peter, "I know about the Lakota doing that. And I once heard at a science fiction convention that California Ohlone do that same wrapping. I'm not sure that the Cherokee follow that custom. Hopefully, she will recognize the gift for what is intended, even if the wrapping was not traditional."

"Like Danaxe said," Anton told him. "We can hope. I'm starting to think it's our stock in trade."

***

One month later, the three sat in a cozy parlor, the men on a sofa, Danaxe on a stool beside John Ross, whose large body filled the great chair. The fire that roared in the fireplace was nearly enough to keep the cold from the freezing winter winds at bay.

The Cherokee leader stared at the book his guests had given him. The 1996 paperback edition of *The Cherokee People: The Story of the Cherokees from Earliest Origins to Contemporary Times*. Ross had not spoken a word since he had begun reading over an hour ago. Next to it lay the proposed Sequoyah State Constitution from the 1905 Statehood Convention, which was rejected in 1906, when Congress decided that opening the land up for white settlement was a better idea. Now, at last, he looked long and hard into each of the faces surrounding him and asked, "Why do you show me these things?"

Chief John Ross was old, and in poor health, although Peter knew Danaxe was doing her best to change that. The anger and despair on his dignified face broke Peter's heart. "Because we hope to change them," he said.

"I do not believe the stories you have told of travelling through time," Ross said. "But this?" He looked again at the book, then pushed it from him so it crashed onto the table beside him. "This, I believe. Reservations, poverty, despair, the young turning to strong drink so they do not see it. What do you think you can do to change all that?"

"The key lies with Lincoln," Anton began, but Peter silenced him with a look.

John did not appear to notice. "Lincoln hates the red man. Even us civilized tribes." He shook his head and looked like he'd bitten something sour.

"I can't tell you how we hope to change the past—your future," said Peter. "But I can tell you this much. When you see Danaxe's picture in the newspaper, be ready to travel to Washington."

The Cherokee man glanced at the nurse beside him, then at the table where recent issues of The Kansas City Star and the Cherokee Advocate lay open. He looked puzzled. "I assume you mean in a context that does not involve a sale price?"

Peter's jaw dropped while Anton's eyes doubled in size. Danaxe merely said, "Yes, Chief Ross, that's what he means. Now, if you'll be kind enough to follow my advice and stay healthy enough to travel to Washington—and make it back home alive—one day soon you and I will gather up all the newspapers that advertise slaves for sale and put them where they belong."

"The outhouse?" Ross asked, with the hint of a smile.

"No," Danaxe said, fingering the silver necklace Chief Ross had given her. "Museums. I especially want to see issues of the Cherokee Advocate there. While there are many from my future who don't know there ever was such a newspaper, there are plenty more who don't believe that Indians kept African slaves. I hope to see to it that those in the new future know both."

There was an uncomfortable pause.

Finally Peter said, "Thank you for your hospitality, Chief Ross. We will leave in the morning."

"Where to?" asked their host.

"North," said Anton. "To the land of Lakota Sioux."

"Are you mad?" John began, but his words disappeared into a fit of coughing. When he could speak again he continued. "Those people are savages!" At the stunned looks of his guests—except for Anton, who was trying not to laugh—he added, "Yes, I know. Many call my tribe that as well. But the Lakota... they're as likely to kill you as speak to you."

The three exchanged uneasy glances. "We are aware of that risk," Peter finally said. "But our plan depends on gaining their trust. So we go."

"Then I wish you well," said John. "May Christ and the Great Spirit both protect you."

Chapter 15

Spring felt more like summer when they reached Fort Laramie, Wyoming. Danaxe thought it looked more like the set of a Western movie than a real place, but then, she'd been feeling that way a lot lately. It was strange, she reflected, as she stretched the kinks from her back after stepping down from the stagecoach, that after more than eight months, the past still felt unreal.

"The place looks more like a California mission than a frontier fort," Peter said, taking in the blocky, squarish building with a high watchtower and nearby stables. "I thought there'd be a wall... uh, stockade around it."

"That's the Hollywood version," Danaxe said. The three gazed at the lone wagon train, getting ready to move west, while settlers loaded the last of their newly purchased supplies and hurried to their wagons. They were more interested, however, in the cluster of tipis outside the fort.

"So, we're just going to walk over to a group of strangers who've learned to hate white folks on sight, and ask them for a ride to Lakota territory?" asked Anton.

"The atmosphere here is likely to be tense," agreed Peter. "Most of the troops are volunteers, since the regulars are busy back east at the party we just left. But the First Peoples we'll meet are probably here to trade."

"Or are working as scouts for the Army," said Danaxe. "Either way, it looks peaceful enough. We have cash for horses, and sugar and tobacco to give as gifts."

"And we have you, a genuine medicine woman, with roots from a faraway land, and skin the color of magic," said Peter.

Danaxe's response was lost in the ringing of a blacksmith's hammer, the stomp of boots and voices calling in a variety of languages as they approached the busy fort. They slowed as they passed the temporary dwellings of the First Peoples—Cheyenne, Kiowa, and Lakota —and offered the greetings they had learned since making their leap backwards in time.

None of the responses were friendly.

"Let's try inside the fort," Anton suggested. "We can see about buying horses; maybe hear some news."

They didn't make it to the inside of the fort. Just outside the main gate, where a drunk guard was leaning against a post, an argument that could have given the Battle of Gettysburg a run for its money was underway.

"Keep your filthy injun hands off of the white woman, you damned half-breed!" a slightly more sober guard was yelling. Two soldiers were struggling with a man dressed in the clothing of a Lakota warrior. Another soldier was pulling a young red-haired woman away from the warrior, though she struggled like a wild cat to stay near him. Danaxe didn't like the way the man was handling the girl, and she liked his leering face even less.

"She's my wife!" yelled the struggling man.

"And he is my husband!" cried the redhead in heavily accented English.

"This warrant says you are one Elizabeth Godwin," said a fourth man, who wore the uniform of a

Union sergeant. "Taken captive by the Lakota at age six. Rescued three months ago—"

"Rescued!" the woman spat into the face of her tormentor. He froze, and then backhanded her across the face. Off balance, she fell hard onto the dry ground.

"There's our cue," Anton muttered as Danaxe ran to the woman and Peter approached the sergeant with a stride that looked more military than anything the actual uniformed soldiers could muster.

"I see no need to strike a woman or violently separate two people who clearly wish to be together," Peter said. "I am sure this matter can be solved peacefully."

The sergeant nearly stood at attention. Then he did a double take, noticed Danaxe and rounded on Peter. "Who the hell are you?" he demanded.

"Concerned citizens," Peter said. "We are on our way to Lakota Territory, and are seeking an escort that will get us there alive, and keep us alive once we get there."

"Or at least increase our odds," Anton added.

Danaxe was still bending over the woman. Momentarily stunned, she lay motionless, and then leapt up, pushing Danaxe away. A ripple of laughter from the soldiers died as Danaxe recovered, danced backward and regained her feet—and her composure—with artistic precision.

"No one touch me!" hissed the redhead.

"I would advise all of you to listen to her," Danaxe said. "And while we are all busy not touching each other, can you two offer proof that you are married? White man's proof, I mean?"

"You uppity, nigger wench--" began the man who had struck the woman.

"I was just getting to that," said the warrior. "I would like to take some paper from my vest, if you folk can keep from getting itchy trigger fingers."

The white men's expressions ranged from confused to outraged, but they kept their hands in plain sight. The mixed race man offered a stained and creased document to the sergeant. "Snowbird and I were married this morning by a Methodist minister in a church about ten miles from here."

"That ain't the name on this document... William Hawthorn," sneered the sergeant.

"He would not accept our tribal names," said William.

Throughout this exchange, Snowbird had remained silent, her gaze to the north, her lips moving in silent prayer.

The sergeant shoved the marriage license back to the groom. "It looks legit," he said.

"She ain't old enough to marry," said the man who had been holding Snowbird. "Our job's to hand her back and let her folks decide."

"How old are you, Snowbird?" Anton asked.

She turned startled green eyes to him. "Seventeen winters, by the white reckoning. But White Cloud has been my husband for two years."

One of the men took a step back. "Let her go then! You think her family wants her back now?"

"Ain't for us to say," began her captor, and now his leer had taken over his face. "But if they don't, I can think of some use for her."

"She's of age and they's married," pronounced the sergeant. He turned to the young couple. "You two best be gone from my fort before sundown." He glanced at the unsettling newcomers. "And if you can take them with you, so much the better!"

***

That afternoon, all five rode out of Fort Laramie on good horses, two pack animals trailing behind.

White Cloud, who had bounced between both worlds for most of his life, spoke easily with Peter and Anton. "Why do you want to meet Sitting Bull?" he asked. "He is not an important leader. And his clan has not been involved with the recent troubles—which, of course, has not stopped the Great Father in Washington from retaliating. White faces are not likely to be welcomed when we get there."

"What about black faces?" asked Danaxe.

"Those are rare enough to be more interesting than threatening," said White Cloud turning in his saddle to answer her. "You should be safe, if your two friends do nothing stupid."

Anton laughed. "Well then, we're all dead."

"And to answer your first question," said Peter. "We believe Sitting Bull will be interested in what we have to say. And that he might one day become an important leader."

Their guide nodded. "He is already a holy man. Part of why I agreed to take you to him is that I would like to meet him myself." White Cloud lowered his voice. "I also hope that he or someone else can help Snowbird. I fear the whites who took her away made her spirit sick."

Behind them, Danaxe was already working on the problem. After riding in silence, in accordance with Snowbird's refusal to speak, Danaxe suggested they rest.

The men agreed easily enough, but Snowbird snapped at her. "I am a woman of the Lakota! I can ride as hard as any man! And twice that of any white man!"

"But your baby is none of those things, yet — and will not be if you do not take care of both of you."

Snowbird's head snapped up. "How did you—?"

"Baby?" said White Cloud.

Snowbird switched to her second language, glaring at their uninvited traveling companions. But it was clear enough she was telling White Cloud that she meant to tell him when they were home, and alone.

"Is it... mine?" White Cloud gulped reverting to English, clearly terrified of the implications.

"How can you ask me that? Would I have returned to you at all if I had been so dishonored? The army men who took me away did no more than force me to speak this ugly tongue and wear those horrible clothes! I only learned of the baby after I had been locked in a room that was like a hole in the earth for more than a month. When I could no longer hide it, the man they claimed was my uncle beat me so I would lose it." Snowbird glared at the travelers. "He said he would brook no injun bastards in his house. When I recovered enough to run, I did."

"And if you want the child who will bless your marriage to live and thrive, you must listen to Danaxe," Anton said.

After that, they traveled in silence for the most part. The dry lands and wide blue sky of Wyoming passed by without comment. Snowbird slowly began to trust Danaxe, though she had nothing to say to the two men. At one point, she started having contractions, and it looked like she might lose the baby. Snowbird then refused to be parted from her nurse, and when the danger passed, all five of them celebrated, and traveled as a single group.

It was in the final days of spring that the party stood on a bluff and gazed down at a sight the time-travelers would remember forever.

They had missed the buffalo hunt, but the celebration in the camp below attested to its success. Meat of various cuts cooked over more than a dozen fires. Music and laughter filled the air. A few women worked to stretch thick furs on drying racks, but most of the camp was in full party mode.

"Can we join them?" Peter asked White Cloud. "We do not have much to contribute. Just some tobacco and sugar."

"And songs," said Snowbird. "And a healer who has proven she is willing to share her knowledge. And stories—never forget those."

"Even the crazy ones?" asked Danaxe.

"Especially the crazy ones."

White Cloud put his arm around Snowbird. "You are also returning a lost daughter to her family, and bringing new life to the tribe. I believe they will welcome you."

As they began to pick their way downhill to the gathering, Anton hung back and took a last look at the panoramic view the bluff afforded them. "This is cooler than *Dances With Wolves*," he said.

Peter looked back with a nearly manic grin. "Way cooler."

Chapter 16

White Cloud's introductions afforded all three travelers a place at the feast, but little else. Sitting Bull—if he was here—was not identified, and those who sought to change history knew better than to ask for him before they had gained the trust of their hosts.

Danaxe, after patiently enduring a few curious looks, fell in easily with the medicine women. It didn't take her long to identify the highest ranked woman, present her with the gift of several pouches of healing herbs, and begin a spirited discussion—all without either knowing more than a dozen words in the other's language.

Peter and Anton presented their carefully hoarded tobacco, along with an intricately carved wooden pipe in the shape of a wolf, made by one of Anton's 21st century friends, to the leader of the hunt, and found a much warmer welcome.

"If only I didn't have to worry about throwing up," Peter whispered after yet another obligatory toke.

Anton leaned against a cushion in the lodge, sleepy, overfed and more content than he'd been since his arrival nearly a year ago. "Go get some fresh air," he told his friend. "And maybe bring me another rib—"

"You've had enough!" Peter snapped, lurching from the crowded tipi, into blessedly fresh, cool air.

Anton looked blearily at the man next to him. "I've heard that at a bar before, but never at a dinner party," he said.

The warrior, a few years older than Anton, with scars visible nearly everywhere not covered by his festive clothing, nodded with what appeared to be perfect understanding. Anton drifted to sleep, contemplating what kind of woodsmoke gave the bison hides that formed the tipi its unique smell.

At some later time, he was shaken awake. "They want to hear you play," Peter was saying.

Disoriented and annoyed, Anton was about to tell Peter he could go play with himself, when he saw that Peter held Anton's treasured fiddle —and not very carefully.

"Give me that!" snapped Anton, now fully awake. "This thing has survived more than we have. I'm not about to lose it now." Despite his angry words, Anton allowed Peter to guide him through the camp, as the firelight, noise and general chaos of the place left him a bit unsteady.

In a cleared space, people were dancing to the music of flutes and drums. The dancing wasn't much like what he remembered from old movies, but Anton could see that at least a few directors had seen and heard something like this, and let it seep into their films. Anton soon found a spot beside a flute player about his own age. For a while, he just listened and watched. When he felt his body swaying in time to the music, Anton lifted his bow and slowly joined in, improvising, blending his strings to the woodwinds and percussion notes around him.

A white-haired drummer looked up in surprise, and then nodded at Anton in the universal language of music. "I get you," he seemed to say. The flute player next to him adjusted his playing so the flute followed the fiddle. There was no obvious feedback from the dancers, but everyone had a good time, and that was enough.

Soon, Peter joined the dance with a young, and, if her clothing were any indication, high-ranked Lakota woman. Anton chose to keep playing, although he knew he could probably wrangle an invitation to dance if he tried. Danaxe stayed with the healers. And so the evening passed into night, and the party continued.

The locals outlasted the visitors, which was a good thing, since the next morning everyone got up with the sun whether they wanted to or not. Nothing was said directly to the trio of outsiders: they simply mounted their horses and rode with the tribe, to what White Cloud said would be their home for the summer.

Snowbird's Lakota mother, Mahkah, a widow with no other living children, had been singing her joy at having her daughter back since their arrival. She wasn't much of a musician, but Anton could not help sharing in her happiness. Life was hard in this part of the world, and so much more so for anyone without family. The return of her only child, now pregnant with her first grandchild, and a son-in-law to help provide for her, would change everything for Mahkah, whose gaunt frame and grief-ravaged face now showed signs of healing. At Snowbird's invitation, Anton, Peter and Danaxe shared the small family's campfire at night and slept nearby, but it was clear that Mahkah was uncomfortable with their presence.

"Do you think it's because we're white?" Peter asked as they rode side by side on their third day with the tribe. "Like maybe she thinks we're going to try to steal Snowbird away from her again?"

Anton rubbed his scraggly brown beard, which had never grown back as well as he'd hoped. "More like we just remind her of the people who took her in the first place. Her son-in-law is half white, and her daughter's hair is redder than yours."

"Maybe she just wants to enjoy her family's return without the presence of outsiders," said Danaxe, riding up. "Mahkah seems pretty high strung these days. Or maybe always."

Anton couldn't argue or even complain. It was just another reminder of how easy it was to create a family—for everyone except him.

Days passed before the trio got their first lucky break. An ill-tempered warrior named Otaktay, which translated into English as the daunting phrase, "Kills Many," punched Danaxe in the face when she was slow moving out of his way. While she regained her feet, Otaktay shouted various curses at her that didn't require translation. White Cloud soon appeared to translate anyway.

"He's saying she's an ugly, bad luck woman," White Cloud said, as a crowd gathered. Most of the women Danaxe had befriended walked at various speeds to surround her. Wakunda, the medicine elder, stopped beside Danaxe to put an arm around her while giving her an appraising look. Satisfied that Danaxe wasn't injured, Wakunda stepped forward to the still shouting Otaktay, and began shouting at him.

"He says the dark woman isn't so ugly on her back in the dirt," White Cloud continued to translate. "Wakunda is telling Otaktay that he is a fool and a disgrace to his family." Otaktay turned and spoke to the clan chief. "Now he wants to claim your friend as a slave."

"Bad move," sighed Anton.

"This is exactly what we need," Peter said, looking excited for the first time in days. At Anton's glare, he continued. "Come on, you knew this was going to happen sooner or later."

"I was hoping for later," Anton said, but he understood Peter's view. While Danaxe and Anton had been busy making friends and learning what they could, Peter had been forced onto the sidelines. Unlike the other two, he had no skills to offer that the Lakota valued, except for a willingness to work—but mainly at things usually viewed as "women's work." Peter's diplomatic and political brilliance had to wait until the three achieved some status—which Danaxe was about to win them.

Wakunda continued to rant at Otaktay, but Danaxe caught her eye and motioned her aside. "White Cloud!" she called. "Please translate for me. Ask this man if he is as skilled with a bow as he is with his fists."

By now the watching crowd included nearly the entire band. Otaktay looked more surprised than angry, but he refused to answer Danaxe. Instead, he looked at the chief. When he only shrugged, Otaktay was forced to answer the question. But he spoke only to White Cloud, not looking at Danaxe. "More," he said. At this point, Wakunda whispered in Danaxe's ear.

"Then I challenge you to a test of skills, Otaktay, son of White Bear," Danaxe called loudly.

And the crowd goes wild, Anton thought, as everyone within earshot reacted with a heady combination of laughter, cheers, gasps and shouts. Anton's only reaction was to wonder how Danaxe knew the name of her antagonist's father.

"How dare this woman—?" Otaktay sputtered, but the chief cut him off.

"A challenge has been issued," the old man said mildly. "You can either accept it, or withdraw your insult to this woman, who is both my guest and a healer who is held in high regard by my sister." He nodded toward Wakunda.

Otaktay called one of his younger brothers to bring his bow.

"If I win," Danaxe said as Peter brought her the two tubes from her pack. "Otaktay will acknowledge me as a warrior of this tribe, and introduce me to Sitting Bull."

Several people were already running to set up an archery range in the flat open space beyond their camp. Others were calling out wagers to one another.

"When she loses, this witch will be my slave," Otaktay retorted.

"If you so insist," growled the chief, "then she must raise the stakes, for they are not remotely even. The woman does not try to take your freedom in what should be a friendly contest."

A stillness descended. "I will stake my horse, if you wish," Danaxe said calmly. "He is a fine animal. I will stake this necklace, though it was a gift from the greatest chief I have met so far in this land." Her fingers touched the jet and silver necklace John Ross had given her. "But I will be no man's slave. Ever."

As White Cloud continued to translate, the crowd murmured approval. The wagers continued, but it was clear the support of the crowd was moving in Danaxe's direction. Otaktay uttered a few curses. "Fine! The horse and the necklace."

"And if I win?"

That seemed to restore the Lakota man's good humor. "I will acknowledge you as a warrior and introduce you to my cousin Sitting Bull." He grinned like a man who knew he would win.

"This just got awkward," murmured Anton.

"Maybe. Maybe not," said Peter. "I don't think there's anyone else with that name. And even if they're related, it shouldn't be a big deal. Unless she has to kill this jerk."

"Then it might be a big deal," Anton agreed.

Danaxe left to change her clothes. The crowd grew restless when she didn't immediately return. When she finally exited the tent, the reason for the delay became obvious. Danaxe now wore the traditional pants and plain shirt of a samurai archer, carrying a long tube, and with a fur covered quiver on her back, with twenty arrows, thirty-nine inches long. As she walked up to the crowd, she stopped and gave a traditional bow to the elders. She then walked to where Otaktay waited; he visibly startled when she gave him the same bow.

The crowd grew noisy again when Danaxe removed her ninety-two inch samurai bow from its case. Otaktay frowned, and looked like he was about to object, but then shrugged, and made a gesture that Anton knew was a ward against evil. He chanted while he strung his bow. Danaxe did the same, although in a different tongue.

There was no need to ask for the location of the targets or the procedures of the contest. The crowd escorted the two combatants to their designated places, while at least a dozen members insisted on explaining what was to happen —in a variety of languages. As the explanations were being given, Danaxe kneeled in traditional fashion on the ground. Peter and Anton recognized she was sitting zazen, the Zen Buddhist meditation, as she chanted to herself, without vocalizing.

Even Snowbird approached, happier than Anton had ever seen her. "Each will take three shots," she told him, pointing at two targets, a pair of stumps. "Otaktay will go first, as he was the one challenged." Snowbird bit back a laugh as she gazed at Danaxe. She seemed almost mesmerized by the calm, sure-footed woman and her bow. Like many of the people Danaxe had helped with medical issues, Snowbird already held her in high regard.

The last bets were made, the chief called for silence from the crowd and witnessing from the spirits, and Otaktay raised his bow. The arrow flew and the crowd cheered as it hit dead center of his stump.

The crowd waited in silence for several minutes as Danaxe continued her razen. People began to whisper as Danaxe rose, walked up to her target, and then turned around and started walking back, counting aloud, "one, two…" each number matching a stride. At twenty five, Danaxe stopped. It took a moment for the crowd to realize she needed them to move. As the crowd made room, Danaxe kept walking until she finally counted, "sixty." She then stuck three arrows in the ground. Lastly, Danaxe strung her bow.

The crowd gasped in a mix of shock and surprise, as it became clear that the grip was only one third up the length of the bow, as opposed to being aligned for the center. Danaxe followed the samurai tradition of knocking the arrow, lifting the bow above her head, and then bringing it down as she fully pulled back the arrow. Without a pause, as she reached full pull, her gloved right hand released. At sixty paces, the impact of the arrow was surprisingly loud, and the arrow had obviously buried its head in the wood.

Otaktay first glowered at the target. He threw

down his bow in a fit of rage. The crowd hissed at him for his rudeness, and closed ranks between him and Danaxe. Then they realized he was not acting in anger. Puzzled, the crowd allowed him to pass. When he reached Danaxe, he stopped, two paces short of where she was standing, obviously thinking. Danaxe stood silently.

Otaktay attempted to mimic Danaxe's earlier bow to him. Danaxe responded in kind. Otaktay started speaking quickly. So fast in fact, that the translator had trouble keeping up.

"Otaktay first says that he is amazed at that shot. He could see the penetration, and he sees also that you hit the target dead center. He wants to know what you would have done if he had taken a shot at sixty paces?"

"Taken another thirty paces and destroyed the first arrow," she replied.

To everyone's surprise, Otaktay laughed, and spoke again. The translator spoke, "Otaktay says you have won the contest—but so has he. He wants you to show Sitting Bull what you can do with that bow. He also asks why is the grip so low on the bow?"

"So I can shoot from horseback."

"Otaktay asks how good you are without that bow?"

"I am not sure what he means by that."

"Otaktay wants to know how well you can fight for yourself without that bow." Peter and Anthony both broke up in laughter. With everyone looking at the two of them, Anton calmed down first.

"Well, I suggest that at sunrise, you come outside and find Danaxe," Anton said slowly, so the translator could keep up. "If she is sitting like she just was, sit back and wait. Then she will do one of four katas, practicing two different styles of combat, from across the western ocean. One is called Tai Chi. The other karate. She alternates between a slow one, and a fast one. Seriously? You don't want to mess with her."

"Mess?" asked the translator. "What does this have to do with cleaning?"

"Ah, sorry. I mean that if you get into a fight with her, you will come up very badly hurt or dead. She has never fought in a contest. And trust me on this, it shows in her katas. At her high speed, you can see that she means every move to land with maximum damage. At slow speed, you can see how every move will go exactly where it is supposed to be."

White Cloud and Otaktay spoke for a couple of minutes. Otaktay stared at Danaxe, obviously studying her. A quick spate of words ensued between the translator and Otaktay.

"Otaktay says he noticed you changed your clothing to use your bow. He wants to know if you need to change your clothes to fight without your bow?" Danaxe shook her head "no," obviously not liking the direction the conversation was going. White Cloud continued, "He also wants to know that if you did not participate in contests, did you at least practice against real people?" Danaxe nodded. "So, Otaktay asks that you allow him to use the same punch as when he hit you in the face, and that you defend yourself without hurting him."

"No," said Danaxe. "I will hurt him, but no worse than when he punched me in the face. It is unavoidable. Tai Chi is primarily used in China as a form of exercise, with the added benefit of teaching you how to defend yourself. If I do as he asks, there will be pain."

The translator conferred with Otaktay, who then laughed. He spoke to the translator, who then turned to Danaxe. "Otaktay notes that it is only fitting that he feels pains from your hands, as he has given you. His only request is that since he did not cause you life-long damage, that you give him the same benefit." Danaxe stared at Otaktay for a few moments, while the translation took place, and at the end of it, Otaktay laughed, and then spoke very briefly.

"Otaktay thanks you for your fairness in returning pain for pain. He is actually wanting to experience first-hand that a woman can do this, rather than spending his life wondering." Danaxe nodded, and reluctantly handed her bow to Anton. She then moved around Otaktay to open a safe place for the demonstration. Again, Many Kills bowed. Danaxe smiled as she took the bait and returned the bow instead of doing it simultaneously. As she started the bow, Otaktay threw his right-handed punch.

Again the crowd hissed. Danaxe took a half step back, and slapping the left side of her head with her left hand in a motion that planted the sharp point of her elbow on Otaktay's middle finger of his fist. A grin spread over Danaxe's face as she felt him try to slow, if not stop the follow through of the punch. Then watched as he went through the Lakota gyrations of non-verbally communicating "Wow —that really hurts!"

After a moment, Otaktay addressed the translator. "Otaktay asks if while on the way to meet Sitting Bull, could you teach him this style of fighting?"

"Tell him that as a favor, tomorrow I will change my schedule. I will start with a slow Tai Chi exercise form. We can start there. Starting with his bow."

When the translator finished, Otaktay turned to Danaxe and bowed slowly. Danaxe matched the slow speed, and very carefully used the moment to start teaching the eye contact of a martial arts bow, a smile crossing her face as she straightened.

Chapter 17

The tipi offered welcome shade from the searing heat of summer. Peter wondered briefly what the name of a state controlled by the First Peoples of this part of America would be called. It would be South Dakota if they failed. The land he knew as Oklahoma would be called Sequoyah if they succeeded, but this land… He hoped to find out today.

Turning his attention back to the endless formalities that the council meeting entailed, Peter gazed at Sitting Bull. As with Chamberlain, Peter marveled at seeing him live and in color. But what left Peter speechless this time was the man's beauty, vitality and laughter. This was not the man of the portraits Peter had seen. There was no air of tragic dignity, no lines carved into his face by pain and loss. Sitting Bull was in his mid-thirties, and only recently made a chief of the Hunkpapa sub-tribe of the Lakota. His warmth and charisma made it easy to see why men followed him. Given the chance, Peter knew he would as well.

The tipi was large, and easily held the dozen or so men who had come to hear Peter and Anton's story. They had hoped White Cloud would remain as translator, but Sitting Bull had insisted on a man from his own camp to translate for those present who did not speak English. Peter found the situation more daunting than he expected, and Anton hadn't spoken a word since the meeting began. Clearly some in this tipi wanted the two white men dead, and for now, only their status as Sitting Bull's guests kept them safe.

The argument wound down. For the third time, Peter went through his dog and pony show. For the movie, he showed "*Dances with Wolves.*" Anton showed the video he had taken of the elders watching Peter's show. Again Peter showed ZNN's Greenland Glaciers report, and then finished with a documentary on Wounded Knee.

Sitting Bull drew another breath from his pipe and at last addressed his visitors. "That is quite a story, my friends," he said in English.

Anton choked and for a moment, Peter was afraid he would laugh. Fortunately, one of the men who wanted them dead spoke before they could commit any social gaffs. "This is just another white devil trick," he said angrily. The translator kept the emotion out of his own voice, but nothing could disguise the young warrior's contempt for Peter and Anton—and their story. "They want our land, so they confuse us with talk of a terrible future, and promises of protection. Soon they will ask you to make your mark on a piece of paper. Then we will be told this land is now their land."

An ancient warrior, seated next to Sitting Bull nodded. "Such things have happened to many tribes already. And now white men are building houses on land that the latest treaty says is ours."

"We need no treaty to tell us what is ours!" shouted the young man who had spoken before.

"This is true," said Sitting Bull in a mild voice. "Yet never has the Great White Father in Washington sent men such as these to us. Men who carry no weapons to sit in council; no papers declaring them to be our friends who want only what is best for us, who then insult us with every word they speak." The leader shook his head. "These men are different, and against all reason, I believe they are speaking the truth."

"A madman speaks the truth," said another elder. "And for him, it is."

Anton finally spoke. "We are madmen," he said. "But the future we speak of will be painfully true for you and your children if we cannot find a way to change it. Those small bands of farmers who begin to encroach on your territory are only the beginning. Your lands will be stolen from you. Many of you will die, fighting bravely for your homes and way of life, but those who live will be penned on reservations, where many more will die of cold and hunger—and despair, perhaps more than anything. And your children—" Peter placed his hand on Anton's back. Anton turned to Peter.

"Things are already heated," Peter said quietly.

"Let him speak!" Sitting Bull told Peter. "His face loses color every time someone speaks the word 'children.' " To Anton he said, "You will be white in truth if this continues! So find your voice and tell us what even your clever-tongued friend is afraid to say."

Someone handed Anton a cup of water. He drank it down and began to speak. "When the soldiers take your weapons, they will take your children as well. Not all of them," Anton spoke into the hissing around him. "Many children will die of hunger and disease on the reservations. And some will grow up to live lives of despair at the injustice and humiliation inflicted on them. But many others will be taken to schools where they will be taught to live and speak and worship as the whites do. Their hair will be cut and they will be beaten, and worse, for speaking their own language. It is in this way that the whites currently in power hope to solve the problems that exist between your two peoples: to make your way of life cease to exist."

There was much angry muttering, followed by shouting. "We did not come here to bring discord," Peter called over the din.

"And yet you have!" For the first time, Sitting Bull spoke in anger. "And still you do not tell us how agreeing to become a state of your union—which is at last doing us the favor of destroying itself—will prevent this terrible future! Or why two strange white men should want to!"

The tent fell silent, and Peter spoke quietly. "If we succeed in making the changes we came here to make, then statehood will protect your freedom to live as you choose. You will not be signing papers initially. Others will write and speak and vote, and sign. You will then be presented with the law. You will be told what must be written, and how you will decide. Accept, and you will elect representatives who will go to Washington, and sit with the men—and soon women— from all of the states, and yours will have a voice equal to theirs. Those who wish to live as hunters, healers, musicians and spirit leaders will be able to do so. Those who are warriors will have to fight under the rules of the United States military—who will be lucky to have you! But some of you must choose to work with those in power who are white—and black and brown, if all goes as we hope—so that they will understand that they must respect your ways and your borders."

"And why must they do that?" asked the elder who had earlier spoken of madness.

Peter knew his uncertainty showed on his face. "That's the part we're not sure of. It depends on changing people's minds; their most fundamental beliefs—"

Into the growling and shouting that started up again, Anton spoke. "You asked a second question, Chief Sitting Bull. Why do two strange white men want to help? Or more accurately, why did three crazy people from the future give up their lives and fortunes to come here and meddle with the universe?" At that, most of those gathered settled back down to listen. The elder smiled, and nodded for Anton to continue.

Anton's certainty fled. "You better take this one," he whispered to Peter.

Peter shook his head. "You're doing fine right now."

Anton gulped more water. "We came here because our world is dying. Because those who have power now, and will have it for the next two centuries do not love the land as you do, nor do they understand the consequences of their actions." He looked at Sitting Bull. "You once said, or maybe will say, that the white man knows how to make everything, but does not know how to distribute it."

Sitting Bull's eyes widened in surprise. Anton pressed on. "That is what must be changed. We believe that if the hearts of just a few people can be changed, our future can be saved." He looked at each of the hard faces surrounding him. "*All* of our futures. But each of us has a role to play." Anton's gaze now rested on Sitting Bull. "Your role involves your love for this land. You will need to teach others to love it as much."

"Teach greedy whites to see that the earth is their mother?" Sitting Bull asked skeptically. "Make them want to stop defacing her with their buildings and their refuse?"

Anton and Peter looked at each other. "Yes,"

they said at once. "We know it sounds impossible…" Peter began.

"Whether they are liars or madmen," said the warrior closest to Sitting Bull. "We need not heed them. When those of their kind come to take our land— or anything else of ours-we will kill them. We do not need the help of these two." There were murmurs of agreement.

Sitting Bull stared hard at the two white men. "Yet my heart tells me we do."

"You should listen to your heart, Sitting Bull," called a new voice.

Chapter 18

Everyone turned to the open flap of the tipi. Many reached for weapons.

"Who comes unannounced to disturb my council?" Sitting Bull demanded.

A man entered the tent with a boy of about nine or ten years behind him. Both held up empty hands in the commonly understood gesture of "we come in peace." Their dress and hair showed them to be Paiute. Before the tent flap could fall closed behind the strangers, two Lakota warriors appeared, both looking confused. One appeared to have been struck speechless, while the others simply said, "They must be heard."

Sitting Bull nodded, waving away his guards. "Be welcome, friends," he told the strangers. At a gesture from the chief, food and drink were placed before the two newcomers, who sat down gratefully. Sitting Bull himself placed his pipe in the man's hands. "You have traveled a great distance to come here."

"Like, all the way from Nevada," Peter whispered.

Anton stared at the boy. "It can't be," he said, forgetting to whisper.

"I am Tavibo," said the Paiute man. "This is my son—"

"Wovoka!" Peter gasped.

Tavibo turned to gaze mildly at the two white men. "Ah, you would be the reason we have travelled all this way. My son has been having dreams—and not always when he sleeps. It was at his—rather frantic insistence —that we came here. Many thanks for not arriving in the dead of winter." It was only after the translator began speaking that Peter realized Tavibo had spoken entirely in English.

The child who would later become one of the most influential spiritual leaders of his time did not look frantic or manic or anything much more than an ordinary little boy. His gaze, when he held Peter's eyes, was the only thing that seemed extraordinary. After holding Anton's eyes the same way, Wovoka settled down and examined his surroundings, but made no move to speak.

"Tavibo, your name is known to us," Sitting Bull said.

"Not in the most flattering manner, I would imagine," Tavibo continued in English. But then, it was unlikely the translator knew the Paiute tongue.

The elder beside Sitting Bull nodded. "Some of your own people claim you have sold your souls to the whites. Others that you are a false prophet."

"Never the first," said Tavibo. "Though perhaps I am guilty of the second. I receive visions; messages I feel called to deliver, even if they are not to the liking of those I speak to. But the boy is a true vessel of the spirits. Of that I am certain."

When all eyes in the tipi were upon him, the boy spoke, and Peter wondered how he could have thought him ordinary.

"Two futures lie before us, Great Chief. Choose the path of war, and everything these two strangers have told you will come true. Worse things as well, for you will die at the hands of your own people and the Lakota will become the poorest and most miserable of all the tribes, although it will be a time of evil for us all. Choose the path of peace, and both our tribes will prosper—and many other tribes as well."

Now Wovoka turned to Peter and Anton, and this time his ancient eyes held anger and accusation. "But not all tribes will share in this bright future. Some will be lost forever. And the dead will not return, as my father would hope."

Peter flinched. "We cannot save them all," he whispered. "From the moment we stepped into that elevator, it was already too late for millions of people. But we want to help! Whoever can be saved, we will do our best to."

"Stop!" the father commanded, and Peter didn't know if Tavibo spoke to him or Wovoka. But he was looking at his son. "Will you speak ill of a man who rushes into a burning home because he could save only half the people who were there? Curse the man who saves your life because he could not save your dog as well?"

Wovoka lowered his eyes. "I apologize," he mumbled.

"I grow weary of this talk of 'saving' " said the young warrior. "The missionaries speak of it often. How has that worked out?"

Peter took a deep breath and decided he could reply without babbling this time. "We did not come here to change your beliefs or culture. In fact, most of the missionaries, and those who believe as they do, will likely come to hate us. Because as passionately as they believe that making you into second class whites is holy work, we believe the opposite." He turned to address Wovoka. "You will be remembered as a great teacher. In the years before I was born, a whole generation of disillusioned young people embraced your words. I and my two friends have been here for a year now. Can you tell us if our presence has changed anything yet?"

Wovoka starred again into Peter's eyes, and then to a distant point just over his left shoulder. "Change? There is change all around you, swirling like a colored mist. Some is bright with hope. Some dark with pain. Some is death. But I cannot tell what has already happened from what will happen."

"Which of the colors is the strongest?" asked Sitting Bull.

"The bright ones," the little boy replied, with the hint of a smile. "Hope, with harmony and chaos all wrapped together."

Peter smiled. "That sounds like us," he said, but the words caught in his throat.

"Let us have feasting and dancing tonight," said Sitting Bull. "Tomorrow we will see what kind of treaty the Lakota can make for two white men to carry back to their Great Chief in Washington."

***

Anton was sitting alone on his bedroll, softly playing the flute that was a gift from a Lakota musician, when Tavibo came and sat across from him. The feasting was done, and most people had found their sleeping robes, but Anton was too restless. Even his beloved music could not bring him peace.

"You are a brave man," the Paiute elder said.

Anton shook his head. "No, I'm not." In the dim light of the stars and the banked fires, Anton saw Tavibo frown. "Ah, that was a social gaffe, wasn't it? Refusing a compliment?"

"Something of an insult, yes," said Tavibo,

although he did not sound angry. "After all you have given up to be here? All the times you have courted death to bring your message to strangers, you truly believe you are not brave?"

"I truly don't know what I am." And as he said it, Anton saw that simple truth for the problem it was. "In fact, I've never known. I never had family or roots. I lived with many families, but I never belonged to any of them. And in a couple of families, the men who were supposed to act as fathers, did not, in the most horrific ways imaginable. I followed whoever would take me, and I guess I never cared where they took me, or I wouldn't be here. And now that I am, I don't know why."

Tavibo opened a pouch and withdrew a small carved pipe and a pinch of tobacco. When all was prepared, he lit it with a twig from Anton's campfire, took a deep draw and passed it to Anton.

Finally used to smoking, and not the least bit worried about living long enough to get cancer, Anton drew a lungful of smoke and passed the pipe back. They smoked in silence until Anton asked, "Do you believe one man can make a difference?"

Tavibo chuckled. "If I did not believe that, I would hardly have come all this way at the behest of my son. Yet you have come from even further. After all you sacrificed to come here, do you, yourself, not believe it?"

"Oh, one man can make a difference. I can think of a thousand bad, scary or ugly ways. Kill one good man or woman. Set a fire. Shoot up a school. Even travel back in time with the best of intentions. I think I mean, can one man change the world in a good way? Even save it?"

"Most likely," said Tavibo, as if it were of little importance. "But you are not asking the right question."

Anton, who had finally begun to relax, groaned. "I don't suppose you'd be kind enough to tell me the right question? No, of course not. It's my journey, so I must do the work, right? Your job is to sit back and push me toward new growth with annoying questions and cryptic comments."

"Is that what the medicine elders of your time call being helpful?" Tavibo seemed genuinely disturbed by Anton's reaction. "If so, I can see why you left."

"Wha—?" Anton's mouth hung open. For once, he was truly at a loss for words.

Tavibo took a long, slow draw from the pipe, and then set it carefully on the ground between them. "You want to know the true reason you followed your friends back in time. And you want to know the purpose of your existence." He leaned forward and took both of Anton's hands and gazed into his eyes with a look of both awe and sadness. "Before you die, my friend, you will know the answer to both."

Then he was gone, leaving Anton to wonder if the whole thing had been a dream.

Chapter 19

Anton, Danaxe, and Peter decided not to establish their own tents or tipis. Peter had read that among the Lakota, visitors were expected to stay in the homes of local families. Unfortunately, he couldn't remember which side of the tipi strangers were expected to stay. They were all clear on the concept of not speaking first, but no one wanted to enter a tipi and start out on the wrong foot by sitting on the wrong side.

Anton, who was clearest on the concept of adapting to local culture pointed out the simplest solution. "It doesn't matter what side. Sit opposite the owners of the tipi. If people are on both sides, start toward the side of the least people, and if they react negatively, go to the other side. Then enjoy the silence. Use the time to look at how they put together their homes."

Peter and Danaxe high fived Anton on his suggestion. They followed his advice to great effect. As local culture required, they slept in a different tipi each night. They followed a pattern so that the members of the camp could anticipate where they would show up next.

Tavibo was waiting beside the tipi when Danaxe left it at sun up for her morning routine. She nodded to him as she walked one hundred paces to a flat spot she had identified the day before. She smiled as she saw Otaktay walk over to join her. She turned to Tavibo and shook her head once as he reached a spot ten paces away. Tavibo simply sat where he was. Danaxe and Otaktay knelt, facing the rising sun.

Danaxe pulled out a set of wooden, strung beads out from under her clothing. Otaktay simply put his hands, palms up upon his knees.

"Myoho renge kyo. Ho ben pon dai ni…" Danaxe started her morning chant. Otaktay started his own prayer.

"Great Mystery, thank you for this day. I thank you for the Universe, which is our tabernacle, our house of worship." When Otaktay finished his prayer, he stood and walked to his tipi. About ten minutes later he returned. Danaxe finished her chant.

Otaktay nodded. Danaxe stood up in one fluent move. Tavibo watched, fascinated, as the two faced each other, bowed, and then started a slow motion version of the Tai Chi morning exercises. Tavibo noted that Otaktay was mimicking Danaxe, who was clearly judging Otaktay's performance, and was using her own motions to get him to correct himself. Tavibo noticed that two of Otaktay's motions were obviously in need of more practice. At which point, the two stopped and bowed again.

Otaktay turned around and started over, building speed as he repeated himself, except for the last two motions, which he slowed down and took extra care to do correctly. Meanwhile, Danaxe kept going, but now at full speed. After a bit of time, she stopped, and waiting for Otaktay to finish his last repetition. Danaxe smiled as he completed the last two forms correctly.

Finally satisfied, Danaxe stepped back, stood straight, and clapped her hands against her thighs twice. Otaktay matched her final stance, and the two bowed to each other. Otaktay walked off, smiling.

Danaxe turned and looked at Tavibo. "Good

morning. Thank you for staying back. He is not used to having anyone other than me watching."

Tavibo smiled in acknowledgement. "So you were both praying to your different gods?"

"I have no assurance that there is a god or gods. I follow this tradition to become a better, balanced person. I strive to make my actions from a place of being at peace with myself, and thus able to deal with others from a place of peace. Not from anger or hatred."

"What are you teaching Otaktay?"

"A martial art called Tai Chi. It comes from a country called China. It is a set of exercises that are practiced in the morning, and it also teaches one how to defend oneself, as well as mental discipline."

"Martial?"

"Yes. As in 'military.' A form, and theory on how to be able to defend yourself."

"Ah yes. Why would you wish to give away your secrets?"

Danaxe cocked her head at Tavibo. "What makes you think they are secret? I teach because he wishes to learn. The task for my level is to teach anyone who asks."

"So you would teach this entire encampment if they chose to attend?"

"Of course. Do you not share your knowledge in the same way?"

"I will share my medicine at need. With some conjurations, there is great power, and so I will not teach everyone all that I know. Wovoka is different. He is responsible, good hearted, and very loving of Mother Earth. Him, I will teach all that I know, and he will do the same with me."

Danaxe nodded. "I cannot say that I have been taught everything about the Buddha, so I do not know if there are dangerous conjurations. I rather doubt it, but not being Buddha myself, I have no certainty. He was a great teacher, and I have applied myself to learning more of his teachings. But I do not see being a Buddhist nun as part of my future. And if I want to get any archery practice done, I must be off." The two nodded, and went their separate ways.

About mid-morning, Peter and Anton left the tipi, each bearing a cup of coffee. Peter noticed Tavibo looking at them, and waved his coffee mug in acknowledgement. Tavibo turned and walked into Sitting Bull's tent. Just as Peter finished his coffee, he noticed Tavibo and Wovoka walking towards him.

Peter called out "Morning. So when is our next palaver?"

Tavibo replied, "It will not happen today. What you have said, what you have suggested, requires time for all of us to think and reflect upon it. I suspect there will be several sweat lodges in use today. I would urge you to join us in this."

Peter looked at Anton. "I read it will be very dark in there." Anton shuddered, and shook his head.

Peter turned back to Tavibo, "Anton does not do well with dark, tight spaces. But I would be very interested."

Tavibo smiled, "Good, we should find each other after sunrise, when the men have finished combing their wives' hair. I suggest you drink a lot of water between now and then. I will go find a lodge to use and prepare."

Peter turned to Anton. "Interesting. I get to streak the village. I wonder if they have ever seen a naked male Jew before."

Anton laughed in response. "Better you than me. Think I need to go fiddle some. I gotta say, just standing here, doing nothing is wearing. Waiting and not knowing is not something I do well. As you well know."

Peter nodded. "Yeah. Yesterday did kinda get under my skin. I know we can't save everyone. But this? We got to get them to agree to come on board with us. And then we get to go back East and save the day, and then argue with Lincoln and everyone else." Peter closed his eyes, trying to avoid seeing all the butterflies and demons in his mind's eye.

Peter spent the morning wandering around, watching people, sometimes watching people watching him. In the distance he could hear Anton playing his fiddle, and from what he heard, it sounded like Anton had a group of playful children in attendance. Later, he saw Danaxe taking riding lessons from Otaktay.

A while later, Peter saw Tavibo walking towards him. He noted that Tavibo had three white feathers in his hair, along with colored beads around his neck, painted symbols on his chest, and leather breaches.

As soon as he got close, Peter spoke. "Can we go by my tipi, so I can dress properly?" Tavibo grinned and nodded yes.

"You have done this before?" asked Tavibo.

"Never. But I suspect anything that I am told to drink a lot of water for, and has "sweat" as part of the name is going to be rather hot." Tavibo clapped Peter on the back and laughed. Upon reaching the tipi. he quickly went inside and disrobed to just pants and shoes, and returned outside.

"You have been drinking water as I instructed you?"

Peter nodded.

"Good. Now drink some more."

Peter gave a half smile and drank from the waterskin in the tipi.

Tavibo stood in the doorway watching. "I said drink. Not suckle."

Peter stared at Tavibo for a moment and took a much longer drink.

"More," was Tavibo's response. "Until your stomach can hold no more. Do not worry, I promise you will not need to make water for quite a while."

Sighing Peter complied.

Coming from the south, as they approached the sweat lodge, Peter noticed a fire to the west of the lodge. In order, working back to the flap of the lodge, there was an earthen mound, and a ridge of dirt, about ten paces long, and just before the entry to the lodge, a pair of forked sticks, with a third stick set across the other two. Under the sticks, sat a buffalo skull, with three small red pouches dangling from each horn. One elaborately decorated water skin bag lay next to the sticks.

In silence, the two made their way to the sweat lodge. One man stood next to the fire, tending it and a pile of stones in the fire. The stones were added to the fire periodically. A group of five warriors stood, watching Tavibo approach them, obviously in a somber mood. One of them, the young warrior that spoke against Peter glared as he approached. Once Peter reached the group, he stripped off his shoes and pants. He did his best to ignore the comments and chuckles.

Tavibo spoke to the warrior as a parent to a

child. The warrior gave Peter one last glare, and then relaxed, dismissing Peter from his world.

Tavibo removed his breaches, picked up sage, and went into the lodge on hands and knees. Peter kneeled to watch, as Tavibo spread the sage on the ground. He noticed that Tovibo went counterclockwise around the lodge, and avoided the center of the lodge, as a hole had been dug there. When Tavibo returned to the entrance, his assistant handed him a smoldering length of braided grass. Tavibo swung the braid in the air in front of him, again going slowly counter clockwise. When he was finished, he crawled outside.

Nodding at the gathered men, Tavibo led the way into the waiting lodge, followed by the five warriors, then Peter, and last in line, the assistant. Tavibo sat to the right of the entry, while the five warriors took their preferred places. Peter realized that they had purposely left him a spot farthest from the door. On his left was the warrior, who protested his presence, and was now doing his best to ignore him. Once the assistant reached his position, to the left of the entrance, Tavibo started chanting. The man who had been tending the fire entered, bringing a heated rock balanced on a forked stick. Everyone except Peter called out "Pilamaye." While the helper was getting the second rock, the warrior to Peter's right leaned over and slowly whispered "pilamaye." Peter repeated the word, and nodded. The first rock went in the center, the next four in the cardinal points, west, north, east, and south. The sixth rock went on top of the first. The helper nodded to Tavibo as he exited.

Tavibo lit his pipe, and passed it around. Peter noticed that everyone was grabbing the smoke, and rubbing all over themselves. Peter followed along.

When the pipe returned to Tavibo, he leaned it against the forked sticks. At this point, the helper sealed the entry.

As Peter sat, cross legged, he felt the heat coming off the stones. He heard water being poured on the stones. The resulting steam seemed to roil in the air, heading straight for Peter. The steam was suffocating. Peter coughed, fighting a rising sense of panic. Tavibo changed his chant to English, instructing Peter to just work on breathing, letting the lodge, the darkness, and the people around him become the arms of his mother enfolding him as a child.

Peter's fear of suffocating disappeared, as a long forgotten memory surfaced. A time when, as a sick child, his mother cradled and rocked him. He found himself rocking the same way. More stones, more sage, more water were added. The hot, thick air seemed to crash in on Peter, who kept rocking and just worked on getting enough air into his lungs.

Tavibo never stopped chanting, often switching to English so he could guide Peter, who was never able to remember the exact words. Other times the others would sing "Tunka-shila, hi-yay, hi-yay." Once he was confident, he could match the singing. He found himself thinking of the family and friends he had abandoned without warning. Trying to forge new friendships, and seeking others. Allies. All the people. All the people he was hoping to help. Tears added to the wetness of his skin. He joined in as they sang the song two times in a row. Peter was blinded, as he didn't know this was the signal to open the lodge entrance. The warriors talked, none of it in English. Some of it sounded serious. Some of it friendly.

Tavibo, out of the blue, asked Peter, "I gather

you have expected this question. These men are curious as to whether you had an illness or injury that you would cut your manhood."

Peter replied instantly, careful to keep his voice level, "Neither. It is a religious custom among my people to do this. It is called a circumcision. We do it to remind ourselves and our, uhm, Great Spirit, that we cherish and keep the Covenant between us."

"Covenant?" Tavibo asked, his voice slightly puzzled.

"A holy written contract."

"Was it written on paper?" asked Tavibo.

"Actually on two stone tablets."

"Ah," responded Tavibo, "That was our mistake in dealing with the White men. We should have signed on stone. This will continue with three more cycles."

For the next go round Peter noticed that the helper simply put the new stones wherever he thought best.

Again the pipe, followed by more chanting. And again the steam kept building. Peter had just about reached the end of his ability to get enough air. He was about to suffocate, and he knew the warrior next to him would do nothing to help him.

Emotionally, Peter collapsed. His tears changed to uncontrollable sobbing. Pictures of what his family was going through in trying to locate him. Shame that he was crying in front of strangers. He took on the soul crushing reality that if he and his companions carried out even part of their plan successfully, billions of people who would have been born between now and when he left would now never be born. Never exist — never living and then dying, never being. Consigned to eternal neverness. Peter heard the chant shift back to

English. Unable to comprehend, he clung to the words and tried to follow along. And then, at the height of his emotional collapse, he found something to hang on to. A place where he found himself standing.

For the third round, Peter raced back through his last emotional collapse, and as he returned to standing, he found he was not alone. Around him were Anton and Danaxe. And a host, a multitude of people. The warrior next to him, standing side by side, facing the future. Together. In his destruction of the universe Peter knew, he had gained a new universe. People whom he needed to care about. People who needed to care about each other to save the future. And again, before he could continue to the next plateau, it was interrupted.

As he returned to the heat, Peter tried to focus on the fact he was sharing this suffocating experience in the dark, he was not alone. He felt gratitude that he was facing his demons, as Tavibo intended. He realized that while the warrior to his left did not like him, his willingness to share meant something. Peter, while suffocating, tried to puzzle it out. Fear of failure tore at his heart, and once again, he started sobbing. When he hit rock bottom, a single word came to him.

Caring.

Peter realized he was no longer suffocating. His fear and sadness were gone. For possibly the first time in his life, Peter knew what he truly had to help make it happen. To get as many people as he could to care, for each other, and for those yet to be born. Every thought, every word, every act needed to have that as the central theme and goal.

Joy filled his soul. Peter saw that part of what had sent him down this path was the realization that even the warrior next to him had been sobbing and crying out in pain. Seeing that he was not alone caused Peter even greater joy. While still reveling in this joy, he found himself blinded by the light of a late afternoon as the lodge door was flung open. This time, the pipe was passed for the fourth time. When the warrior to his left passed the pipe, he turned to Peter and whispered in his ear.

"When the last smoker cleans the pipe, and sets it down, we will say "Mitakuye oyasin." It means "all our relatives." Then the ceremony is complete." Surprised, Peter nodded his understanding. When the time came, Peter joined in the closing phrase.

Peter followed the procession, counter clockwise to the exit. Peter raised his head, eyes closed, and inhaled the cool, fresh air. He joined in rubbing his body with dry sage, and drinking cold water. He put his pants and shoes back on. The family he was staying with respected his silence as he worked to come to grips with his newfound knowledge.

Chapter 20

The follow-up council meeting was held three days later. In the meantime, Anton, Danaxe, and Peter found themselves approached by individuals and small groups and peppered with questions. All of them centered on finding any reason to trust whites — especially their leaders in Washington. Some left these conversations looking thoughtful, some still angry, and a considerable number left looking confused and anxious.

The council was held outside as no tipi was large enough to fit everyone. Some four hundred plus people were in attendance, seating themselves in a large ring, three to five people deep in places. Sitting Bull and the elders sat on one side of the ring. Tavibo, Wovoka, Anton, Danaxe, and Peter sat across from him. Sitting Bull stood, and all the very quiet conversations stopped. Even the children in attendance were still.

"You have all had a chance to speak with our guests, who have journeyed far to talk to us. I and our elders have had a chance to sit and listen to Tavibo and Wovoka." Sitting Bull sat back down.

Tavibo stood up. "I have met each of these three guests. I can tell you that Anton's heart stands with all children everywhere. Including ours. Danaxe is a woman of the earth, wanting harmony between the earth and all that live on it. Peter is a dreamer. He has big dreams with which he hopes to change what he considers to be nightmares of the future. In my dealings with them, they have been honest, and I have only heard them speak with one tongue." Tavibo sat.

With a gesture of his hand, Sitting Bull invited Peter to speak. Peter took a deep breath and stood. He looked around the ring of people, and tried to judge the mood. Danaxe reached up and held his hand for a moment. Peter squeezed it in acknowledgement.

"I admit much of this is my waking dream. It is why my companions are with me. But to steal the words of a beloved spiritual leader from another time and place, 'I have a dream.'" Peter paused. "I want the United States to exist with honor, and no stains upon it. Where all of us are treated fairly, equally, and with respect. Where we can all listen to each other's stories, and learn from them.

"I only see one way that this will work. We need to form six new states. Three of them will be First Peoples. The first one will undoubtedly be Sequoyah, and the other two will be based on the lands around here. The other three are to be for the former slaves. They will form two states to the west of here, and one to the south in Nebraska Territory." When the translator sitting next to Sitting Bull finished, Peter noticed a warrior coming to his feet. Peter stopped.

"How will you make these states? What guarantee will we have that the white man will not simply come and take them away?"

"How will you be sure? Because it will be illegal in the most fundamental sense of the word. You would not be living as a sovereign nation, surrounded by a larger, more powerful nation. You will be citizens of the United States, and your people will have complete control of your state for a set time. That is how I see it coming to be. You give up your nation, to turn it into a state with the same rights that the other states have. And more importantly the protections of a state." Peter paused, but no one stood up, so he continued.

"So how do we get this done? We agree that we will work to make this happen. We arrange for your Chiefs and Elders to come east to meet with certain people. We work to get Congress —our elders —to change the language of our Constitution, the biggest of all our signed words. That language would make you, your children, and all your future children, citizens of the United States. You will then be declared a territory. President Lincoln will appoint a governor. You will work with him to write your state constitution, and set out how all your laws will function. When you have completed all the work, Congress will then grant you statehood, and you will stand as equals among equals."

A woman rose and spoke. The translator said, "And then all these white men can move here to establish cities and towns as they please?" Peter noticed the many soft voices around him reacting to her words. Peter smiled and looked around the ring.

"That is really what is at the heart of this. Normally, the answer would be yes. They could. One of the changes for these six territories, and then states, would be claiming the right to control who can settle, including being able to tell any white no. Not permanently. In my religion, the standard time would be forty years, but if we can get twenty-five years, that will give you the time you need to get your political power built up. You will have to let any United States citizen travel through your territory, but you will have police and militia to keep track of them, and make sure they keep moving. One of the fundamental differences between the three First People states and the others is that land will not be owned by individuals, but by communities. I would expect that in your states, no white would be able to just go anywhere. They would have to apply to the community and accept what they are given."

As the translator finished, another warrior stood. Peter realized he was the man who had sat next to him in the sweat lodge. Much to Peter's surprise, the warrior spoke English. "I noticed that in the sweat lodge you struggled with powerful demons. May I ask what they were?" Dumbfounded, Peter stared at him for a moment. He glanced at the sky, and noticed an eagle flying over the encampment. Peter looked the warrior right in the eye and spoke with quiet strength in his voice.

"My demons were grief. The first was that in order to speak to you, here and now, I left my family behind, with no way to tell them where I was going, and that I am all right. My second grief was my fear that I and my two friends will not be powerful enough to make these changes happen. That we, I, would fail, and I grieved for what would be lost as the world died all around us."

"So how did you overcome your demons?"

"I sweated. I faced them. I refused to give up. Instead, I felt the strength to be gained by joining with you in sweat, and sage, and tobacco, all of us facing the struggle of life together, and the strength to purposely gather together, to find the strength together to face any and all demons. Tavibo saw me first. But I saw you as a possible brother in arms." Peter paused for a moment. "And I saw you see me. I will never forget that moment. And as I stand in this circle. I see you all as such. All." Peter locked eyes with as many people as he could. "My strength is now centered in the lodge for all time. In the ground beneath my feet, and in all of you gathered to hear what I have to say."

For a moment there was complete silence. Then the young warrior spoke again.

"Yes. I see you. I did not want you in that sweat lodge with me. I agree that it has brought us together. I agree with Tavibo. You bring us nothing to sign. You bring your vision, and you ask for our help. I have seen the strength of your demons. I see the strength in you. I am glad we sweated as People should. And I say that in this, I will stand with you." Peter nodded thanks. The warrior walked over to where Peter stood, and sat near him. The susurration returned. Peter remained standing. People started rising one by one to ask questions.

In response to the questions, Peter covered topics that included the creation of a state militia, taxation, Sequoyah's proposed constitution, issues based on a growing population, the possibility of towns and even cities forming over time, farming, ownership of land versus leases… At some point, Peter's memory failed him as it seemed like he was assailed by all the questions that attentive adults and children could bring to bear. As midday arrived, a group of women and their children brought food and water to those in attendance. Quiet finally descended.

Peter sat down, exhausted. While sitting and finally eating, he looked around. Sitting Bull's half of the ring was much thinner than Peter's half. Peter was aware that Danaxe had been spending time with the women of the camp. He realized that many, if he understood the rankings written in clothing, who were medicine elders were on his side of the ring.

Peter caught Danaxe's eye, and then pointedly looked at a number of the women in question. In return, Danaxe looked back and nodded. Peter looked at Anton, who in turn pantomimed eating popcorn. Peter smiled, appreciating the humor. He started to relax. While there had to be people who disagreed, no one displayed anger, or disgust.

After a while of watching, Peter laughed as he finally recognized what the conversations reminded him of. The cafeteria of any politically active college. He felt someone staring at him, looked around the ring, and saw Sitting Bull. As Peter settled his gaze on the Holy Man, he nodded at Peter with a very slight smile.

Peter turned to Danaxe. "Wow," he said. "I don't think I'll remember one third of what I just said." Danaxe smiled, and opened what Peter thought of as her first aid kit, revealing a cellphone.

Smiling, she said, "I'm sure we can come up with a transcription."

Without a clock, Peter found it hard to judge time, but finally Sitting Bull stood. "From what I have heard, this is where I believe us to be. We are not being promised statehood. We have three people who believe they might make it a reality. They cannot promise us that, and refuse to do so. They do say that if they can, they will. As part of this, they ask that we start writing this State Constitution. And in so doing, we must account for what power belongs to the State, what power belongs to the Counties, and what powers belong to towns and cities that the future will force us to do, upon our choosing.

"That we write all of this so the People own the land, and not any individual. That as a result, we will be allowed to choose two people to speak for us in the

Senate. And based on the number of our people we will
be able to vote for people to stand for us in the House
of Representatives. That they will speak for us as a
People. That with the Negro states, we would have
allies, to double our voices.

"That as part of this, we would have a time to
ourselves, for at least the first generation, run our
affairs without interference. That we could control who
lives here, but must in turn allow anyone to pass
through our lands. We will have the right to defend
ourselves within the rights of a state to form a militia.
To do this, we must await a mysterious signal to go east
to a place called Gettysburg. It is this last I do not
understand."

Peter stood, noticing that people who had
started to murmur quietly, stopped immediately, and
their full attention swung back to him. He purposely
stood silent for at least a hundred heartbeats.

"There are several reasons for this meeting.
There is a man I want you to meet, a General Howard.
If there are no states for Native Americans, but only
reservations, this man will be forced to conduct a war
against you. He is a Christian, but unlike many of the
Christians you have encountered. He will carry out
orders that he considers evil. He will do so, because he
considers this current war to be a greater evil. And he
will do everything in his power to prevent a repeat of
this Civil War.

"If, on the other hand, you both meet, and can
reach an agreement, he will become your greatest ally.
He just needs another way forward. Part of that is this:
you need to know that in any war with the United
States, you may win a battle here or there, but you will
never win a war. I want you to stand on a battlefield

where more people died in three days than you have warriors. I want you to understand what you are facing.

"And while I get that you are willing to die, what I know is this: I need you to live. I need you to live so that you can teach the people of this land that in any decision, we must look seven generations ahead. I need you all alive to show that there is another way to judge progress. And it is not just me that needs this. Ultimately, this world needs your wisdom. So yes, please commit to this vision. From there, I hope to get your people involved with Congress to make these things happen. For what it is worth, John Ross of the Cherokee has already promised to do so."

Peter went back to sitting. As his sweat lodge partner started to stand, Peter put a halting hand on his arm. "Hello, I am Peter. Your name is?"

Laughing, the warrior stood. "Hard Arrow." In the time it took for the introduction, Otaktay stood up. In deference to the older warrior, Hard Arrow sat back down and listened respectfully.

"I believe this going to Gettysburg is a good thing." Otaktay pointed to Danaxe, "All here know of the contest between this woman and myself. She showed that with awareness, a woman could hurt a Lakota warrior. So now I practice with her in the morning to learn her ways as a warrior. Afterwards, she takes lessons from me on how to ride as a Lakota warrior. She has nearly matched my skill with a horse. I have come nowhere near her skill using my bow against her foreign bow.

"So I say this. As this woman warrior has shown better skills than me, it is wise to travel to Gettysburg, and see the truth that the white man is better equipped for war than we are. If true, we lose no

honor in finding another way to fight and survive."
Otaktay sat down.

For several minutes, silence reigned. Sitting
Bull stood up. "I ask you all to stand with your
thoughts between me, and Peter. We have talked well,
and I would know where people stand." Sitting Bull sat
down and waited for people to shuffle towards him, or
towards Peter. Shortly, it became clear that most
favored Peter.

"I see that most of you would walk the path that
Peter suggests. While I see that some of you would
walk my path, you are merely waiting for me to state
my path. Once Peter tells us the message to start the
path, I will walk the path to Gettysburg, and meet with
this General Howard. I will send warriors to start a
conversation with Chief John Ross to learn of what he
has done to prepare for this state of Sequoyah. If told
how, I will contact these law-speakers Peter talks of to
help us write a state constitution. My last question is
simply this. What is this mysterious message you speak
of?"

Peter laughed as he stood. Pointing at Danaxe,
he replied, "When you receive a newspaper with her
picture, that will be the time to head east."

Chapter 21

The first snow was falling when the three returned to the East Coast. Their mood matched the weather, for despite their successes—not to mention adventures—there was nothing left now but to wait out the four months until "Our American Cousin" debuted at the Ford Theater, and with it, the final discovery of how much history they could actually change. After resting for a few days, the trio started running errands. Peter and Anton went to their various lockboxes. Danaxe went to confer with her attorney.

As she was led into Mr. William Barnwell's office, the first thing she noticed was a table, sporting her patents. Mr. Barnwell stood, smiling, as he greeted her.

"As you can see, Miss Davis, your models turned out quite well. I had several sets made. Your patents were completely approved a couple of months ago. Your antibiotics were the first to be approved, about a month after you left. Dr. Smith and I have started up manufacturing and sales as soon they were approved, and the Union Army was the first major customer. As of now, you have twenty-four approved patents. We have been licensed to sell to the Confederates, under the promise that ten percent of their purchases would go to Prisoners of War.

"Miss Wight was actually quite helpful, as she found a chance to introduce me to Miss Dorothea Dix. She has used the sulfamides, and has found that they do reduce the number and severity of infections. We are in the midst of sending a tenth shipment to her. She also reports that the incentive spirometer to be effective. We have a number of doctors who are ordering chloramphenicol, both in the Army and here in New York City. I am happy to say, you are officially showing a profit, and that it will likely grow much larger in the future."

"This is indeed excellent news," Danaxe said. "Thank you for your fine work, Mr. Barnwell." Outwardly, Danaxe was the picture of nineteenth century woman of means: well-dressed, calm and gracious. Inside she was as giddy as Peter had been when he left the Lakota sweat lodge. This was her dream of living history. Real, but the way she would have directed it.

She spent a relaxing afternoon with Mr. Barnwell, discussing her long list of patents, and their various stages of acceptance. Then Danaxe surprised him (although perhaps not as much as she expected) by dropping off another set of papers, complete with drawings. Mr. Barnwell looked at the first page. "What does this autoclave do?" he asked.

"It will allow for sterilization, and a number of industrial processes. So it will be useful in industry, and not just medicine," Danaxe replied.

Mr. Barnwell stared, and then thought about it. "Yes, I imagine that will be quite the money maker." She left with a bank draft in the amount of $11,142.63.

Danaxe then went to Brooklyn, to the home of Dr. James McCune Smith. She found his wife, Malvina, at home.

"My husband will return soon," said the older woman. If Danaxe had found Dr. Smith intimidating at first, his college-educated wife was equally a force to be reckoned with. "Will you join me for tea in the parlor?"

"Yes, thank you," Danaxe murmured.

Malvina served the tea herself, but looking around the comfortable, tastefully furnished home, Danaxe guessed there were servants about somewhere. If Malvina was bothered by any changes in her husband's work, political views or the sudden presence of a young white woman in their home, nothing in her manner indicated it.

"I have had few opportunities to speak with educated women," Malvina said. "Especially women of my own race."

"I, as well, Mrs. Smith," said Danaxe. "Perhaps we might hope that such things will change."

"You and your friends seem to bring change with you," Malvina said with a knowing smile. "Young Miss Wight, more than anyone."

Danaxe wondered how much James had told her. She stared into her teacup, as if hoping for answers. Suddenly she blurted out, "I hope she has not brought any unpleasant change. By that I mean… that is to say..." Danaxe faltered, and then drew in a cleansing breath. Malvina raised an eyebrow, but offered no other reaction. "I fear that in my efforts to make the world a better place, I may have unintentionally created difficulties for those who least deserve them. The presence of a young white woman in your home, for example?"

Malvina nodded. "I worried about that myself, when we first employed Catherine, three years ago." At Danaxe's puzzled expression, Mrs. Smith smiled. "Catherine Grellis, our maid. From Ireland."

After Danaxe managed not to choke on her tea (more from surprise that she had missed that bit of historical trivia than anything else) Malvina continued. "Fortunately, Brooklyn has an impressively varied population, and a tendency for people to mind their own business. If you are concerned that a much younger, attractive white woman might be a threat to my marriage…?" Danaxe concentrated on her breathing. "I might indeed worry about that—but fortunately for my marriage and my husband's soul, Miss Jenny's tastes do not run to men."

This time, Danaxe nearly poured tea down the front of her dress. Malvina caught the cup before in crashed to the floor. "Really, Miss Davis! I did not know it was possible to surprise you." Malvina's smile took the sting out of the situation.

"That does explain a few things," Danaxe said weakly.

"I trust you will keep this between us—" Malvina began, and then stopped as a series of loud footfalls climbed the steps to the front door.

Danaxe managed to get to her feet and facing the door before Jenny came through in full tornado mode. Then she flung herself at Danaxe, who just barely managed to keep from being knocked over.

"Oh Danaxe! It is so good to see you! Did you notice the handwriting of the last three letters I sent you! And Sergeant Typton says I am a natural reader. We finished all of William Shakespeare's plays. Say, those English people spoke real strange. And now we are going through _Paradise Lost_, and I have read so many books. And did you know that the Hindi have their own alphabet, that it is older than ours?" At this point, Jenny took a much needed breath.

Danaxe laughed as she took the girl by her hand and led her to the sofa. Malvina left the two of them to catch up with each other. Jenny showed no desire to slow down her rapid delivery as she recounted all she had accomplished and learned under Dr. Smith's tutelage. The two were so engrossed in conversation, they failed to notice Dr. Smith's arrival until Malvina called them to dinner.

Danaxe smiled as she noticed that Jenny calmed down once she had sat and displayed her new-found etiquette. The main topic at dinner was Dr. Smith's appraisal of Jenny's growing list of skills, both academically and medically. Dr. Smith also included a report he had taken from Sergeant Typton. During all of this Jenny, just smiled and nodded. When he finished, Danaxe spoke up.

"As I understand it, Jenny, you spend your mornings with the good sergeant, and then report to Doctor Smith for the afternoon?" Jenny nodded. "So Doctor Smith, if you would not mind, I would like to join the two of you in the afternoon. I may miss some time to work on my patents, but there are things I would like to show both of you."

"That would be an excellent plan. How long do you expect to stay in New York?" asked Dr. Smith.

"I imagine until sometime in March, so almost three months," replied Danaxe. Jenny grinned. The rest of the evening was taken up by catching Danaxe up on the war, mostly concerning Sherman's March and the rumors of panic in the South, including rumors of desertion in the Army of Virginia. Danaxe pretended to be hearing it for the first time. Around 9:00, Jenny excused herself to catch up on homework, and sleep. Dr. Smith kept Danaxe company, as she waited for a carriage to take her home.

"I must tell you, Miss Davis, those medications

of yours are really saving people. I have even heard that some amputations were put off, and there are surgeons that I know of who are actually saving limbs."

"I am glad to hear of that. There are some things I can show you as well that will help. Just a friendly warning: I have plans for you and for Jenny. Change is coming soon." Danaxe smiled at Dr. Smith.

The doctor sighed. "Of that I have no doubt. May I enquire as to when?"

"After I and my companions leave New York." Danaxe was spared any further questions as her carriage arrived.

***

The next morning, Danaxe, Peter and Anton gathered around the breakfast table.

"Well gentlemen," said Danaxe. "I have my schedule figured out. I will be spending my mornings working on more patents. My afternoons will be taken up with Jenny and Dr. Smith. How are the two of you faring?"

"Well, we should have a couple of Pinkerton guards knocking on the door anytime now," said Anton. "We've about a dozen more banks to visit. Then we look at what else we can do for investments. How about we invest in your patents? Would that help?"

"Actually, that might be a good idea. I have my first bank draft." Danaxe showed it to Anton and Peter.

Peter whistled in appreciation. "First payment after all the startup costs? Nice!"

"In 1864 dollars, that is," said Anton. "Funny, I'm having trouble remembering things uptime."

"I guess we're finally adjusting," said Danaxe.

The three went to the bank for Danaxe's draft, and from there went their separate ways, with Anton and Peter going about their investments, pouring over their newspapers on their tablets and comparing them to the actual downtime copies.

Danaxe spent her mornings working on drawing up new patents, and her afternoons and evenings in the company of Jenny and Dr. Smith. Things went rather well, until the afternoon when Danaxe's contribution to the education of Dr. Smith and Jenny was the copper, intrauterine device. After explaining how it worked, Dr. Smith became visibly outraged.

"I find this to be most unbefitting any good woman!" he said with as much anger as Danaxe had ever heard from him. "It is for the Lord to decide when a conception should occur."

"Then the Good Lord can come down and Himself ensure that child is fed, clothed, raised, and educated!" Danaxe replied. "Until He does that, you know what will happen, Doctor. We must not let the world population grow unchecked. And now is the time, as I already explained to you that the increased population contributed to the climate change that caused me and my friends to come here."

Before Dr. Smith could respond, she added, "You and I both know of places right here in Brooklyn where a child's life is brutal. Their families overrun and forced into abject poverty. Then there are the streets with all that horse manure. More people means more manure, more horses, more disease, and we end up right where it all comes to an end. Here and now Doctor, here and now, is where all this can be changed."

"I believe I am done for the day. Jenny, Miss

Davis, I will see you two at supper. Miss Danaxe."
After a stiff bow in Danaxe's direction, Dr. Smith left.

Jenny finally spoke. "I fear that is smoke coming out of his ears. Supper shall be most interesting tonight." Jenny paused, and then continued, "Where exactly are you and your friends from?"

Danaxe just stared at Jenny, and then literally smacked her hand against her forehead, as she realized she had totally fubared her cover story for the second time. After a quick set of calming breaths, she answered Jenny's question. "The only answer I will give is this. I was born in the Year of Our Lord, 1996. I have great-great-grandparents who are alive today as slaves. In the year 2025, things will go horribly wrong. I am here with my friends to prevent that from happening. More than that, I cannot tell you. Repeat a word of this to anyone, and our relationship ends. Understood?"

Jenny sat back for a moment in obvious contemplation. Typical Jenny, she energetically jumped out of her seat, and hugged Danaxe, saying "That explains why you know so much more than doctors! Your secret is safe with me."

Danaxe returned the hug, and whispered in Jenny's ear, "Malvina told me about you. Your secret is safe with me. And her. For the record, it's totally natural. You hear me?"

Jenny blushed hard. She managed to stammer out, "Thank you." Any further conversation was prevented by Malvina's call to supper.

The conversation at dinner was initially a bit wooden, as Smith got over his anger. Jenny simply ignored it, and spoke of her day, describing her difficulties in learning Handel's "Surprise Symphony."

"Sergeant Typton is trying to instruct me not to simply play what is written, but to "feel" it. And I am simply unable to do it. With all this reading and writing in two different languages, I thought the point was absolute precision." Jenny's voice was petulant as she finished.

Danaxe responded, "You have dealt with hundreds of patients. Have you noticed that no two patients bodies are alike? Nor their symptoms from the same disease?" After Jenny's nod, Danaxe continued, "As a musician, your job is to put your own twist, to show us your emotional take on whatever you are playing. Variations in tempo, loudness or softness, even adding gracenotes."

Jenny nodded, "Like embroidery, adding your own changes to a pattern."

Another uncomfortable silence descended. Catherine brought in desert: apple pie and thinly sliced cheddar cheese. As Malvina did the honor of slicing the pie, and passing the slices around, she looked her husband in the eye while addressing Jenny, "I have some suggested reading for you. Ask Sergeant Tipton to find you a copy of a play by Aristophanes called *Lysistrata*. As I was not sufficiently far away, I could not avoid hearing my husband's reaction to, what was the phrase? Birth control? I will be having a discussion with my loving husband. I believe you should be able to finish the lesson tomorrow."

Danaxe tried to avoid looking at Smith, but she couldn't help but notice he looked defeated.

***

March quickly arrived. Too quickly for Jenny who valued both her lessons from Danaxe, and her friendship. On the day of the departure, Jenny and Dr. Smith arrived at the brownstone to bid Danaxe, Peter and Anton farewell. From Dr. Smith there were formal handshakes all around. Jenny gave Danaxe her usual rambunctious hug and smiled coquettishly at the two gentlemen.

As Danaxe shook Dr. Smith's hand, she made a point of looking into his eyes and said, "Soon Dr. Smith. Very soon."

The doctor sighed. "My life was a good deal more calm and orderly before I met you, Miss Davis. But I find I do not miss those days in the least."

Chapter 22

Anton, Danaxe, and Peter enjoyed their train trip to Washington D.C. Their four Pinkerton guards sat at either end of the train's first-class car. They chatted quietly amongst themselves, until they spied the unfinished Washington Monument.

"Five hundred and fifty-five feet," said Anton. "It won't be finished for another twenty years."

"Unless... Butterflies," said Peter. After a moment of brooding, he smiled. "You know? I think I like it better this way. One of the perks of time travel."

Silence descended again as the train slowed, and finally stopped. Again, it was Anton who broke it.

"Well, this is where we remake history." Peter started to glare at Anton, but then broke into a grin as he realized no one else in the car would know what was planned for this fine, first day of spring. As they stepped off the car, their Pinkertons took up surreptitious positions around the trio. Quickly, they collected their luggage, and found a horse drawn taxi, which they then rode to their boarding house. Upon arrival, they checked into their separate rooms. They met for supper, keeping to themselves, and ate in silence. After dinner, they went for a walk.

Peter broke the long silence. "Tonight's tour is locating Secretary William Seward's house. In Lafayette Park as I recall."

Anton teased him, "Right. I saw you look up the house on your tablet. As I recall."

Peter smiled. "Yep. We have twenty-four days to get things done. But I want to get eyes on Seward's house first. Then check out Kirkwood House, where Vice President Andrew Johnson is staying. We'll have to find a play to attend at Ford's Theatre, preferably in the box where Lincoln sat, so I can measure the chair."

"Why measure it? Wouldn't it be easier just to get a replacement chair made?" asked Danaxe.

"Huh, hadn't thought of that. But I don't know that we have enough time."

"Hey, isn't that what money is for?" said Anton. "Pay triple and it will get done much faster."

"How are we going to find out where the theatre gets their chairs from?" Peter responded.

"We got four Pinkertons. I bet one of them can come up with a plan." Anton grinned.

When they arrived at 17 Madison Place, the three of them gawked for a couple of minutes. The glow of kerosene lamps shone behind mostly shuttered windows. Peter started walking again. "The next one is easy to remember —1111 Pennsylvania, Kirkwood House, the hotel where Vice President Johnson stayed." The walk was rather short. The three found a table open in the bar. Anton collected two beers and a claret, and brought them to the table.

"So 10:15 that night was pretty much the kickoff time, but I think we need to have people in place earlier than that. Maybe 8:00?" Peter looked at his two friends, who both nodded.

Anton interrupted, "Hey, do you think George got drunk at this table?" Peter stared at him for a moment.

"You mean Atzerodt?" Peter responded. Seeing Anton nod, Peter continued. "I doubt it. He was talking to the bartender, asking questions about Johnson. Danaxe, have you decided on how to take care of

Booth?"

Danaxe nodded. "Hard and fast. Problem will be his gun hand. You normally want to control the wrist and hand first, then the arm. But that derringer he used, it's too small. And I'm betting he will pull the trigger in surprise. If he doesn't, I will. Then he will try to pull his knife. I'll just emoji him." Both Anton and Peter stared quizzically at her.

"I'll just smack his head against the wall until he passes out."

"Where will that pistol be pointed when it goes off?" asked Anton, picturing all the horrible ways that could end. Danaxe pointed at the ceiling.

She paused for a moment, gathering her thoughts. "Okay, here's a twist. I am an unknown Negress, and Booth is a well-known, white, male actor. Come trial time, it will largely be his word against mine. I propose that I train our Pinkertons in some uptime forensics. Namely finger and palm prints. We don't have to establish the big picture, just that my palm prints won't be on either the gun or the knife, but his will be. We need them to safeguard the evidence, maintain the chain of custody. The only person worth interviewing will be Major Rathbone. He actually tried to take on Booth after the shooting. Took several knife wounds in the process. Then we wing it with the Lincolns at the White House, and wait for the Pinkertons to bring in the other two conspirators."

"Huh. Hadn't thought of that. How are you going to teach them?" asked Anton.

"I have a copy of a paper on viewing objects with a microscope. That should be enough for a start." replied Danaxe.

Over the next couple of weeks, arrangements

were made to hire a total of twelve Pinkertons. Four for each of the three protectees. Danaxe spent a couple of days researching and found she actually had obtained two documents. The first one, an English translation of a paper written by Professor Paul-Jean Coulier in 1863, and a second one that a Mr. Thomas Taylor wrote on the use of a microscope for identifying fingerprints on objects. When asked about the date of "July 1877" on the latter article, Danaxe feigned surprise, and told the Pinkertons it was an apparent typo.

Peter and Anton set out to find where the Ford Theatre acquired their furniture, only to discover that Lincoln sat in a wooden rocking chair.

Anton scratched his head, while Peter made barely audible, angry sounds. Anton ventured, "I don't think we can armor that chair. It will tip back, and make it damned uncomfortable to rock." Peter just nodded his head, and kept swearing under his breath.

The trio tried to relax as April 14th approached. They bought a row house on Pennsylvania Avenue, and established that as their new headquarters. Danaxe found that she needed to chant more. Anton let Danaxe practice a couple of times on him so she could set up a kata. Fortunately, she didn't need to use a wall for the practice. The crick Anton had in his neck was bad enough. Peter took to going to the library and reading incessantly. Anton kept getting more and more wound up. Enough so that the next time Danaxe offered to teach Anton meditative breathing, Anton was desperate enough to take the offer.

Slow inhale.

Slow exhale.

Chapter 23

On April 14, Anton, Danaxe, and Peter took their now accustomed table for supper. Silently, they sat and ate mechanically, without enjoyment. Just adding fuel to keep their bodies going. Anton and Peter were dressed in jackets, waistcoats, and bow ties. Anton sported a top hat, his clothes in medium grays, while Peter wore what Danaxe thought of as the father of the bowler hat, and his clothes in a dark blue. Danaxe dressed all in black, and flat black at that. She wore no visible makeup, but she had used something to remove all highlights from her face.

Once supper was finished, they silently left their house and walked slowly to Ford Theater, arriving shortly before curtain time. The misty fog of the evening matched their somber mood. Anton and Peter went to their seats. Danaxe was alone in the back of the theater where she could move unnoticed.

Peter went to the tavern and satisfied himself that the four Pinkertons were there, pretending to drink. They confirmed that they had checked in with the other two teams, and that everyone was in position. Peter returned to the theater and met with his contact on the staff. Peter confirmed that a pitcher of cold lemon water, glasses, and a plate of sweets would be available for Danaxe to pick up.

He caught up with Anton and settled in next to him. At 9:55, Peter's cell phone buzzed its alarm. Anton followed Peter to their hiding place in a closet full of carefully rearranged cleaning supplies.

Meanwhile Danaxe went to collect the tray, only to find a white woman holding it. Careful to sound properly respectful, Danaxe quietly said, "Ma'am, I was sent here to collect that for President and Madam Lincoln."

The woman turned, and upon seeing Danaxe, stated frostily, "I know all the staff here, and you are not staff. We do not hire colored women to serve the likes of the President. What do you think you are doing?"

"What I was told to do by my employer, ma'am." Danaxe kept her eyes demurely lowered, but kept her adversary in sight. "Mr. Tormey will arrive shortly and…."

"Don't you sass me, gal! snapped the woman. "I am looking forward to meeting this fictional person. I will give him two minutes. And then I will have the police deal with the likes of you." Danaxe kept her face calm and concentrated on her breathing, trying to regain her pre-mission calm.

***

Peter, looking at his watch and became increasing agitated. He whispered to Anton "You ever know Danaxe to be a minute late?"

Anton looked scared as he hissed, "Fuck — butterflies!"

Peter hurried back to where the tray was awaiting Danaxe. When he spotted the woman confronting Danaxe, he froze, losing precious seconds, as he fought down his panic while trying to remember her name.

Feeling relieved, he scolded, "Why are you

bothering Mrs. Fields when she has important work to do?"

Danaxe watched as the woman turned, and then smiled as she assessed Peter. "Sir," she said with grave politeness, "who is this Negress?"

Peter looked around in an exaggerated fashion, and leaned over to Mrs. Field's ear and whispered, "She is a root woman. I am introducing her to Madam Lincoln. We are hoping that she might be able to help her with, uhm, let us say some feminine matters. And she is already late."

Mrs. Fields gave Peter a look that could have frozen the Potomac in summer. "A root woman. Of course." She looked at Danaxe as if she were an exotic animal. When she turned back to Peter, he wished he had studied charm as well as science.

"You are not the first snake oil man to approach the First Lady, but I must say, you are the most original." Mrs. Fields smiled suddenly, her gaze even colder than before. "I will leave you and your *surprise* for the President to manage." Peter nodded his thanks, suspecting that their escape was due entirely to Mrs. Field's eagerness to share this salacious bit of gossip with the rest of the staff.

Danaxe picked up the tray, and curtsied. Her practice with surgical trays allowed her to do so without disturbing the contents. "She might not do more than gossip," she whispered once the woman had gone. "But she might go to the police, or even Lincoln's bodyguard."

"Nothing for it now," said Peter. "Just hurry--and pray."

Faster this time, Danaxe headed for the stairs, balancing the tray in her left hand, while she put on a bluetooth earbud with her right. As she passed Peter and Anton's lookout perch, she heard Peter say, "Stop at the door for a three count if you can hear me."

Danaxe followed the instructions, and used the time to put herself in a hyper-focused state of mind, drawing in cleansing breaths as she had done so often in Kabul. She then opened the door and stepped inside.

Danaxe noticed that Mary Lincoln quickly glanced back and saw the tray and then returned her attention to the play. Major Rathbone, on the other hands, watched her warily for several seconds. Danaxe quickly and efficiently set out the glasses and sweets, and very quietly filled the glasses. She stood behind Lincoln, against the wall, closed her eyes, and chanted silently. The comedic moment of the night was fast approaching.

Peter's voice in her ear was jarring. "Usher at the door."

Danaxe opened the door at the knock, glanced at Booth's card, and whispered into the usher's ear, "Yes, he is most certainly welcome."

After a seeming eternity she heard, "Booth is at the door. He just loosened his knife in the sheath. Pulled the board out from under his jacket and left pants leg. Board in left hand. Door opened. Derringer out...."

Quietly and quickly, Danaxe went into horse stance facing the side wall of the booth. As John Wilkes Booth moved into the box towards Lincoln, Danaxe launched into action. She adjusted the course of her hands just as the would-be assassin noticed her. His pause in forward motion made Danaxe's job a smidgen easier.

With her right hand, she grabbed his right hand,

her forefinger going over his, twisting the barrel away from Lincoln and towards the ceiling. Her left hand grabbed Booth by the top of his neck. She used her entire body's weight as she slammed his face into the wall, breaking his nose. John's hand involuntarily clenched and fired the derringer into the ceiling. She heard the board, meant to block entrance into the box, hit the floor.

Without missing a beat, Danaxe switched up her hands, re-grabbing Booth's neck in her right, while she reached in front of his left arm above the elbow, and grabbed his left wrist with her left hand. As he tried to pull the knife into a fighting position, she took control of his wrist, and alternated between slamming his face into the wall, and redirecting John's knife into his thigh. After the third slamming of his face, Booth went limp. Before letting Booth drop to the floor, she slapped Booth's knife hand over her left thigh, causing the knife to drop behind her.

In the middle of the fight, Mary had started screaming, followed by many others in the theater.

With Booth on the floor, Danaxe felt herself return to the world. She realized that despite the derringer's small size, her ears were ringing. She looked at Booth, both marvelling that she had stopped so quickly, while her Buddhist/Nursing persona felt enraged and shamed. She told herself, *Okay, we've been here before. We'll work it out as usual. I still have work to do*. She realized that Major Rathborne had reached her side. Before he could speak, she said "Please sir, whatever you do, do not touch that knife." As she spoke, she laid out Booth on his back, surprised to find she was panting, her voice barely audible.

"What is the meaning of all this?"

Danaxe turned and found the president of the United States staring at her. The shock of seeing a living and enraged Abraham Lincoln left her briefly paralyzed. No time for breathing, her time in the mountains of Afghanistan returned.

"Mr. President, this is John Wilkes Booth. He was here to assassinate you. Meanwhile another assassin is backing out of killing your vice president, and if all went well, is now in the company of four Pinkertons, enroute to meet you at the White House." Danaxe stopped, suddenly out of breath.

At that moment, two Pinkertons rushed into the box, which had now reached maximum occupancy. She gulped air and pushed on as everyone else moved back. "These Pinkertons are here to make sure you remain safe, and to establish and preserve the evidence. Also, another team of four is making sure Secretary of State Seward does not get stabbed, and they will bring that accomplice straight to the White House. Any questions, Mr. President?"

Lincoln absently hugged Mary and seemed to gather his thoughts.

"Who are you, and how did you come to know all of this?" he demanded.

"My name is Danaxe Davis. I can answer your second question only when we are alone at the White House. That knowledge must be safeguarded." Danaxe quickly turned to Major Rathbone and spoke, "Please accept my assurances that this is no reflection upon you, sir. All I know of you is that you are a fine and honorable officer." She turned back to Lincoln. "Mr. President, I and my two companions will answer every question you have. At the White House."

"Everything?"

"Yes, Mr. President. Initially at least, this needs to be for your ears only." As the roaring in her own ears, partly adrenaline induced, and partly from the gunshot not twelve inches from her ear started receding, Danaxe finally noticed the noise coming from the audience. "Mr. President, you have hundreds people concerned about you. You might want to let them know you are unhurt."

Lincoln, without missing a beat, turned around like it was his own idea.

The president waved, and then gestured with his hands as if to say "please sit." It took a moment, but most audience members regained their seats and fell silent.

"Thank you, friends. I appreciate your concern. I am unharmed." He gestured to his left, turning slightly as he did so. "It was just a slight political fracas that got a might heated. As is my custom, at the end of the fracas, I am still standing." As he paused, he purposely glanced behind himself, and looked down on Booth. "Also, as is my custom, my opponent is feeling and looking right poorly at the moment, and I suspect he will be some time in regaining the ability to carry on a conversation." Lincoln paused for the cheers and applause to die down.

"I fear I must take my leave, as this requires me to attend to a number of details. I thank you heartily for your kind concerns, and I expect that you will be hearing from me tomorrow." President Lincoln turned around to look at the proceedings. "I hope we will be able to leave soon?" he whispered.

While Lincoln was speaking, Danaxe had kept her eyes on the Pinkerton men, nodding in satisfaction at the way they carefully collected the pistol, knife,

board, scabbard and belt, and stored them in small
boxes. Each box had a piece of paper glued to the lid,
and the Pinkertons dutifully noted both the date and the
object in each individual box, along with their names.
Quietly, they stepped out into the hallway. Meanwhile,
a man was attending to Booth's wounds.

"Doctor?" asked Danaxe.

"Army surgeon," he answered.

"What do you think of his chances?"

"I've seen worse. His nose will never be the
same again. I palpated, and I find no depressions in his
skull, and so that is a good sign. Looks like what you'd
find after a typical drunken brawl."

"Thank you, doctor." Danaxe replied. The
surgeon turned and studied Danaxe. He glanced at her
hands. Even in the low lighting of the theater, the blood
on her left hand was evident.

"You did this?" he asked. Danaxe nodded.
Much to her shock, the surgeon grasped her hand and
shook it firmly. Danaxe matched his grip. "I thank you
for making sure I was not treating the President.
Someday, I would like to see how you managed it. This
man is rather well muscled himself." The surgeon
turned back to bandaging Booth.

"Surgeon, I believe my party and Miss Davis
here need to be leaving. Can you let us know when we
can get by?" asked the president.

The surgeon stood up and made room. "You
ladies may want to hike up your skirts, and do not come
in contact with the wall. There is a fair amount of
blood." Mary and Major Rathbone's fiancé, Clara
Harris, both paled, but lifted their dresses accordingly.
President Lincoln's party plus Danaxe reached the
hallway. Lincoln grunted when two Pinkertons, and

two more men who seemed quite relieved to see Miss Davis, had joined the party, and followed the cavalcade to the president's carriage. At the president's insistence, Danaxe accompanied him. At her insistence, the two Pinkertons went with the president's carriage as well. Danaxe introduced Anton, Peter, and the other two Pinkertons, who all went into their hired coach.

Except for sobs of relief from Mary, with occasional attempts to ask for explanations, which quickly disappeared into more sobs, the ride was quiet. When Lincoln wasn't affectionately calming Mary, Danaxe watched as he evaluated her. She gazed back at him steadily.

Just as the carriage reached the White House, Mr. Lincoln spoke. "You have seen the elephant, have you not?"

"Yes sir. Two tours in Afghanistan as a nurse in the US Army. My specialties included Trama and Surgical. You would not have heard of Afghanistan. Another answer for your ears only." Danaxe noted that President Lincoln was not fond of being put off, although it was only a small grimace that ever showed.

The two parties from the theater arrived at a White House that was fully lit, and a staff that was quite stirred up. Mr. Lincoln sent Mary to bed with a brief embrace. He next turned to his official bodyguard.

"William, please accompany these Pinkertons and their two prisoners to the nearest military prison cells. Check in with the Ford Theater, and see what they have done with John Wilkes Booth, and get him to the same prison."

"The actor?" an incredulous William Crook asked.

"The very same. Tried to shoot me." The

President gestured at Danaxe, "Miss Davis made sure I was not hurt. Booth took a whipping at her hands." Of the eight Pinkertons, only four followed Mr. Crook. Lincoln turned to Danaxe. "More of your mysterious ways, Miss Davis?"

Danaxe unapologetically looked the President in the eyes. "Yessir. I am afraid it is. No more answering the front door of the White House for you."

Lincoln snorted. "I never have."

Danaxe nodded. "That's true. That would have been Truman. Still, some changes I will vociferously argue for." The four remaining Pinkertons left the room, taking stations around the White House.

"Why am I not surprised?" Lincoln seemed unable to make up his mind whether to be angry or amused. In the end, he settled for exasperation.

He then turned to two young men, his secretaries. "Gentleman, clear my calendar for tomorrow morning and go to bed. I am not certain when I will be available. I will call when I need you." The two men glanced at each other, and then reluctantly bid their president goodnight.

Lincoln sat in the chair behind his desk, and gestured for the trio to sit.

"Miss Davis, you promised answers." Gesturing around the room, "I see no other ears than mine. Do parlay away." He frowned as Danaxe smiled back, and stood without speaking. She walked to the door, and rapped on it three times in quick succession. In response she got first a single knock, and then two more in quick succession. Danaxe repeated the two quick knocks, and stood by the door.

"I cannot say for certain, but I believe two men named John are trying to overhear this conversation. I have instructed the Pinkerton outside the door to chase them away." Lincoln watched her stand there without comment. After a couple of minutes, there were two slow knocks. Danaxe knocked once, and returned to her seat. Peter and Anton stood silently behind her. Danaxe took a deep breath and began to speak.

"The two prisoners you saw are the other two would-be assassins. Their original plan was to kidnap you, Mr. Johnson, and Secretary Seward. Once the Army of Northern Virginia surrendered, that plot turned into assassination. The hope was that great chaos here in Washington might get the Confederacy off their knees."

"That tells me their story. Says not a word about how you know all this. Not nice forgetting to tell the authorities." President Lincoln scowled.

"Ah, but Mr. President, we would not have been able to help if we were locked in one of Miss Dix's cozy sanitariums, could we?" she said.

"That does not bode well for your coming statements." Lincoln looked at Peter and Anton, and then back at Danaxe. "Are your two friends mute?"

"No, Mr. President," said Peter. "But thank you for asking. You see, up until now, with each question, you have looked mainly at me; sometimes at Anton. Only after we remained silent did you turn back to the person with the answers. Who also saved your life."

"And your point is?" Lincoln sounded angry.

Peter took a deep breath. "That being the tall white man, you seem to think I am the one in charge. We three travelled a long way, both to save your life, and to change assumptions like that."

"I am not sure I like where this is headed," said Lincoln. He turned to Anton. "What might your role be in all this?"

"I mostly stand back and make them look good," Anton said in his best deadpan.

They were rewarded by a bark of laughter from the president.

"Well gentleman," said Danaxe. "Time to put our tablets on the table."

"Do you not mean cards?" Mr. Lincoln asked.

Peter and Anton reached into their jacket pockets and produced their tablets. Peter added his smartphone. Danaxe reached into the back bottom of her bodice and pulled out her smartphone and added it to the pile on Abraham's desk. He looked at them.

"Those are children's bricks, not cards!" Lincoln actually looked disappointed.

"I understand," said Danaxe. "I am going to make an outrageous claim. When you hear me state I have outrageous proof, you will come to the opinion that I am a charlatan, a swindler, a trickster, who wants something from you. Well, to be honest, we have some requests. But we will get to those later. I will start with why we are here. And from where. You asked if I had seen the elephant? Yes, I have."

She continued. "I served in the US Army as a Lieutenant. Yes, you heard me correctly. An officer. I was an officer because I was a nurse, with specialties in both surgery and trauma. I served two years near Kabul, as a nurse who was willing to take front line assignments when the medics and the helicopters could not keep up with the casualties. I have been under both artillery and rifle fire. I have had to fire my own side arm to protect my mates on more than one occasion. I am in point of fact a veteran."

At this point, Lincoln looked again at Peter and

Anton, caught himself, and returned his attention to Danaxe. "This had better begin to make sense soon!"

"Yes, Mr. President. As to why am I here this night? Let me show you." With that, Danaxe stood up, picked up a tablet, powered it back up, fiddled with it, and called up the ZNN report on the Greenland Glacier collapse. Put the tablet in front of Lincoln and hit play.

Anton, Peter, and Danaxe sat back and watched as Lincoln's face became incredulous, then studied, and finally worried as the report wound down to graphics of the impending flooding from a six-foot rise in sea levels over the next few months. Lincoln looked up.

"What did I just see?" he demanded.

"We call it a video. Single pictures make portraits. Take thirty-two such pictures in a second, and record the sound and you get what you just watched. We have the technology, the science to share that across the entire globe instantly."

Lincoln stared at the tablet for a moment. "Can you set this 'tablet' to show the part of this regarding the history of the glaciers retreating?" Peter responded by standing and retrieving the tablet, and resetting the video to the part where the history of glacial retreat in Greenland was displayed.

Lincoln rewatched for about ten seconds, and then called out "Here, can you make it stop here?" Peter immediately reached over and hit the pause button.

Lincoln looked Peter in the eyes, and said, "These are dates. Has there been a change in the reckoning of years?"

Peter swallowed nervously, "No, Mr. President. When this was released to the world, you had been dead for 160 years." Lincoln unpaused the video and watched it once again.

"And this flooding will destroy the world? The Lord promised fire next time, never water." Lincoln was obviously appalled.

"Destroy the planet? No. End all human civilization as we know it? That it will do. Most population centers tend to be close to water. Some of our technology is not so helpful."

"What technology? And what do you mean by 'not so helpful?'" snapped Lincoln.

"That climate change that the reporter was referring to was made by us," said Peter. "Mankind. Too many people did not want to believe it, and so we ended up doing too little, too late. You are aware of coal?"

Lincoln snorted. "Dirty stuff to burn, but handy when the alternative is to freeze to death. I see nothing to connect it to that glacier."

"Well, you know that it is dirty. A good place to start. We refer to it as a 'fossil fuel.' It releases carbon dioxide that was in the atmosphere from some sixty plus million years ago. The earth's current system cannot reabsorb that. So, being a gas that is excellent at capturing the heat energy of the sun, we ended up allowing it to heat the planet enough to destroy our civilization."

Lincoln looked at all three in front of him. "So based on your knowledge of history, you have come back to dictate terms. Wait, 160 years as of... 2025?...." Lincoln looked off into the distance, obviously trying to put his thoughts together. Suddenly, he put his face in his hands, and rested his arms on his knees. His shoulders slumped.

Lincoln looked up at Danaxe, and stared into

her eyes for a moment. He harrumphed, and straightened up. "So, your big historical change was keeping me alive?" Danaxe nodded. *Lincoln was actually getting this!* "So as of tonight, what you think of as history has changed?"

This time she drew in a breath and whispered, "Yes."

"So does that mean that now no one knows what will be upon us tomorrow?"

Danaxe couldn't help it: she laughed. "Yes and no. This is a big world, so I would say that across the Atlantic and Pacific Oceans, little will change tomorrow. But there have been small changes since we arrived. Especially here in the United States, and as time goes by, more and more will change. I am certain that if we assist in creating new events, we will become less and less certain, and that will speed up to the point where we will be as you put it, clueless."

"Well Miss Davis, do you have plans that you will be carrying out?" Lincoln asked sharply.

Danaxe smiled. "Off course we do. Sitting here talking to you right now is one such plan. If you are worried we are going to take over the world, have no fear. We lack the means. We have as much respect for the Constitution as you do. But we have a vision. We need people of steadfast character, such as yourself, to first agree, and then work to make our visions real. I have no illusions that the three of us have all the answers, much less know how to accomplish the changes what we believe are necessary."

"Well young miss, it has been a very long night, and I have not even had the chance to express my gratitude to you and your friends for saving my life. Tell me how I might reward you for that, and perhaps we might discuss these changes you want tomorrow."

Danaxe hesitated, and for the first time, looked at Peter and Anton for help. She couldn't miss Lincoln's chuckle of satisfaction.

"We do have a few requests--" Anton began.

"Let her ask," said Peter.

Danaxe recovered her poise. "My first request, is that my picture be taken, and printed in at least one local newspaper, and that I and my partners against crime be publicly credited with stopping the plot to decapitate the Union's government." Danaxe paused, and once she realized no response was forthcoming, she continued. "My second request is that you allow me to work with your wife on a possible treatment for her maladies." Lincoln stirred, but remained silent. "Last that you include us in your schedule as much as you can. We need to work with you to keep that glacier intact, and it will not be easy, as the issues are complex."

Lincoln studied the threesome for a couple of minutes. "Why, as I see it, you already have the answers. I see no need for me to paddle in waters I have no knowledge of."

"Mr. President, it took an entire planet full of human beings to kill our civilization. It might only take one nation to steer us away from it. As to why we cannot do it alone? Just to be clear Mr. President, in our world, Booth killed you at 10:15 this evening. And in the end, your wife's grief broke her spirit. We, all four of us, as you pointed out, are in uncharted waters. So about those favors?"

Lincoln sighed. "More like boons. Why just your picture in the newspaper? Sounds to me as if you all have some things already up your sleeves."

Danaxe smiled. "Yessir. We most certainly do. It is our signal to a few individuals that we succeeded in our quest, and they need to come meet us and a few other people. We expect that they could arrive as soon as early June."

Lincoln stared into space for a moment. When he turned back to Danaxe, he stated warmly, "Well then, you will be pleased to note that I have decided to grant all three of your boons, but I demand one in return. You three shall sup with myself and Mary, say, at one o'clock tomorrow afternoon." Danaxe smiled at the lack of a questioning lilt at the end of Lincoln's statement.

"On behalf of my two companions and myself, we accept." Peter and Anton were both nodding eagerly. Lincoln stood up, heavy with weariness. Peter and Anton bowed awkwardly, tried to turn it into handshakes, and finally turned to leave the White House, with Danaxe walking between them.

As the three left the White House in silence, their hired carriage pulled up, and they were joined by two Pinkerton guards. Another pair were on the carriage, one next to the driver, and the other standing on the back at the doorman's station. They entered the carriage silently. And then they all collapsed.

Chapter 24

The next morning, Anton made it all the way to the kitchen before the memory of the previous night hit him—at which point he dropped the mug of coffee Peter had just handed him. "Sorry," he said, although he knew he didn't sound it. "It's just... we did save Lincoln last night, right?"

"As far as I know," said Danaxe, helping Peter clean up the mess, while Anton just stood there. "We'll have to wait for the evening newspaper to be sure."

"Or, we could just show up at the white house at 1:00 this afternoon, like we're supposed to," said Peter, pouring Anton more coffee.

"Holy shit!" Anton shouted. "We're having dinner at the White House! With Abraham fucking Lincoln!"

Peter put his hands protectively over the cup that Anton was now trying to reach. "No coffee for you until you get it all out of your system!"

"Fair enough," Anton muttered, while Danaxe smirked.

"You should talk, Peter," she said.

"How much coffee did you spill?" Anton interrupted, as he sat at the breakfast table and tried to take it all in.

"None," said Peter. "I just knocked over some furniture last night after I gave up on falling asleep."

"So that's what I heard. But you've been calm?" Anton asked Danaxe.

"I think I got over my excitement by the time we got home last night," she said evenly, and then had to set down the spoon she was using to drop strawberry preserves on her biscuits because her shaking fingers were making the jam fly.

Anton stopped on his way to the oatmeal warming on the wood burning stove, and gave his friend an affectionate hug. "Glad to see you're human after all."

"Must meditate more," Danaxe muttered as she left the room.

When she returned a few minutes later, Peter and Anton were tucking into their breakfast of oatmeal with raisins and dried apricots, and hot biscuits. Danaxe took her usual seat, and Anton poured her a bowl of the thick oatmeal.

Once the illusion of normalcy was established, Anton broke the silence. "So I assume today's business plan is all about Butterflies?"

Peter nodded and swallowed. "I hope to start by getting a real Secret Service established. After that? Maybe let Lincoln take the wheel? He seems pretty good at it, from what I've read." He shrugged and resumed eating.

Anton considered whacking Peter with a dishtowel, but decided to clean the kitchen instead. After that, they tried on their best clothes, and then changed outfits a few times, despite having chosen what they would wear to such an event over a month earlier.

The trio and their hired guards reached the White House at exactly 1:00. To keep the staff from officially noticing their arrival, they sent one of the Pinkertons to get the head of the current Presidential Protection Team, a very fit middle-aged man, dressed in proper afternoon attire. Anton thought he could count at least three different weapons, and was betting he had at least two more on him.

Peter stepped forward. "Hello, I'm Peter Tormey. I am the one who hired you gentlemen."

"My name is Richmond Pearson," said the older man. "I know who the three of you are." He glanced at Danaxe, seeming unsure how to address her. "That was very impressive, what you did last night, Miss Davis. And I am impressed with the plan you had us carry out. How may I assist you today?"

"We are putting you in charge of what will now be called the Presidential Protection Detail. At some point, your new boss will be the Secret Service."

"Secret Service? The men in charge of finding counterfeit currency?"

"We thought they might also be good at providing a serious threat to anyone who wants to hurt a sitting President, or former President."

Richmond took a deep breath, and cocked his head. "You ever consider checking with someone before changing their lives?"

"You rather President Lincoln was shot last night?"

"Of course not," Richmond growled. Peter looked up to stare him in the eyes.

"We need him. Alive. I have inquired about you. I believe you are the man for the job. Are you up to proving that true?" Peter kept staring Richmond in the eye. Richmond matched Peter, stare for stare for at least a full minute. Pearson then broke the stare and physically relaxed.

"Yes, I am. What exactly do you have in mind?" Richmond kept glancing between Danaxe and Peter, not sure who was going to speak. Danaxe broke the silence.

"As I have had the experience of being a protectee, I will be giving you pointers on how to be sufficiently paranoid. For example, do you have two men on the roof with a pair of binoculars, and who are highly capable sharpshooters themselves?"

Pearson looked startled at first, then thoughtfully studied the roof and front of the White House. "You have a very disturbing way of looking at the world Miss Davis."

"It comes naturally from losing a friend to a sharpshooter. In short, your job is to figure out how someone could kill President Lincoln, and to prevent it. And just to make your life interesting, we three will occasionally try to practice an attempt. I call them live action drills."

"Starting when?" Richmond responded, unhappily.

"I will leave that as an exercise for the student," Danaxe finished with a smile.

The trio strolled off to the official entrance to the White House, where they were met by a tall African American man. All three recognized him as Peter Brown, President Lincoln's personal butler. He led them to the dining room, pausing just shy of the door, turned to the group, and spoke very quietly, so as not be heard through the closed door. "I would like to express my personal thanks for saving Mr. Lincoln last night. I have no words to convey the debt of gratitude I owe the three of you."

Embarrassed, the three merely nodded. Brown opened the door and led the three into the room. Mary remained seated, as President Lincoln rose, and shook hands with all three and directed them to their seats.

Danaxe found herself seated next to Mary. The butler then summoned dinner to appear around the table.

Mrs. Lincoln, no longer able to contain herself, addressed Danaxe, before anyone touched their food. "Miss Davis, my husband tells me that you have a possible treatment for my condition?"

"Yes, Mrs. Lincoln. I suspect that your body has difficulty in absorbing an essential nutrient, necessary to make your blood healthy. This causes problems with your circulation, and how much oxygen reaches your brain. I believe a simple dietary supplement will clear up the problem. Your migraines and issues regarding temperament should lessen rather dramatically, perhaps over the years go away altogether. I will not pretend I can guarantee that last will happen, but I am hopeful."

"How is it that you know of these things, while others here do not?" Mary asked.

"I cannot say, madam. Perhaps I was gifted with better teachers," replied Danaxe gently.

Anton had given little thought to what to expect from the White House kitchen, circa 1865, but found the dinner of soup, chicken, vegetables and bread rather plain. Still, the quality was evident and it all tasted wonderfully different from the foods the travelers had grown up with. Since none of uptimers knew what to expect from a private meal with President and First Lady Abraham and Mary Lincoln the day after history as they had known it ceased to exist, they decided to just listen and speak only if spoken to.

Conversation was, considering the circumstances, surprisingly ordinary—except for the part where their host was Abraham Lincoln, who insisted on entertaining his guests with amusing stories. Anton couldn't decide which he liked better: the two he knew from a lifetime of studying Lincoln, or the three he had never heard before. If it hadn't been for the weight of responsibility, Anton would have been alternately jumping out of his chair in excitement and rolling on the floor laughing.

Mary, with a look of long-suffering patience, interrupted her husband to change the subject to talk of their impending summertime retreat to the governor's house at the Soldier's Grounds. *Embarrassed by his behavior, or just trying to get him to eat?* Anton wondered.

As dinner wound down, over a dessert of berries, heavy cream, and brown sugar, President Lincoln finally addressed the business of the day. "Miss Davis, at or about two o'clock, I will grant your first request. A photographer will take the picture you have requested. His companion, a reporter with the *Evening Star* will conduct a brief interview with the four of us. I understand there is some difficulty in printing a picture, but after negotiation, in return for an exclusive, in which we four agree not to talk to any other reporters for a week, they will have that photograph and the interview in tomorrow's edition."

Danaxe smiled and nodded. "I thank you for your quick and complete handling of the matter, Mr. President, although I do have a question. How do I make sure I get at least a half dozen copies?"

Abe, the person, not the President, laughed. "I rather suspect you can sweet talk that reporter yourself, without any help from me."

As dinner was cleared away, Danaxe and Mary went to the kitchen to go over with the staff how to prepare and serve the new addition to Mary's diet. The three remaining gentlemen retired to Lincoln's office.

Anton noted with appreciation, the quiet and unobtrusive way the Pinkertons shadowed the President as he changed rooms.

Upon reaching the office, the three sat down in comfortable silence for a moment. Lincoln broke the silence. "I trust today, we will cover your plans for the United States? And the world? And that this time, you gentlemen will be allowed to speak?"

Peter and Anton managed not to laugh—barely. "Yes, sir," said Peter.

"And will we need those infernal tablets again?" Peter and Anton glanced each other, looking mildly surprised.

Anton responded first. "Well Mr. President, that depends on whether or not you believe us, which would require further proof from us, or if you have technical questions, for which we have access to better teachers than ourselves. Why do you call them infernal?"

"Frankly, young man, iffen' I was the master of those tablets, and came back in time, I might well be looking to rule the entire roost, me being superior and all." If Anton harbored any doubt about this leader's ability to change the world, Lincoln's icy expression would have removed it.

Peter answered, for which Anton was grateful. "Mr. President, that is the furthest thing from our thoughts. We, my friends and I, are counting on your cooperation. But to rule? We are just three citizens of the United States, trying desperately to save humanity. We have suggestions, and frankly, we have put quite a bit of thought into them since we arrived in 1863, almost two years ago. We know how history played out after your death, but we are in totally new territory here, with a chance to solve a lot of problems by heading them off."

"Such as?" The president's tone was sharp, but at least he sounded interested.

"Well, sir, freeing the slaves, for one," Peter began.

"I thought y'all might be in favor of that," Lincoln said, his sardonic humor resurfacing. "Given the company you keep."

Peter laughed, causing Anton to answer. "Definitely! But, in our history, emancipation created a lot of unexpected problems for the Negroes. Those plantation owners, having lost the war, won it in the long run by extrajudicial means. And it got ugly." Anton paused for a moment, wondering if he truly had the courage. "I was going to suggest the use of an infernal tablet, but actually, I know a song that tells the story."

Lincoln cocked a bushy eyebrow at Peter. "Is he any good?"

"Very," Peter replied, smothering a laugh.

"Then by all means, proceed," ordered the President of United States.

"What did I just get myself into?" Anton muttered, but then assumed his full professional mode.

"Southern trees bear strange fruit
Blood on the leaves and blood at the root
Black bodies swinging in the southern breeze
Strange fruit hanging from the poplar trees
Pastoral scene of the gallant south
The bulging eyes and the twisted mouth
Scent of magnolias, sweet and fresh
Then the sudden smell of burning flesh
Here is fruit for the crows to pluck
For the rain to gather, for the wind to suck

For the sun to rot, for the trees to drop
Here is a strange and bitter crop."

As Anton sang, Lincoln started to relax, but by the third line, he was sitting upright, looking horrified. "When was that song written?" he rasped when Anton finished. "How many?"

Peter replied, while Anton caught his breath. "In 1937, it was a poem written by Abel Meeropol. Then a singer by the name of Miss Billie Holiday made it famous in 1939. As for how many, I honestly do not know for sure. I have heard estimates ranging anywhere between 2,000 and 4,000 between 1866 and 1964."

Lincoln put his face into his hands. "What have I done?" he moaned.

Anton forgot himself. He stood and rushed to Abraham Lincoln, who for a moment, wasn't the president and a personal hero, and put his hand on the distraught man's shoulder.

"What you did was fight to preserve a nation that might one day allow all people to live freely and with respect for each other's humanity," he said. "When you died at the hands of an assassin, that dream was lost. None of that was your fault, Mr. President."

Peter stood and joined them. "We came back to help you avoid much of this, for as many as we can save, both from death, and scores of years of degradation, predation, and humiliation. But, sir, this was nothing you did."

Anton steadied his voice and continued. "Sir, after your death, President Johnson, and some senators and representatives, used their political might to make this happen, with the support of a fair number of like-minded Northerners. While abolitionists, such as the Quakers, were great on ending slavery, they were rather lacking in realizing that they, too, had been corrupted. To hold slaves, you have to regard them as less than human, and those Southerners were great arguers for that hellish lie."

"In our world," said Peter, "by the eightieth anniversary of your assassination, the future country of Germany murdered some twelve million civilians. Their crimes? Six million, like me, were Jewish, three-and-a-half million were Gypsies. The rest were a combinations of people who preferred to love people of the same gender, espoused different political systems, or otherwise recognized Germany as the evil it was. This and a host of other reasons, is why we are with you in this room."

At that moment, Danaxe, was ushered into the office by one of the servants. Quietly, taking in the mood of the room, she took a seat. A moment later, Lincoln pulled his face from his hands. Spotting Danaxe, he smiled.

"Miss Danaxe, you have the finest timing of anyone I know. Last night, you saved me from a most fatal migraine, and now your two friends have handed me a moral one. So as the good nurse, what are your recommendations?" Danaxe looked at her two friends quizzically.

Anton went first. "I sang *Strange Fruit*."

Peter followed, "President Johnson, Jim Crow, and yes I went there. The Holocaust." Danaxe nodded, and looked satisfied. She looked President Lincoln in the eyes, and smiled.

"It is quite simple President Lincoln. We wage a political Civil War, the one that our South won in the timeline we left. It used laws, hangings, and terror to spread a Whites only political and economic system that stretched from the South, along the Mississippi River to the Canadian border. Except this time, we kick ass." For a moment, Lincoln looked dumbfounded. Then he laughed and pounded his desktop a couple of times.

"Miss Davis, I find in you a delightful set of contradictions. May I ask how you fair with sailors in language?"

Smiling, Danaxe responded, "I am not sure about sailors. But I did nurse U.S. Marines sir, and taught them a thing or two." A knock on the door, and one of Lincoln's bodyguards appeared in the doorway.

"Mr. President, a reporter and a man with a camera are here to see you. They are listed on the visitor's log. It might take a minute or two for the photographer, as we are checking the camera to make sure there are no surprises."

Lincoln cocked an eyebrow at Danaxe, and responded, "Pray let them in as you can."

Immediately following after the Pinkerton's announcement, a distinguished, middle aged gentleman, sporting a wide mustache, with a matching beard trimmed to the width of the mustache entered the room.

"President Lincoln. Good to see you whole and hale. Mr. William Wallach has dispatched me to conduct the interview for the *Evening Star*. I am Crosby Noyes." He held out his hand to the president, who shook it vigorously. "I must tell you sir, very little can either surprise or enrage me these days, much less cause me to push younger reporters out of my way, but the events of last night has done all three. There are rumors flying about everything: who tried to shoot you, reasons why—"

"Oh, surely that cannot possibly be raising too many eyebrows," Lincoln interrupted. "Plenty of folks want me dead."

"That is sadly true, Mr. President, but that is just the problem," said Noyes. "So many possibilities and everyone guessing, er, that is to say—" For the first time since entering the room was at a loss for words. "I do apologize if I sounded in any way disloyal, Mr. President. I meant no offense."

"None taken," Lincoln said amicably. "I am quite aware that I have enemies. But the last twenty-four hours have made me a good deal more aware of my friends." He glanced at the three time-travelers, and then back to the reporter.

"While we wait for Mr. Jeremiah Gurney, Jr., I'd like to set the record straight over exactly who this country has to thank for your miraculous survival. There's been some crazy talk that a Negro was involved, but of course it would make more sense if they said he had been the shooter. Others say it was a Secessionist actor named Booth who attacked, and a woman who jumped up and fought him off. Of course that would be just plain lunacy—"

The President cleared his throat, all warmth gone from his manner. Danaxe stepped forward. "Just so you understand at the outset, Mr. Noyes, this is the young lady who took down John Wilkes Booth, whom, last I was told, cannot speak coherently yet. I was given a report by his jailers. Broken nose, possible fracture of the front of his jaw, and he lost at least four teeth. He will be able to walk, but is expected to have a permanent limp favoring his left leg." His gaze shifted to Danaxe. "Where you stabbed him repeatedly, Miss Davis."

Danaxe took a couple of minutes to take quiet cleansing breaths.

She was saved from having to respond immediately by Noye's response. He found a chair, and sat down, landing heavily as he visibly deflated.

"Mr. President, this will prove to be the most incredulous story ever told in the history of the United States. You are telling me that a Negress just accomplished the greatest rescue of a sitting president, while the rest of the government stood by and let it happen?"

"Yes, Mr. Noyes, that is what I am telling you."

Noyes stared into the distance for a few moments, seeming to run through a list of possible responses. "Miss Davis," he said at last. "Please accept my apologies for having completely devalued your contributions to this situation. I trust you can demonstrate how you accomplished this rescue?"

Anton laughed, while rubbing the back of his neck. "She practiced on me just two times, to establish how she would carry out her attack for this event. Friendly warning, she did not use a wall to practice planting my face into. Just the grip she had on my neck, and the force she used to propel me into an imaginary wall took a few days to recover from. The bruises lasted a week, at the very least."

Noyes nodded as he appeared to take in Anton's comments. He then turned to Danaxe. "I suspect a single demonstration will suffice for my needs. Please understand that as a gentleman, I find it hard to ascribe as how someone of the fairer sex could do such a thing. But as you seem knowledgeable about the business, I am willing to be educated."

Danaxe smiled. "I understand. I suggest we get

the demonstration over with, and that will inform your conduct of the interview." Noyes nodded in agreement. Danaxe turned to Anton "You look a bit heavier than Peter in both weight and heft. This time, I need you to play the wall." Danaxe demonstrated for Anton how to catch Crosby's shoulders on his palms to simulate the impacts against an imaginary wall. She then turned to Noyes, and asked "I assume you use pencils for recording interview answers?" Crosby nodded again. "I need two unsharpened pencils." Noyes diligently handed over two.

Danaxe handed back Noyes two pencils, one for the stick, and one for the knife, slipped under his belt to the left of the buckle. "Please accept my apologies in advance for any bruising."

Noyes laughed. "Miss Davis, given my stated doubt in your abilities, any bruising is my own responsibility. Unlike Booth, I shall not be surprised as he was."

Danaxe smiled wickedly. "What makes you think I am not aware or prepared for that fact?"

Noyes smiled and gave Danaxe a slight bow. Over-acting, he got himself in the agreed on starting position, while Danaxe dropped into horse stance. As with Booth, it was over in seconds.

With the demonstration finished, Noyes sat down heavily into his chair. He ran his hand over the back of his neck, and then undid his shirt cuffs to look at his wrists. He held them up to show his wrists, and then stopped, staring at Danaxe.

Danaxe, upon releasing Noyes just froze where she was. For two minutes, everyone stared at her as she stood there, eyes blank, and nostrils flaring. Danaxe shook herself, stood up from horse stance, and took an additional minute doing cleansing breaths. Then suddenly, she came back. She looked around, obviously regaining her senses. She looked at Noyes, and asked solicitously "Are you okay? I mean are you unharmed?"

A bit nervously, Noyes replied, "Well as you can see, both my wrists are bruised, and I am willing to bet that my neck has similar bruises. Which, if you do not mind, leads me to suggest this. Along with a picture of you, we publish pictures of my bruises? It would give greater weight to your statements about your confrontation with Mr. Booth."

Danaxe expended another minute on cleansing breaths. "Yes Mr. Noyes. That makes complete sense. And makes that page much more salacious for future sales."

"Miss Davis, are you all right?" Lincoln asked.

For a moment, Danaxe stared at him, obviously taking in the question before responding. "This is the first time in my life that I have rehearsed inflicting harm in a specific situation, well deserved as it was, and then do an after-action rehearsal of the same. I suspect, in the next couple of days, I will have the same reaction as the first time I had to use a firearm to kill someone in defense of the people I was there to heal." Shaken, Danaxe returned to her seat.

A few minutes later, Noyes began his interview. With impressive calm, all three flatly lied, claiming to overhear snippets of conversations that lead them to put together a narrative of the attempted decapitation of the Union Government —- President, Vice President, and Secretary of State. This was followed by the actual events at the Ford Theatre, and then the reports of the two teams protecting Vice President Johnson, and

Secretary of State Seward.

In the midst of all this, the photographer, Jeremiah Gurney Jr., was allowed in, and quickly introduced. In the interest of not overloading President Lincoln's office with smoke, Noyes suggested that photographs of his wrists and neck be taken elsewhere. Peter spoke up and arranged for eight copies of the newspaper be delivered to the White House. Danaxe posed in front of the single part of the wall of President Lincoln's office that was mostly bare, and had her picture taken, without a smile.

After Noyes and Gurney departed, the president addressed his guests. "I gather we have grave matters to discuss. Miss Davis, are you prepared for this?"

Danaxe paused for a moment before responding. "Yes Mr. President. I understand how my reaction might look, but at the end of the day, I understand the uniqueness of the situation. And yes, I have my wits about me."

"I am gratified to hear that. Any opening thoughts on how to resolve my second migraine?"

"But of course, Mr. President. Allow me to lead you to your third migraine. Given the plantation owners' resolve to fight a political second stage to the Civil War, the first step is to totally block their readmission into the Union until they approve certain Amendments. On a personal level I am honored to be in the same room as the man who pushed through the 13th Amendment. As I understand it, Senator Thaddeus Stevens has written a proposal for the 14th Amendment."

Lincoln nodded, and replied, "Yes, he has."

Danaxe took another breath. She had worked her entire life to get to this moment, and was not going to give into a full-scale stress reaction until she was finished. "What gets passed, in our future, isn't even close to what he proposed. We have the text of the 14th as passed. We also have the text of the correcting 15th Amendment. Together they get across Negro males as citizens in theory. Trust us on this, due to your death, it does not work. Negro males were hit with literacy tests, and poll taxes. On top of that, women were not granted the right to vote until an additional fifty-five years and four amendments had passed. No offence Mr. President, but can you name one reason that I, as a Negress, having served in the US Army should be prevented from voting?"

Danaxe watched as Abe Lincoln started with an immediate response, paused for a second thought, and then dug for honesty.

"You personally? I would have no issue. With my wife, whom I love dearly and deeply, I would have a problem."

"So, in your life, you have never met a man who was emotionally challenged? Given your experience in an Indian war?" Lincoln glared at her briefly, but then changed his glance to stare at the floor. He looked back up at Dan axe and responded.

"I have known more than a few men from that experience of whom I would doubt their ability to vote rationally. At this exact moment, given your previous arguments, I might have to include myself." For the first time, Dan axe saw a shrunken Abe Lincoln, who was viewing himself in a new light.

"Just to be clear, your wife is suffering from several possible medical issues. Using a woman who clearly has a medical condition to judge all women is not based on the rationality of science. It is the practice of religion, in a governmental position, which is specifically forbidden by the 1st Amendment. In these discussions, it is no accident that I am the one talking. My male colleagues and I chose this style of argument on purpose. On medical issues, in this room, at this time, I am the supreme authority by my ability to solely argue from the imprimatur of science.

"I can also conduct this conversation from two other angles. I am the only person who can speak for the Negroes, as I am the only person in the room who is Negro. We also need to discuss the Indians. I refer to them as the First Peoples. That is because they were here before us. And to put it bluntly, as a nation, we need them to help lead us away from the future we came back to avoid. I look upon you not as just the President that preserved the Union. I look to you to expand who is included in that Union, so that we have multiple voices and viewpoints to safeguard that future."

Looking every inch the President, Lincoln stared Dan axe in the eye. "Bit early to think you've treed a President, is it not?"

Dan axe grinned as she matched him eyeball for eyeball. "I am not looking to tree anyone. Well, except for one Nathan Bedford Forrest and his future allies. I am pleading with you to save us all. We need the First Peoples to teach us how to think seven generations ahead. To see the earth in a new and wondrous way. To know that to protect us, we must protect that earth. Last but not least, we need everyone's voice, European, First People, Negro, Asian, men, women —whoever is here to work together so that our society works for everyone equally."

"And besides," Peter added with a grin. "Think

of all those arrogant people whom you can ruffle!"
Lincoln stood up and paced around his office.

"You three are surely enough dumping a bit
much all at once. Is there a particular reason for any
hurry involved?" Lincoln stopped pacing, and waited to
see who was going to respond first.

Dan axe smiled when Anton stepped up.
"Actually, first up is we need to keep at least ten
Colored regiments from being disbanded. We need
them to become mounted rifle units to become the core
of the militia for six new states. And everyone in those
will need a Henry Repeater rifle."

"And what six states would those be, young
man?" Lincoln asked.

Anton thought for a moment, and looked to his
friends. "Well Sequoyah is the obvious first one, and
that for the First Peoples. Nebraska for former slaves.
The Dakotas to supply two more states, one centered on
the Lakota, and the other centered on the Cheyenne.
Figure Montana and Washington for the former
slaves."

"Any other states you have in mind?" Lincoln
asked crossly.

This time Peter jumped in. "Well in the future,
if two territories are added that are not connected with
the rest of the United States, you might want to
consider that the local indigenous populations have a
say in the matter, equal to everyone else."

"We have two more coming?" an incredulous
Lincoln asked.

"Maybe. It is a new history we are trying to
write Mr. President. Who knows? Maybe it will be
four. Or none," Danaxe responded.

"Actually," said Peter, "before you were

elected, Russia tried to sell us Alaska. We bought it in 1867. If the same offer comes along in this new future, would suggest that you purchase it. We have an alternate view how to safeguard the First Peoples there."

"So with all these complications you are using to give me a third migraine, do you have suggestions as to timeline? Or more demands?" Lincoln crossed his arms, looking much like a father dealing with recalcitrant teenagers.

"Suggestions sir. Very, very strong suggestions. And yes, we do." Anton narrowly avoided actually squeaking. He continued. "First off, those ten colored regiments I mentioned. I suggest getting them to Kansas first. Not sure where we will need them to go after that." Danaxe followed up.

"Next we need amendments. How many I do not know. The first to establish that anyone within the territory of the United States, including reservations, is a citizen with full rights, regardless of gender, race, color, or previous condition of servitude, and upon reaching twenty-one years of age, will be guaranteed the right to vote. For the future, we need to separate big money, corporations, and politicians. We have some time on that." Peter stepped in next.

"And this very same summer, while all of this is going on, we need a Segregated States Act." Peter stopped, taking in the glares from Anton and Danaxe. "Although, my friends, think Sanctuary States is a better term. All Indian reservations become counties within their given states or territories. As such no white person may move there without the permission of the State or County government for a period of twenty-five years."

Quizzically, Lincoln interrupted Peter. "Why only twenty -five years? I thought the Biblical precedent was forty years. So most of the adult slaves who would have been the leaders all died off?"

"Because of that word segregated," Peter responded. "The idea is that at the end of the day, we do not want six states to be viewed as "whites not welcome." It is more designed so that those states make it clear that those people have something to say to the civic body, have their economies entrenched, so that unscrupulous people cannot come and steal from them."

"What do you reckon needs entrenching?" asked Lincoln.

"Owning all the local businesses," Danaxe offered. "Having schools and colleges and trade schools. Most all government positions. Enough so that they keep their position as members of said establishment."

Lincoln sat down, leaned back, and splayed his legs under the desk, put his hands behind his head and stared at the ceiling for a while. The three other people sat back and tried to relax. Peter smiled to himself as he caught Anton matching Danaxe in a quiet meditative breathing exercise. Lincoln sat back up, appearing to have reached a conclusion.

"I find myself largely agreeing with what you have proposed. I take your pointed hints about seven generations. That is about when that glacier split in Greenland?" Lincoln paused, and acknowledged the three nods with one of his own. "And I see your point about the Sanctuary States. I cannot recall you mentioning what happens to territories where they already have a sizeable white population, like

Washington Territory."

"Yes," Danaxe said, "that is true. We figure that anyone who is already there stays there with all the rights of a citizen. However, they will shortly find themselves outnumbered, and outvoted. And not able to bring in any more so-called family members."

Lincoln nodded approvingly. "Well, that is enough for today. Keep an ear open for sudden requests, including your personal presence. I gather I will be spending some time with Thaddeus Stevens over all this. I will need a copy of the two 14ths, and the 15th." Lincoln, watching Danaxe stand with an impish grin, looked a bit nervous. Danaxe pulled an obviously brand new toy cap gun out from under the back of her bodice.

"Well, as good guests, having purposely migrained you, we should now work to share your pain. As your butler has not interrupted, I happen to know that Mary is out on a walk." As she finished, Danaxe pointed the cap gun at the ceiling, and pulled the trigger, and then yelled at the door to the office, "BANGITY BANGITY BANG!!!" As she started her last syllable, the door opened as a Pinkerton came through the door, pistol starting to clear his jacket. Seeing it was Miss Davis, and Lincoln was watching with open amusement, the large Irishman was reduced to blasphemy.

"What in the name of the Father, the Son, and the Holy Ghost do you hellishly think you are doing. This is in no way a joke!" yelled Richmond Pearson. Lincoln, behind Danaxe started chuckling. Richmond turned his glare on the President. Lightly, and gently, Danaxe spoke.

"Breathe. Big, slow breaths. I warned you there

would be drills. This is the first one. Lesson one: are you sufficiently paranoid? That is the question you and yours must ask yourselves a dozen or more times a day. I apologize for scaring you, but that is what unplanned drills are for. To expose you to the realities of what can happen." Richmond was near to being his usual tacit self.

"Understood. I will apologize in return as I will be confessing my sins regarding the language I am keeping to myself as I ponder your actions." Richmond stated flatly.

"I was a Lieutenant once. And I have either heard or used every word you are thinking. When you are past the adrenaline rush, let me know what you feel you have learned, and how you are going to deal with it."

Richmond nodded. And then turned to President Lincoln, who was still chuckling. "Mr. President." And then left the room.

The threesome stood up and said their goodbyes. As Peter, the last one out, turned to close the door, Abraham Lincoln broke up in full roaring laughter.

Chapter 25

The next few weeks seemed both hectic and slothfully slow. Meetings with the President and others every two to three days, as Anton, Peter, and Danaxe got to witness how "the sausage was made."

It was a time of letters. The first one was from John Ross, requesting that Confederate Brigadier General Stand Watie be delivered a message informing him that his presence was required by the "People of Sequoyah," and that he be escorted home to make sure he arrived safely. A letter arrived from Chamberlain, which the three read together over dinner.

April 20, 1865

Madam and Gentlemen,

I trust that all has found you well. As you might have guessed, your first hint was a bit shocking. You were obviously aware of my promotion. I noticed that when I was being bandaged prior to being retired to the hospital tents, the ambulance driver insisted the bandages be removed so that he might apply a "sulfa powder." He added that this was being done to prevent any possible infections. While I was recovering from my wound, I inquired and was told that it had been invented by a "Dan R. Davis." May I presume this is the same Miss Davis that I was introduced to? If so, Miss Davis, while I did not mention you, the doctors and surgeons would like to meet you and extend their gratitude. This miracle powder, and the companion pills are credited with saving thousands of lives.

Due to exigencies of the War, at the time, I was not able to read your second prediction on the correct date, but given that it was dated a mere three days before the third missive, I read them at the same time. Living it was more than exciting and overwhelming, but nothing compared to reading it in your missives.

I must admit to still being somewhat discomfited by your missives, and your prediction of Miss Davis's photograph appearing in the newspaper. On one hand I am grateful to you all, especially your efforts in saving President Lincoln. On the other hand, I wonder what you will be doing with President Lincoln, and now General Howard. Your information was too accurate by far, and now I find myself worried about what such knowledge of our future could do in the wrong hands. I fear that if you are not morally fastidious, I have unleashed a great evil upon the world. I would find an answer helpful in quieting what I hope are simply the jitters of one who has seen the hell of this last war that is finished, and do not care to see a new one erupt.

> *Cordially yours,*
> *Major General Joshua Chamberlain*

Anton spoke first. "Man has a point. Lincoln said nearly the same thing the next day. Why not have him at Gettysburg when we introduce General Howard to the onion. Might calm his jitters."

Nodding, Peter responded, "And maybe convince him to help."

Danaxe stared off into the distance briefly. "Actually, he ended up being President of Bowdoin College in Brunswick, Maine. Sounds like someone who could be helpful finding us people to establish colleges in the Sanctuary States." Danaxe searched for a tablet, and quickly found an article on Chamberlain. "Interesting. He stated he didn't suffer any infections. Wonder if that means he doesn't have to spend the rest of his life using a catheter and urine bag."

Peter and Anton both shuddered and grimaced. Peter went to write the letter. Danaxe committed to passing on John Ross's letter to President Lincoln the next day.

Letters came from Jenny regularly. One was four pages long, and the first two were completely unreadable. The next two pages confirmed Danaxe's suspicion that it was Hindi, written in the traditional Devanagari script, and was the same letter as the English version. More letters came from Danaxe's patent attorney, with follow up questions for her third batch of patent applications. The most troubling issues involved specialty stethoscopes, that did not require hard plastic membranes. Danaxe did not feel up to trying to get all the steps from oil to plastic membrane, as she would be required to submit physical models of everything involved.

The month dragged on. The first of the United States Colored troops were on the move. Danaxe, as she visited with Mrs. Lincoln on nearly a daily basis, had been informed by John Hay that all six of the Colored Cavalry Regiments were heading towards Kansas. Along with enough infantry regiments to take them back up to full strength. Danaxe was also told that the Federal 3rd Colored Troop Regiment was being joined by veterans who requested to be allowed to make up the regiment's losses. There were rumors that the 54th Maine Volunteer Infantry Regiment was asking to be federalized and sent to Kansas, and that volunteers who were not accepted for the 3rd would be used to bring the 54th back to full strength. The 67th United States Colored Troops (formerly 3rd Regiment Missouri Colored Infantry) had been federalized. Work was ongoing to organize one last regiment, and replacements to bring all units to full strength. The request for all Henry Repeaters to be turned over was denied. Soldiers were being allowed to keep their issued firearms if they bought them, and the Repeaters were very popular.

Peter and Anton responded with a quick series of telegrams with the Henry Rifle Company. At the end of a very tense week, Anton and Peter celebrated at their favorite tavern.

With each beer, they toasted their way through all their achievements.

Anton lead with "80 grains powder!"

Peter followed with "More barrel and tighter grooving!"

Which of course led to the favorite toast of the night, Anton's "No brass but the idiots behind us!"

Over the next week, Peter and Anton poured over the proposed contract with the Henry Company, delivered via telegram. At the end of the week, they signed a contract for ten thousand rifles, at a minimum production rate of 500 rifles per month to start, rising to 2,000 per month by the end of July, and peaking at 2,500 no later than September. As part of the deal, Henry Rifles agreed to only sell the rifles to Peter and Anton for the next ten years, but they kept full rights to the patent. When the conversation turned to the finances, the conversation became much more sober, despite the beer.

Anton reflected ruefully, "Well it was fun while it lasted, but that leaves us with only a couple hundred thousand." Peter nodded.

"Of course, that means we head to the next level. The Long Range Foundation."

Anton softly banged his forehead against the table. "Really, you want to bring this up again?"

Peter glared. "Yes. This is when and where the race to climate change begins. We're going to get crushed by England in particular for the next seventy years. They have the population to drive fossil fuels forward no matter what we do. You know it. I know it. Danaxe knows it. Our best bet is to harness the best technology commercialists, plus Tesla, to develop an alternative technology path, that gets ignored until it produces money-saving results. Hell, have Edison invent the lightbulb and the phonograph, but then invent tube technology. Then solid-state electronics, and finally, the silicon chip.

"By 1920, we'll be needing one tenth the electrical output. If Danaxe's plan with Jenny works out, the population of the entire globe will be lower to begin with! Take Tesla. Point out the problems with projected power, and then show him the photovoltaic solar cell. And wind turbines. And lithium ion batteries. Hell, throw in turbine generators, water reservoirs for energy storage. Bags under deep water. Ocean turbines. Hell, his disc turbine will be an energy saver to begin with! He'll glom on to that faster than flies on the horse manure we keep trying not to step in! And lead to the technology for silicon chips that Edison needs for that final step. And after we give Edison a lesson in humility, we'll have a money-making proposition that Bill Gates would hate our guts for!"

"When you're in this kind of mood, there's only one solution," Anton said. He headed for his room with a bottle. The one with the bourbon label.

Chapter 26

Peter felt like he was melting inside his fashionable summer suit. "Our reenactors garb wasn't this miserable!" he complained as they headed for their row house after another long meeting at the White House.

"And whose brilliant idea was it to build the nation's capital in a swamp?" Anton retorted. Neither would admit that the sticky heat wasn't their worst problem. More than a month had passed since the end of the War, and John Ross had yet to appear in Washington. Meanwhile Sitting Bull had sent word ahead that he was en-route, but the rumor mill was saying he would be delayed by Congress for "security reasons"—which was their political opponents' way of saying armed Lakota warriors would never set foot in Washington so soon after an assassination attempt. Of course, Sitting Bull would never go into the heartland of his enemies without at least eight or ten of his most trusted warriors, which everyone in the government knew. They were asshats, but they weren't stupid.

"There are two men following us." Anton flicked his eyes across Pennsylvania Avenue.

"Pinkertons," said Peter.

"I thought the Pinkertons were working for us!"

"The ones *we* hired are. I have no doubt about that. But clearly someone else hired a different group. Come on, you knew this would happen. Three people no one's ever heard of show up in Washington, spread money around, get cozy with the President and start advocating for policies that must sound like science fiction to these folk—"

"I was thinking more along the lines of a bad comedy, but yes, I take your meaning." Anton sighed. "I was expecting to be dragged into an alley and beaten; maybe shot outright, but these guys…"

"Oh, hell," said Peter, suddenly changing direction. "I'm sick of this cloak and dagger bullshit! If the meetings don't kill us some hired thug will. Let's just see if we can buy them a drink and discuss it first!"

"Like civilized men?" Anton asked, struggling to keep up with Peter. "Are you sure that's a good idea?"

Peter strode resolutely through light traffic, to where their two followers had paused, looking momentarily confused. "Good!" said Peter. "They were nice enough to stop in front of a bar!" While not quite as upscale as he would have preferred, the tavern looked safe enough; the type to serve low level political functionaries, journalists, and a few of the more prosperous craftsmen. Everyone walking by seemed weighed down by the heat, and few took any notice of anyone else's business.

"Gentlemen," he cried to the two confused detectives. "The day is hot, and since you've been paid to learn all you can of myself and my friend here, you might as well do it in the comfort of this tavern, over a mug of cold ale."

"We're buying," Anton added helpfully as a well-dressed matron walked past them, keeping her skirts well above the dirty walkway. Two young boys followed obediently behind her.

"Your pardon, sir," said the younger, pasty faced man, who looked like his best skill was fading into the woodwork. "I believe you have us confused with someone else."

Peter waited a beat, and then exchanged a look with Anton.

"Forget it, Nathaniel," sighed the second man. He was tall and distinguished looking with a fashionable beard that was still too ordinary to stand out. "They know who we are; we need to know who they are, and I, for one, could use a drink." He fixed Peter's gaze with sharp, intelligent eyes. "Your friend did say you were buying, sir?"

"Absolutely." Peter led the foursome into the cool, dim establishment.

They stopped beside a long counter, and Peter bought beer for the group. Then all four took their drinks to a corner table in the back. Peter and Anton took seats against one wall, affording them a clear view of the establishment. Their two guests moved two chairs so that everyone had a wall at their back.

"My name is Peter; this is my friend Anton. But you already knew that, Nathaniel?" Peter glanced at the pasty looking guy. "And…?"

"Richard," said the taller man, who seemed to be in charge. "Pleased to make your acquaintance." Richard offered his hand. Peter and Anton took turns shaking it, while Nathaniel merely sipped his beer and looked around the room.

The beer was cool and foamy, and for a few moments, everyone drank in silence. Finally, Peter spoke. "We are aware you won't divulge the identity of your clients. But perhaps you could tell us what you were asked to learn?"

The two detectives exchanged a glance. "Frankly," Richard said, "anything we can. No record exists of either of you before two years ago, yet you have been very... Busy in those two years."

"Patents, investments, travels to Injun' country," Nathaniel spoke up. "Plus, the continued company of a nigger woman who claims to have saved —" Richard shot Nathaniel an angry look. Peter wished Richard had not silenced his partner. While much of the country still believed Danaxe's role in saving the president was some kind of stunt perpetrated by the Radical Republicans and others took it as a strange joke, far too many people were saying nothing at all. It felt to Peter like the calm before the storm. He wanted to hear everything Nathaniel had to say—even if it meant wanting to take a bath afterwards.

"We presume nothing and have no wish to be indelicate," Richard said. "But the three of you make for an interesting... team. And now you have the ear of the president of the recently re-United States. Surely you can understand why any number of parties would wish to know more."

Anton nodded. "We were just discussing that ourselves. Is there any betting going on? If so, we'd like a piece of the action."

Nathaniel choked on his drink while Richard laughed. "Quite a lot, actually. As well as a desire among many to know if your influence could perhaps be... purchased. Only in small matters, I assure you. It is clear enough that your political affiliation is rather radical, and cannot be swayed."

"Understatement," muttered Nathaniel.

"It would depend on what those matters were," Peter said. "You have correctly noted that our political allegiance is set. But if someone wishes our help in a way that does not conflict with that allegiance, then we are willing to listen."

Richard reached into a pocket of this vest and withdrew a calling card made of fine linen paper. It had an address from a part of the city Peter was not familiar with, and the name "John" scrawled beneath. "Please contact this man," Richard said. "I assure you, it will be to your mutual benefit." With that, the strangers took their leave.

Anton and Peter watched them exit the building. Then, after a hasty check to see if any other patrons were moving or looking their way and finding none, they looked at each other and shrugged.

"Let's give this to our own Pinkertons," said Peter, still holding the card.

Anton nodded and stood. "Let's get back to base; maybe hear some good news about John Ross and Sitting Bull."

"The one time 'Indian time' is just not helpful," Peter said as they left the bar and continued down the street. "With John Ross in poor health, and all the hotheads Sitting Bull has to contend with... Hey, what the—"

They had been walking past the entrance to an alley. Suddenly, both Peter and Anton, were jerked off their feet from behind, and dragged down the alley by two large men. A third, who seemed to be in charge, was no less dangerous-looking. For a moment, Peter expected to be asked questions which they would be reluctant to answer, when a fist crashed into his stomach. Doubled over in pain, unable to stand upright, he could do nothing to fend off the blows to his face which followed. From the grunts and cries of pain that punctuated an almost precise, rhythmic thudding of raw meat being smacked hard coming from beside him,

Peter could tell Anton was receiving the same treatment.

Peter's assailant suddenly released him. Stumbling against the alley wall, and leaning there for support, he realized Danaxe had joined them. Peter noticed she was dressed for a fight, with an unbuttoned riding skirt. If Peter's gut didn't feel like a crab was trying to claw through his stomach to the outside while pythons crushed all of his joints, he would have laughed at the expressions on their assailants faces, as they approached a ridiculously easy fight with a black woman. Their expressions changed, as with absolutely no wind up, she kicked her first target in his solar plexus with the heel of her shoe.

Her next target threw a roundhouse punch, which she used to throw him, and then followed through by landing on him. This knocked the breath out of him leaving her ready to take down her third target. He, however, had wisely fled the scene.

"You guys alright?" Danaxe asked, barely breathing heavily.

"I think so." Peter felt his face and winced. "Ice would be good."

"And aspirin," wheezed Anton. "Why haven't we patented that yet?"

"I've got everything you'll need at our house," Danaxe said, with what Peter guessed was more confidence than she felt.

"What are you doing here?" Peter asked as they limped out of the alley back to Pennsylvania Avenue. This time, passersby did notice them, and at least one woman hurried her children past with a look of disdain. "And by the way, thank you."

"One of our Pinkertons told me there were two

men asking questions about you two and claiming to work for the same company. But our guys didn't know them." At that moment, George, head of their personal security, came running up.

"I saw a man in a black coat and blue pants running. Was he part of this?" George gasped. Danaxe nodded, as she took charge of her breathing.

"Good." George gulped, and regained his breathe. "I told my two partners to take him into custody. Do you need a doctor?"

"I have it from here," Danaxe said. "If you could rouse the gentlemen in the alley, and find out who sent them and what they want, that would be helpful."

"Done!" said George, clearly disgruntled over missing the action. But not, Peter noted, over receiving instructions from a black woman. He was getting better.

"And," George added, "Go straight home. I will be sending a detail. You folks have done a fine job of looking after the president, but you seem to have forgotten to look after yourselves. You were targeted."

Back in their comfortable house, Peter and Anton lay on their beds while Danaxe administered basic first aid. The exceptionally fine scotch that the first lady had sent after the assassination attempt would also help very soon, but for now, they needed clear heads.

"So... Nate and Dick?" asked Anton. "Set-up?"

"Could be," said Peter, glancing at the card Richard had given him.

"Probably," said Danaxe. "We'll know more after we check out this address. But it's not impossible that more than one group is after you or us." She paused, looking more pensive than usual.

"Oh, crap," said Peter. "Our run-in took you away from Mrs. Lincoln, didn't it?"

"I was grateful for the rescue," Danaxe said bitterly.

"She was having another bad day?" Anton asked, moving the cold compress Danaxe had applied to his face so he could see her.

"To put it mildly. It's not her mood swings that bother me, or even her headaches, which I was so sure I could cure completely!" Danaxe sighed. "I guess we all deserved some humility training, after our grand plans. It's just that I was such a fan of Mary Todd Lincoln. So certain that she'd been maligned by history —that if she'd been a man she'd have been venerated. But the sad fact is, I think she really may be mentally ill. And I don't think I can cure her."

No one had anything to say for a while. Than Danaxe got up, and poured Peter and Anton each a double scotch, and a single for herself.

"You two just need to rest, and you'll be fine," Danaxe said a while later. "For now, we should probably each have a guard assigned to us. I don't think we've seen the last of people wishing us harm."

"I just wish I could stop feeling like we might deserve it," sighed Anton. "We know that history can be changed; we've changed it. But we have no way of knowing how many people we've harmed, or prevented from being born or even killed."

"I feel the same way," said Peter. "But…" He trailed off, suddenly realizing he had no answers. His anxiety over John Ross and Sitting Bull seemed ready to overwhelm him, and the pain of today's attack only made it worse. Danaxe brought him another stiff drink and he gulped it down. "I really hope we didn't come all this way to make things worse," Peter mumbled as sleep finally took him. "Could someone please turn on the air conditioner?"

An unknown amount of time later, Danaxe shook him gently awake. Her gentleness didn't help much with the pain that hit him full force in almost every part of his body.

But the paper she held out to him did. "A messenger just delivered this," Danaxe said. Anton had apparently already read it because a grin lit his battered face.

Peter took it, waited for his vision to clear, and read. Chief John Ross had arrived in Washington that morning. Poor health had slowed his journey, and he was requesting the presence of his favorite nurse, but hoped to be ready to meet with the President within a few days. Danaxe was already packing her medical bag.

Peter tried to stand. "I'll go with you."

"Back to bed," Danaxe said, easily pushing him down with one hand. "I've an escort waiting. Get well, so you can finally be in a meeting where something good happens! Both of you."

Peter found he had no energy to argue. But he was feeling a lot better about everything.

Chapter 27

The next day proved busy. Breakfast was followed by a meeting with the Pinkertons.

"I had your assailants arrested by my Presidential Detail." Richmond Pearson opened his jacket to expose the original long, five pointed star badge of the Secret Service, "And we have been grilling them steadily. Calls of nature, and food yes, but sleep not so much." He paused at Danaxe's frown. "Yes Miss Davis, I share your misgivings. Am I being paranoid enough? That attack was not a robbery, and under the circumstances, I did not feel time was on our side. I have telegraphed some friends with whom I have worked in the past, and they have confirmed that we are holding one Corporal Ray John Williams, on medical discharge from the 3rd Tennessee Cavalry. We are working on identifying the other two." Anton and Peter exchanged looks. Richmond continued.

"I see you know that regiment. I can confirm that he is acting on the directions of one Nathan Bedford Forrest." At this juncture, Peter reached for his wallet, and Danaxe went to fetch her purse. Richmond paused, looking obviously puzzled, as the spectacle reached its conclusion when Anton accepted five dollars each from Peter and Danaxe.

"Bet?" asked Richmond. Anton smiled. "All right, it sounds like you know more than I do about what is going on."

The trio looked at each other for a moment.

Anton responded. "I have some ideas. Forrest has likely been approached to head up a group that will one day be known as the Ku Klux Klan. They are what we call a White Nationalist group, that wanted economic and political control over anyone who was either Negro, Jewish, or Catholic. Since they controlled both the political and economic systems, they were in a position to keep these people, especially the Negroes, poor and powerless. While we finally passed laws to end this, they were largely unsuccessful, as they found other tricks to keep them down.

"Because he was described as a "wizard at cavalry," he has been titled the Grand Wizard of the Klan. He and some of his friends are smart enough to understand what Sanctuary States will mean. Sending troops to Kansas probably has them in a panic. Much like Fort Sumter, out of fear that Lincoln would abolish slavery in '61. And equally unnecessarily I might add."

"I take it this was something of a surprise?" asked Richmond.

Anton and Peter stared at each other. Anton spoke. "Actually yes. We anticipated that we had at least another one or two years before they made their move. They will become violently rabid and vicious in their reaction to Negroes seen as equals. We anticipate that they will use unconstitutional laws and violence to harass, subjugate and terrorize Negroes. And I suspect that will end up spreading to attacks on the Sanctuary States. Including their allies, the First Peoples."

"You mean the Indians?" corrected Richmond.

"No, we meant the First Peoples. The ones who were already here when Christopher Columbus arrived, mistakenly thinking he had reached India, and not China. Hence the sobriquet 'Indians.' "

"I see." Richmond looked off into the distance for a moment. "I wonder if a hundred men assigned to

the Presidential Detail is enough. I was thinking of
twenty men for the President. Ten each for the Vice
President and the Secretary of State. Now I need to
assign fifteen to the three of you. Leaving me forty-five
to run investigations of possible threats. Speaking of
being paranoid enough, why were you not guarded?

"Well," said Peter, "with Danaxe around, I felt
safe, and we never thought we would be targeted." He
looked crestfallen, as he caught up with how big a
mistake he had made.

"Yes, I see you are learning to be sufficiently
paranoid," a somber Danaxe replied. "I presume that is
probably a good number to assess your actual needs. If
the three of us agree to spend at least two days a week,
all together or only just one stepping out, would that
allow you to cut down your detail? Keep in mind I am
totally aware of my surroundings, and as a protectee
capable of taking care of up to three opponents at
need." Richmond appraised Danaxe for a moment.

"What type of dress are you currently wearing?"
Richmond asked pointedly.

Danaxe grinned as she stood up, took a couple
of steps back to get some room and demonstrated a fast,
hard snap kick to the face. Richmond stepped back,
Danaxe's foot a hair's breadth from his face, her skirt
split to allow the full range of motion she needed.

"You have a deal. I will drop your detail to ten
permanent, and a couple of others on an as needed
basis. But there is one other issue. I understand you
practice a form of archery you refer to as either 'yumi'
or 'Kyodo'? At an archery range?" Danaxe nodded.
"As I understand it," Richmond continued, "you could
be in there with as many as nearly thirty other archers?"

Danaxe simply nodded.

"You do realize, that is a threat issue too big for us to guarantee your safety? That a situation like that is, in fact, custom made for an assassin? A group of fine, upstanding citizens practicing an ancient sport? An approved, au courant form of physical fitness--which happens to be potentially deadly? By the time we recognized the intentions of an assassin, we would be too late."

This time, Danaxe cocked her head, and arched an eyebrow. "I will contact the archery club involved. I believe that with, uh, sufficient financial incentive, I can arrange to be the only person present at certain times."

"How often do you need to practice?"

Danaxe, uncharacteristically turned and paced back and forth for a few moments, obviously thinking. "First, I must congratulate you, as you have proved more paranoid than I. Therefore, I accept your offer. As for how often I need to practice, I expect that I will need at least five days a week."

"In that case," said Richmond, "I would suggest that you devote a portion of your considerable wealth to purchasing or creating a private archery range. I can have one of my men look into it today."

"Yes, please do," said Danaxe, wondering why she or Peter or Anton had not already thought of it.

Richmond continued. "As for 'John,' his real name is Theodore Roosevelt, Sr. He has a daughter, Anne, with a medical condition that has left her largely crippled. A 'Dan R. Davis' has come to his attention, via the New York Pinkertons who are of the belief that you two gentlemen, and not our dear Miss Davis herself, are the inventors of all these new medical miracles." Richmond bowed in Danaxe's direction for emphasis, and continued. "I am of the opinion that he means no one any harm, but that he intends to invest, with an eye towards taking you over."

Peter and Anton laughed. Danaxe and Richmond looked at the two, with Danaxe throwing in a glare.

Anton kept chuckling, so Peter stepped into the breach of decorum. "I have a list of lawyers who I am sure can steer us clear of entrapments. Besides he was, uh, I mean *is,* a philanthropist. I am sure that once we can correct his understanding of our relationship, we could be of use to each other."

Richmond looked thoughtful for a couple of minutes. "Yes. I suspect you are right. If I might make a suggestion?" He waited until all three nodded. "I will meet with him in person later today. I will suggest that he meet with you, say tomorrow after dinner?" When the three nodded. Richmond bade them farewell and left. The three then, along with their Pinkerton escorts arranged for a large coach, and went to meet John Ross at the boarding house where he was staying.

When they arrived, they found Chief Ross, along with another Cherokee. John was dressed in white shirt with collar, waist coat, and black, pressed slacks. Another man, dressed similarly, albeit his shirt was red, stood up as they approached. John remained seated, and called out, "Hello! As directed I brought company. May I introduce Stand Watie. Stand, this is Anton, Peter, and Miss Davis. The three I've told you about, and the ones who arranged that safe passage and escort home for you."

General Watie stood up and shook hands, including Danaxe's when she proffered it. While everyone else sat down, Danaxe went to John, visually assessing his health as she walked. "You were late, John. How often were you sick on the way here?"

"He was feeling poorly more often not. Especially after we started riding. Damn fool refused a cart," Stand growled.

"We have a house with some unused bedrooms. You are both welcome to join us. I have my equipment there. And you will be in time for a late dinner," Danaxe said with a smile.

Stand helped Anton and Peter pack their belongings. Danaxe settled their accounts with the boarding house. Stand spent the ride looking around, and while it was not his first city, it was his first visit to Washington. The process went in reverse at their home. Anton settled into the kitchen, while Danaxe examined John, leaving Peter and Watie alone in the parlor.

"So, John tells me you arranged for that safe conduct?" Stand asked.

"Yessir. Well, Danaxe did actually. I assume that John told you of our plan for Sequoyah?"

"Yes. And I do not believe a word of it."

"I can understand that. Did he mention going to Gettysburg? To meet with General Howard?"

"Yes. And I am curious as to the point of that meeting."

"To convince you, General Howard, General Chamberlain, Sitting Bull, Chief Joseph, and anyone else who shows up to not only agree with the idea of Sanctuary States, but to get behind it and push. President Lincoln is agreeably inclined to do this, but we will need help. For example, did that missive to you mention keeping your men together?"

The former Confederate general nodded. "Yes. Out of respect to John, I told my men that upon my return, we may be called up. I did not explain beyond that. No offense to you and your friends."

Stand Watie looked puzzled as Peter gave a bark of a laugh. "None taken. To be totally honest, I cannot even imagine what it feels like to be you in this situation and in this conversation. At the end of the week, we will be in Gettysburg. One of the reasons is that Sitting Bull and Chief Joseph have never seen the way our armies fought. They have no clue what they are facing."

Watie gave his own snort in return. "You white men fight in crazy ways. That Henry rifle you Yanks have makes it even stupider. You should not have used it in volley fire formations. Against that rate of fire, you need to spread out. Some moving while others fire, and then switch roles. Reload on the run perhaps."

"I promise, you join in this enterprise, you will be the one figuring it out."

"With a Henry?"

Peter smiled in response. "One like no other. We should have the first ones by the end of the month. We have someone working on a new version, and it is being tested as we speak."

Stand smiled for the first time. "If you make good on that promise, I may be amenable to changing my mind."

In the kitchen, Anton effectively announced dinner would be soon as he started singing to help him to keep track of when to do what in his cooking. Stand listened for a few minutes.

"What is a pissa pie or uhmoray?" a curious Stand asked.

"It's "pizza" with the 'z' sound, and it's *amore*. Both words are Italian. Pizza is a food, and "amore" is

Italian for love," explained Peter.

"May I assume he is making this 'pizza'?" Peter simply nodded. The two sat down in the parlor and enjoyed the aromas wafting out of the kitchen.

Danaxe joined the two men and sat down. Peter recognized from her lips moving that she was chanting. As Stand took a breath to speak, Peter raised his hand to catch his attention, and shook his head. Danaxe was in such a state of concentration, Stand's presence slipped her notice, as she pulled out a tablet and earbuds. She spent the next half hour using her tablet. Stand's face was pointedly curious, but he remained silent. Peter knew she was listening to something, but had no clue what. Anton's singing stopped. She pumped her fist in triumph, looked up registered Stand's presence, and uttered "Crap!"

Peter laughed. "No worries, mate! He'll be finding out about it all soon enough.

A bit frustrated, Stand asked "How is John? Is he well?"

"Yes and no," answered Danaxe. "He has a heart condition. The good news is I can treat it. Get him to change his diet and take the medicine I prescribe, and he could live for several more years."

Watie hung his head in relief. "Thank you from the bottom of my heart. While he and I have disagreed, I have never hated him. May I ask what you were doing with the thing in your hand and that other... whatever it is in your ears?"

Danaxe thought for a moment before responding. "I lack a piece of equipment to make a proper diagnosis, and I lack practice in doing it the old-fashioned way by just listening. So I listened to John's heart. Then I used this to store what we call recordings, that can capture sound, pictures, or both. I listened to some recordings of known heart problems, and found one that sounds just like John's heartbeat. So I know what is wrong, and I am able to help him."

Stand sat back and stared at Danaxe for a moment. "I suspect that there is something you are not telling me." Danaxe and Peter both nodded.

"We'll show you and everyone else the answer in Gettysburg. That way you will have at least one reason to go there," Peter said, with a plainly mischievous smile.

"Dinner is served," Anton announced from the doorway, rendering a deep, mocking, bow.

Danaxe went to bring John to dinner. She returned a few minutes later, with an obviously relieved patient. Danaxe was unconcerned about her patient eating the pizza, as she knew that working from scratch, Anton's would be safe for John. Dinner was a success. In response to John's questions, Danaxe laid out what he needed to do, plus how she would keep him supplied with digitalis as a medication.

***

After dinner the next day, the three left to meet Mr. Theodore Roosevelt, Sr.. A doorman answered the front door, and initially refused to let any of the Pinkertons into the house. Anton, Peter, and Danaxe stood mute, as the head of their detail, explained.

"I am Secret Service Agent Adam Van Vorst." He paused as he opened his jacket to display the Star of the Secret Service on his waistcoat. "I am the head of your guests' security detail. I have been personally assigned by President Lincoln. You will let us enter, and make sure the place is safe for them to visit, or, you can explain to Mr. Roosevelt yourself that you refused them entry." After some sputtering, the doorman allowed two agents to enter. After a moment, one stepped back out. One of them made the agreed on hand gesture, signaling that it was safe for the three guests.

A butler led them to the library, past one Secret Service Agent. Peter noticed the second one was by the stairs. When they entered the library, he saw that outside, there was one agent each at the two windows.

In front of them stood a man the same height as Danaxe, dressed formally, including a silk cravat. "As you might surmise, my name is not John. I am Theodore Roosevelt. I am here to discuss business with Mr. D. Davis. And you are?" Roosevelt paused.

"I am Peter Tormey." He shook Roosevelt's hand.

"I am Anton Pozda," He pumped their host's hand quite eagerly.

Roosevelt looked puzzled.

"I am Danaxe Davis." Danaxe extended her hand. And left it there. After some thirty or so seconds, Roosevelt cautiously reached out to shake her hand. Unlike Peter and Anton, neither of whom had tried for a knuckle breaker, Danaxe tightened her grip. Visibly surprised, Roosevelt tried to match Danaxe. She only stopped after Roosevelt was unable to tighten his grip any further.

Roosevelt took back his hand, flexing it slightly to take out the sting. He gestured for the three to sit, and sat down himself, heavily with a big sigh.

"Well, I am rather confused. Just to make sure I understand this, Miss Davis, *you* are the person who has now filed some twenty medical patents under the name "Dan R. Davis?"

Danaxe smiled at Roosevelt. "Yes sir. I am most definitely that 'Dan R. Davis.' Your reaction is precisely why I chose to file under that name."

Roosevelt leaned back in his chair, and stared at a point in the ceiling for a couple of moments.

"Forgive me Miss Davis. May I ask how you have the knowledge to put together all these patents? That sulfide and the chloramphenicol are life savers. How did you know how to compound them?"

Danaxe stared off into the distance for a moment, considering her response. "At this point, this is what I can tell you. Depending on our relationship in the future, I may decide I can tell you more. I was trained as an army nurse. Precisely whose army is immaterial, but it was one that saw my possibilities. By your standards, I am a doctor who worked in settings where people who were about to die went for a chance to stay alive. I worked as a battlefield nurse, who saved the lives of people of who had wounds you could not even begin to imagine, with procedures and technologies beyond your imagination. I served two tours of duty in a war, centered around Kabul. As for those twenty patents, I have plenty more where that came from."

Roosevelt sputtered. "Kabul?"

"I am aware of your daughter's spinal issues. I may be able to help with that. The biggest problem is that it will take time to spread what I know. Which brings me to another project in which I believe you could be most helpful, as I am looking to start six colleges, two for medicine and biology, and four for agriculture and technology. With the two medical colleges, I can not only start on making very specific braces and other tools, but we will be able to train doctors to know how to use them. I have a gentleman in mind to work on recruitment, but as I recall he has little experience in raising funds for a charity."

Roosevelt stared at her for several minutes. "I must admit, none of this is what I expected when I woke up this morning. And having heard this, I am frankly stymied as to what to do next. Or where to go from here."

"What surprises you most. That I am a woman? Or that I am a Negress?" Danaxe demanded.

Roosevelt, sounding confident replied, "Both. Equally. I notice you do not call yourself a doctor. Why is that?"

Danaxe laughed. "Because at this point, whatever my knowledge or skill, I am just a highly trained nurse. I have nothing that shows I meet the current standards. I expect to rectify that in the future. You are in a position to help make that possible. I have a simple proposal."

Roosevelt raised both hands, indicating non-verbally "And that would be…?"

"You have known products in front of you. I am hampered by having to make enough money to find people skilled enough to build the models that the Patent Office requires. I do not yet have the reach to expand the markets to other continents, such as Asia, or Europe, or Africa. You do. Think what you could make if those markets were opened." Danaxe raised her hands, as if to say "And what could you do there?"

Reminiscent of Lincoln, Roosevelt leaned back, and found a new point in the ceiling to stare at. Reacting faster than last time, he responded. "So you are suggesting a licensing agreement of some sort, with a look to exporting?"

"Yes. I propose a modest five percent licensing fee. At first. Once you successfully expand the market overseas, I will drop that licensing fee to 1%. I need you to arrange to do some other projects, which will help with the development of more patents."

"What other projects?" Roosevelt asked suspiciously.

"Projects that show I am not an anomaly. Projects that you actually have some experience with. For the licensing, you must split either your hiring or your contracting with suppliers as per the license to be split evenly between Whites and Negroes. Once your sources match the census numbers between the two, you can reduce the number to match same. That you assist in developing training programs with the same numbers for the skills your workers need. That includes management. If you can do this, we have another project in mind."

Roosevelt responded testily, "And why should I do that?"

"Because you cannot comprehend how a Negress is capable of these patents. And there will be more. If you are involved, then you can profit from them, and they will be produced faster. My income will go up, which I will use to foster other projects. And ultimately, we will use you to develop the most important project. The Long Range Foundation."

Roosevelt paused to rub his temples. "I am afraid to ask, but, what is this Long Range Foundation going to do?"

"So far, the patents are regarding medical supplies. My two friends have a long laundry list of industrial patents that they can add to the list. I do medical. They do industrial. Show us you can supply the world with much-needed medical supplies and expertise, and we can show you how to truly build a better world."

Silence prevailed. Danaxe realized that Roosevelt had reached his limit to process the conversation. Suddenly, Roosevelt demanded, "Are you insane?" He looked at Anton and Peter, who both shook their heads.

"From your viewpoint, yes. From my viewpoint, no. It comes down to this. I am producing patents at a rather slow pace. If you put your energies and money behind the effort, then I can put out many more patents, faster," countered Danaxe.

"Do you expect me to trust you can do all that you have suggested?" Roosevelt, with some suspicion in his voice.

"Of course not. I urge prudence. Can you make money off the patents I have already submitted? The biggest problem is lack of capital, and the second is the lack of people trained to perform the work. Can you solve those issues? Yes or no?" Danaxe fired back.

"Well of course I can, otherwise you would not have received an invitation." Roosevelt's tone sounded much less annoyed.

"Good, let us start there. Once you see that works, and why, you will understand the importance of follow up patents. Research will be required. In my culture there is a saying that you need a tool to make another tool. I have done my best, but there may be holes in what I have. Mr. Tormey and Mr. Pozda, will be producing industrial patents." Her companions nodded as she spoke.

"So to restate, you have known patents in front of you. Get them international. I have more patents to offer. These two will add theirs. Prove you can make the requisite copies without any attempt to steal them. I am asking for a rather low licensing fee. Not because I am stupid, but because I know I will have more money than I can eat. The demand will be there. The other issue is training. In manufacturing, and in changing doctor's minds, as well as other issues, but at the end of the day it comes down to trust. I understand your lack of trust. I am making incredible claims. You have seen twenty of my patents. Do you have the ability to ramp up production on the twenty patents I have?"

Roosevelt stared directly at Danaxe for a few moments. "I can definitely increase local production. I have connections I can reach out to for other countries. Based on what you have patented in hand, I can get there in two to four years. I am more than a bit concerned about your requirements about hiring or training equal numbers of Negroes. I am an industrialist, not a charity."

"Simple explanation. Much to your surprise, I am 'Dan R. Davis.' Not either of my two white companions. The fact is that both Negroes and Negresses, and white women can match you in the contest of life."

Roosevelt rocked back in his chair, and crossed his arms. He looked at both Anton and Peter. "Gentlemen, you have been entirely absent from this conversation so far. What say you? And why should I trust Miss Davis?"

Peter and Anton looked at each other for a couple of minutes. Anton spoke. "Well Mr. Roosevelt, it is like this. Miss Davis was in the military. She is a university graduate. She has access to a wealth of knowledge she can use. Peter and I have equal access to knowledge in different areas. If you accept the current offer, you will have more money than you need to develop the causes you wish to champion. If you reach that point, we have another level to interest you in. By December, 1866, 1867 at the latest. At that point, we will lay our cards on the table. As to why doing it that way, that will soon become apparent. Technology is not always our friend—and in point of fact, can be literally poisonous. For bona fides, you have a proven area where you can benefit."

Roosevelt sat back and looked Anton in the eye. "And who actually owns the patent? If I pay to develop it, should not I own it?"

Anton laughed. "Seriously? Without us, you have nothing. We have ownership, and you get first licensing rights. Nice try. This is not about making money hand over fist. It is about something more important. Prove we can trust you, and then we will discuss what this is all about."

Roosevelt briefly templed his fingers in front of him. Suddenly, he stood up, walked to the door, opened it and called out.

"Adam Van Vorst, please enter the library!" The agent in front of the door followed Mr. Roosevelt into the room. He stopped behind Danaxe, his hands clasped behind his back.

Roosevelt retook his seat, and smiled at Adam. "Any insights as to how serious I should take these three? You are a Pinkerton, are you not?"

Adam studied Roosevelt for a moment, and then responded. "Yes Mr. Roosevelt, I am a former Pinkerton. Miss Davis here prevented John Wilkes

Booth from assassinating President Lincoln. That is a fact. Miss Davis has been treating Mrs. Lincoln medically. While Miss Davis has been often frustrated in doing so, I have talked to the staff. Madame Lincoln is in fact improving both in her health and her state of mind."

Danaxe turned in her chair and stared at Agent Van Vorst. He continued, "I am an agent of the Secret Service. My exact assignment is to assure the safety of Miss Davis, and these two gentlemen, by direct order of President Lincoln. The president, who has preserved the Union, has seen fit to listen to their political advice. As to what advice he is actively taking, those are details that I am not at liberty to discuss with you.

"As to my opinion? When any of these three speak, pay close attention. As a bodyguard, I keep my eye on Miss Davis the most. I am not a gambler. But if it would make you feel better, I would gladly bet $50.00 on anything she has to say."

Roosevelt studied Adam for a moment. "How long have you been with the Secret Service?" he asked.

"About a week."

"And before this?" asked Roosevelt.

"The Pinkertons were paying me and a few others to do so surreptitiously." All three, Anton, Peter, and Danaxe turned to stare at Adam.

Roosevelt continued to stare at Adam. "Van Vorst? Any relationship to Sturtevant?"

"My family arrived around 1630, before he was Governor of New Amsterdam, but no one claims kinship. Still possible, I suppose."

"Well as one New Yorker to another, I will take your word under serious advisement. Thank you for stepping in." Secret Service Agent Van Vorst nodded and left the room. Roosevelt looked at the three remaining in the room in front of him. "You seem to inspire loyalty, from people who have no reason to be so loyal for nefarious reasons. I will accept your initial proposal. I assume you will want your own lawyer to draw up the papers?"

"Yes," said Peter. "We will be traveling at the end of this week. I would imagine that our attorney should be able to have something for you by the end of the following week. Should we send it to your New York address, or are you planning to stay here in Washington?"

"New York. My business here is completed. About those six colleges. Whom did you have in mind?"

"I will be discussing the proposition with the gentleman I have in mind by this weekend," said Danaxe. "If he accepts, would it be possible to give him a letter of introduction, and have him contact you directly?"

Roosevelt nodded.

The trio stood and said their goodbyes. Roosevelt made a point of shaking Danaxe's hand, to signal the successful business meeting was formally finished.

**

Once everyone was in the carriage, and the security detail was draped around the vehicle, Peter and Anton broke into an excited discussion about their plans for the Long Range Foundation.

Sitting across from them, Danaxe stared out the window, her mind replaying Adam's comments about

Mary Lincoln. For some minutes, Danaxe tried to put together the puzzle in her own mind. Upon the umpteenth failure, she turned to her left, and addressed Adam.

"So, would you be so kind as to tell me the current gossip about Mrs. Lincoln?"

Looking puzzled, Adam responded, "I did not figure you to be much into gossip, Miss Davis."

"I am not looking for gossip for gossip's sake. My relations with the first lady are as troubled today as the first day I met her. According to what you told Mr. Roosevelt, the staff, and I presume her family has seen a miraculous turn around. I am trying to figure out why that is the case."

Adam nodded. Danaxe waited patiently for him to consider his reply. "As you realize, I have not spent a lot of time around the White House. Much of it was learning what little the Secret Service has in the way of policies and procedures, and what it means to also be Federal Police Officers. In briefing me about the three of you, the subject of your treatment of Mrs. Lincoln came up. As I understand it, you have her eating a preparation of baker's yeast. I have also been told you have taught her ways of calming herself during her spells of great agitation." Adam paused as Danaxe nodded.

Adam continued. "While she still becomes agitated, it has wound down from what was once an hourly occurrence, to maybe once in two or three days. When she does become agitated, she uses your lessons to calm herself. And to everyone's surprise, she has taken to apologizing. Unless you have an appointment at the White House. On those days, just minutes before you arrive, she is struck by one of her infamous headaches, and becomes extremely agitated. Does this gossip help you?"

Danaxe nodded, and spent a few moments staring out the window, trying to puzzle out her relationship with Mary. *Well, when all else fails, go to the source.*

"Actually Adam, I am going to thank you by complicating your day. After we drop off Peter and Anton, at home, I need to make an unannounced trip to the White House. Preferably via the servant's entrance."

Adam grinned, "Your reputation for direct action precedes you. I suspected that this would be your reaction."

Danaxe turned to address Peter and Anton, and was surprised as she realized they had actually stopped their conversation, and focused on listening to her and Adam.

Anton, trying to lighten the mood, broke the silence first, "Go get'em, tiger!"

Danaxe flashed a thumbs-up in response.

***

As Danaxe breezed through the White House kitchen, the butler, Peter had a big smile, and said "You'll find Mrs. Lincoln in good spirits in her upstairs parlor, reading calmly." Danaxe nodded in response.

Danaxe paused at the open parlor door. Mary was sitting in her favorite carved rosewood parlor chair, appointed with blue cushions. Her hair was arranged in braids on both sides, and she was wearing her favorite lavender dress. As was her custom when she did not wish to be disturbed, Mary was sitting with her back to the door. Danaxe considered various opening gambits. She wanted the truth, not a confrontation. A healing, not a rift. Danaxe remembered how she approached her mother with the news of her joining the Army. Smiling at the memory, Danaxe decided to start the conversation with Mary in the same manner.

Danaxe walked silently to Mary's side, knelt down to the left of Mary's four tiered dark lavender satin dress. Reaching up to clasp Mary's hands on the book. Danaxe spoke softly. "T'is great to see you in such a calm state." Danaxe watched as Mary's face froze, and paled slightly.

"Well, thanks to you, I do seem to find more times of calmness." Mary paused for a moment.

Danaxe decided to interrupt. "Yes. Everyday. In fact, only when you know that I am coming do your headaches return. That is the reason for this unannounced visit. I have a favor to ask, as a daughter to a mother. Why, when you know I am to visit you, do you grow so agitated. Have I caused you some harm?" Mary dropped the book, and broke down into sobs. Danaxe rose up on her knees, hugged Mary, and started rocking her. Danaxe refused to let go, and whispered in Mary's ear, "When you can talk, please tell me what is between us."

Danaxe kept cradling Mary, and rocking, losing all track of time. Mary finally stopped sobbing, and returned Danaxe's hug.

Mary patted Danaxe's back, and sat back, fully erect. "Well Miss Davis, you grab that chair, and we shall have a little chat, just the two of us." As Danaxe sat as directed, Mary pulled a handkerchief from the inside of her left sleeve, and wiped her face.

"Since you have started me on eating prepared

baker's yeast, taught me both meditation and the breathing techniques, I have been the calmest, and most pain free that I can remember. My greatest fear is that of being abandoned. I have lost two children, and I almost lost my husband. My behavior has been so terrible, I am…" Danaxe noticed that Mary was taking the time to control her breathing, and calm herself. Picking up where she had left off, Mary said "I am afraid that you will abandon me, and I will return to my former ways. That without you, I cannot keep up this good behavior."

Danaxe said softly, "I am a nurse. Not the cure. The yeast, and teaching you how to maintain your calm, is the treatment. I could disappear today, and as long as you keep up this regimen, you will be much as you are. Yourself. You are not a horrible person. You have an illness. Your body has difficulty absorbing a particular nutrient, called vitamin B12. The yeast basically overloads your body with it, so for the first time in years, if not your whole life, you are finally absorbing the right amount for your brain to get enough oxygen. If your symptoms start to reappear, eat more of the baker's yeast."

Danaxe leaned forward and took the first lady's hands in hers. "Mrs. Lincoln, you are one of the strongest women I know. You can succeed at this. As for abandoning you, I have no intention of such. Yes, I will have to leave Washington, and probably live somewhere out in the plains. I have hope that we will maintain our friendship by both correspondence and visits. I hope that is sufficient to calm your fears."

Mary used breathing for several moments, fighting back more tears. When she succeeded, she answered, "Yes my dear, that is more than sufficient.

Furthermore, if we are going to continue these kinds of conversations, I will call you Danaxe, and you will call me Mary." Both women stood and exchanged hugs.

"Well Danaxe, what say you about visiting our rose garden?"

Chapter 28

As soon as the train came to a full halt in Gettysburg, the luxury cars erupted with motion as a half dozen former Pinkertons, now Secret Service Agents, disembarked. Fanning out, they secured the area around the last two private cars. Station personnel led fourteen nervous horses to the nearest pickets. More Secret Service Agents debarked, followed by Anton, Danaxe, Peter, Chief Ross and Stand Watie. Two of the agents gathered the luggage, met with the arranged drover, and headed for the Union Hotel to claim their rooms.

As soon as the carriage was unloaded, the horses hitched to the carriage, and the security detail arranged, the cavalcade set out towards the site where Pickett's Charge broke against the wall. The weather promised another hot summer day, but the morning air was comfortable. Since on this trip, no one was having to care for any wounded, Danaxe chose to sit between Peter and Anton, as they kept hanging their heads out the windows to see the sights. John Ross was content to look out the window at the countryside they were passing.

Danaxe was the last to exit, as Watie insisted on handing her out properly. For a moment, everyone stood silently

Peter broke the silence. "Good morning. General Howard, General Chamberlain. Sitting Bull, it is great to see you again. And you as well, Tavibo. Wovoka, I look forward to hearing what you have to say." Peter turned to the two First People he didn't recognize. "My name is Peter Tormey, this is Chief John Ross and Chief Stand Watie. These are my partners Anton Pozda, and Danaxe Davis." As Peter was talking, the security detail started to unload and set up folding chairs and small tables.

Sitting Bull smiled as he listened. "This is Chief Joseph the Elder of the Nez Perce, and I am grateful to introduce Chief Black Kettle of the Cheyenne."

Black Kettle nodded stiffly, before speaking. "I am told that you warned Sitting Bull about John Milton Chivington's cowardly plans. And as advised, we pulled back our camps so that they were not discovered. I am not pleased with what we have lost, but I am grateful for our lives. I am here today to listen to your words. I must say from the start, I am weary of treaties with white men, and I do not trust any of them anymore."

Nodding, Anton responded, "Yeah, if I was you, I would not be particularly trusting of me or any treaty. What we propose here today is an end to all treaties." Anton turned to Chamberlain, and continued. "General Chamberlain, Chief Watie, Chief Joseph, Chief Black Kettle, and General Howard have not been fully informed of who we are, and why we are here. Sir, if you would be so kind, and being the Wounded Lion of the Union, pray tell these gentlemen who we are. Let me know what you want me to show. It looks like our detail has enough shade to set you up with a tablet."

In response, Chamberlain twirled his mustache for a moment. "I can see why you might want me to do that." He turned and addressed the group. "General, Chiefs, if you would be so kind as to join me." As the group passed Anton, Black Kettle turned his head and stared Anton in the eyes. Anton nodded and gave the chief a slight smile. He then walked back to the carriage, and pulled out a 15" tablet, powered it up, and opened the video folder.

Chamberlain gave a brief description of how, not far from where they were sitting, he had first met Anton, Peter, and Danaxe, followed up by their description of how they had arrived at Gettysburg. At this point, Chamberlain reached for the tablet. He glanced at the screen.

"Which one do you want first? Peter's film of you two, or Greenland?" asked Anton.

Chamberlain responded quickly. "Peter's film, if you please." Peter grinned as he noticed that Sitting Bull was keeping his eyes on Chamberlain's every move.

"Okay. That will be the picture of bright light at the bottom right. Tap it with your forefinger," instructed Anton. Chamberlain followed the instructions, and held the tablet to allow the group to watch and listen. Black Kettle kept shifting his gaze between the tablet and Peter. After a few minutes, Chamberlain looked to Anton.

Anton replied before Chamberlain could speak. "Touch the screen anywhere, and a long black bar will appear at the bottom of the screen. In it will be what looks like an equal sign. Tap it and it will pause." Chamberlain put the video on pause. He explained the size of the smartphone that Peter used, noting that the devices worked using "Ben Franklin's electricity." Chamberlain followed Anton's instructions. "Did you want to play anymore of that?" Chamberlain shook his head. "Right. Check the top right of the screen. If there is an "x", tap it. If not, tap the middle of the screen and it will reappear, along with the bar at the bottom."

Chamberlain touched the screen, and then asked a question.

"And which picture for Greenland?"

"Top left, with a blue and white square with ZNN in it."

Chamberlain paused before tapping. "And this, gentlemen, is why they came back in time." Peter noticed both Black Kettle and Howard frown at Chamberlain as he then tapped the screen. After about thirty seconds, both Howard and Black Kettle called for Chamberlain to stop.

"What are those?" Black Kettle demanded. "And what magic allows you to see the tops like a bird?"

Chamberlain explained what a glacier was, and about the ice sheet on Greenland, and the location of Greenland. Anton stepped in and explained airplanes. When he was finished, Chamberlain tapped the screen once, traced a line on the bottom, and hit play. The group watched the documentary for forty-three minutes. Chamberlain closed the video and handed the tablet back to Anton, who powered it down.

General Howard, obviously curious, "What force powers those devices? Electricity?"

Anton nodded, and explained, "Yes. We have a hand crank generator, which gives us a great arm exercise. We also have a couple of panels that convert sunlight into electricity. Later, we will get lazy and develop a powered generator."

A series of questions erupted. At one point Black Kettle turned to Sitting Bull and asked aggressively, "Do you know of this Greenland, and how tall these ice sheets are?"

"Yes," said Sitting Bull. "That is why I went to

the library yesterday. The people there were helpful in finding books. They called them 'encyclopedias.' The ice sheets are anywhere from over one to one-and-a-half miles thick."

"So this would be as if all the snow I have ever seen in my life melted all at once into the oceans of the world?" asked Black Kettle. Sitting Bull nodded.

"And you white people caused this to happen?" Black Kettle glared at the four white men sitting and standing among the group. Howard and Chamberlain looked to Peter and Anton for an answer.

Peter spoke up first. "Yes and no. It is true that whites, meaning Europeans developed the technology, but they shared it around the world. The United States, as it was the wealthiest country at the time, had one twentieth the population, but produced one fifth of the dirty smoke. China and India were catching up, and were starting to surpass the United States for dirty smoke."

Watie interrupted, "I have noticed on the few occasions that my unit went through a town with a train station, the stations and the closest buildings were all covered with a black powder. Is this from the dirty smoke you speak of?

Nodding Peter replied, "Yes, that is it exactly. We call it pollution, and that is the problem. As time marches on, coal and other dirty fuels like oil will cause the world to heat up."

"So once more, those of us who are not white will suffer because you cannot acquire or use any self-control whatsoever?" said Black Kettle.

Anton leaned forward in his chair. "Just for the sake of keeping this short, it was not just the whites. The biggest problem is that in the United States we left, a certain group of people did not believe in science. And politicians, because of bribes by the big oil companies, ignored the science. That is why we are here, because now is when that machinery is being invented and used. This new machinery that uses coal, and oil is being added, and at some point, something called natural gas will be used, which helped the population of the planet reach over eight billion people, causing us to burn even more fuel."

"And what does that have to do with us?" Black Kettle demanded.

This time Danaxe responded. "In my world, I am looked down on. First for being a Negro. Secondly for being a woman. My political voice is largely muted. Your voice, Black Kettle is completely muted. And that is a problem. We believe that the way to save the future, is to save you and me, in the here and now. That is why we are here."

"How do you plan to make this happen?" asked Chief Joseph.

"By showing you and General Howard what your two futures look like in the world I came from," replied Danaxe. "If you do not mind, I would like to rearrange your seating. General Howard would you sit in the middle here? Black Kettle, would you please sit next to him? And finally, Joseph, would you sit next to Howard on the other side?"

Peter continued, "Black Kettle, this tells the story of Howard and Joseph's son, then Chief Joseph the Younger, sharing a piece of ugly history, another Indian War. Neither of them know what it is. Sitting Bull is a part of this history, but you will not see him in this story." To Chief Joseph the Elder he said, "Your son, Joseph, was trying to reach Sitting Bull in Canada.

And you, General Howard, won the war by stopping him, but I believe you lost your soul in so doing. And you Black Kettle, had been dead for twelve years. And my apologies, but Chief Joseph, they refer to your tribe as "Nez Perce," not the proper name, Niimíipuu"

With that, Anton hit play, and the movie "*I Will Fight No More Forever*" started.

Chapter 29

For the next two hours, Anton, Peter, and Danaxe sat and watched the group take in the movie. General Howard looked severely uncomfortable after about ten minutes. Chief Joseph was in tears almost from the beginning. When they reached the scene of General Howard explaining to Captain Charles Erskine Scott Wood that he knew he was following immoral orders but stayed for his fear of a second civil war, Howard lunged at the tablet. Danaxe caught it in time and handed it over to Chamberlain. Chamberlain first paused, and then took the video back to the beginning of that scene.

While Chamberlain was taking care of the tablet, General Howard, visibly enraged, stalked off towards the stone wall that General Pickett's charge had failed to breach. Danaxe waved everyone else back as she went after Howard. She waited at his side in silence for a few moments.

When he regained control, he turned to Danaxe and spoke. "You, your friends, and every one of these Indians must all hate me. Hell, I hate me right now."

Danaxe shook her head. "No. If it had not been you, it would have been someone else. The only battle I saw of the Civil War was the clean up at Gettysburg after Lee left. I have been in battles, but I have never been in one so big that a thousand men died in five minutes. I cannot even imagine the nightmares you and Chamberlain are experiencing now."

"That was so craven of me. In your world, I must be burning in hell."

"I seriously doubt that. For a number of reasons. Look at it this way: by coming back to this time, I will have killed more people than you. Redeem me by letting us redeem you. You are not called the Pious General for nothing."

Howard looked into Danaxe's eyes for what seemed like hours. He nodded his head and reached out to shake her hand. The handshake wasn't quite as firm as the one with Roosevelt, but it conveyed all the conviction of Howard's will.

Howard returned, and the group finished the movie. Joseph the Elder cried as he watched the actor playing his son give the famous "I will fight no more forever" speech. Howard put his hand on Joseph's shoulder in obvious sympathy. At the end of the movie, Chamberlain recovered the tablet, closed out the movie app, and handed it back to Anton.

Danaxe knelt in front of Joseph. "We do not actually know if he made that speech. There is some disagreement about that. For me, that is the history as I would like to believe it happened. Chief Joseph, can you see your son making that speech?" Joseph nodded, while the tears continued streaming down his face.

Danaxe then looked at Howard, who was crying as well, completely shamed by what he saw as his portrayal in the movie. She turned her gaze to Black Kettle, aware that he had been watching her during this exchange.

"You can see Joseph's tears for what will be done to his son and his people. That is Howard's hand on his shoulder trying to comfort him." Gesturing at Howard, Danaxe continued, "Howard's tears are different. His come from shame. His come from knowing how cruelly he hurt innocent women and children simply because of the color of their skin. He cries because he knows he would have done this. He cries for Joseph's children. Indian children. If there is a white man in this world that you could possibly learn to trust, might Oliver Howard possibly be that one?"

Black Kettle studied Howard hard. "General, are any of those tears for Joseph's children?" Howard, clearly unable to speak, nodded.

Black Kettle studied Danaxe in the same fashion he had just studied Howard. "And you think you can change all this?"

"Yes. We already have. You are here and alive. We can do more. But we cannot do it alone. Without the rest of you, nothing will change. We need your active help and support."

Anton spoke up. "Well folks, I suggest we take a break and eat. I find I plot better when my thoughts are louder than my stomach."

While the group had been talking, tables had been set up with food. Half the protection detail was standing around and eating. The fare was simple. Black bean chili, cold fried chicken, fresh biscuits, with butter and strawberry preserves, along with local pickles, and a fresh strawberry pie. Coffee, tea, and cool water were all available. The three, along with their guests gathered around the table. Pensive and exhausted, everyone ate in silence.

Chapter 30

It wasn't until everyone had finished eating, while a couple of the security detail cleared the table, that conversation restarted. General Howard broke the silence.

"Black Kettle brought up one major consideration. Can you change history? And how did you save Black Kettle? Exactly what did you three do?" he asked.

To everyone's surprise, Sitting Bull responded, looking at Black Kettle. "Those three told Tavibo and myself what was going to happen, and asked us to evacuate as many of you as would come. True, there were some deaths. But your nation still lives. As for the land, that is another matter. Also…" he said as he stood up, and retrieved his saddle bag, "I know history has been changed because of this." Sitting Bull retrieved the newspaper that Anton and company had sent him, with Danaxe's picture attached to the newspaper announcing that she had prevented Lincoln's assassination. He handed it to Black Kettle, who then handed it to Howard.

Howard spoke for Black Kettle and himself. "Thank you for your efforts on behalf of President Lincoln. I fail to see any proof of changing history."

Anton retrieved his tablet, and pulled up a video. "This is, I believe the first ever major movie put together. It was what we call a silent movie. You'll see words instead of hearing sounds. The movie was called "Birth of a Nation," and hopefully will never be made now. It was based on accounts from still living witnesses as of 1914." Anton passed it to Howard, who hit play, and watched the first filmed reenactment of Booth's successful assassination of President Lincoln. Black Kettle and Chamberlain watched alongside. When they finished, they passed the tablet to the others. Black Kettle asked "I must admit you did predict some of the attacks at the beginning. So why did they change after about a week, and the predictions no longer work?"

"It is the nature of time travel," said Peter. "If I tell you an enemy is going to do something, and you do something different as a result, your enemy will do something different. We cannot make accurate predictions about the new future. The best we can do is keep our eyes on people we know about." He then turned to Howard and asked, "I assume you and Chamberlain have read the accounts?" Both Howard and Chamberlain nodded.

"And those three predictions all worked out," said Chamberlain, although your last prediction did not seem to entirely play out as written. I am not in any pain whatsoever. Nor did I require a catheter thankfully. Since nothing had changed, I do not see how that was different."

"I'm afraid that was me," said Danaxe. "You mentioned a powder was used on your wound?"

"Yes. They also gave me a ten day course of sulfamide pills. So no, I was never cursed with an infection, and the surgery went fine. So fine, that they were surprised I lived. I was given a battlefield promotion, that they then could not take back."

"That General, was a butterfly. I patented the powder and the pills. Being simple to make, it was simple to patent, and then distribute. My understanding was that its use was not universally adopted. That is why your personal future was changed. Thankfully."

"Ah." Chamberlain noticed the quizzical faces among some of the others. Reaching back to his days as a professor, he gave the same explanation that he had been given.

"So these changes by my enemy would be one of those butterflies?" asked Black Kettle.

Danaxe nodded.

Peter reinserted himself. "Getting back to my point, gentlemen, what was your take on those reports of the assassination attempt?"

Howard nodded as he spoke. "Very well timed, in three places at once. And as I recall, the attorneys for Booth and the other two are claiming that your accounts of how you knew of the plan are false."

Danaxe smiled as she responded, "Based on advice from counsel, I decline to comment. I believe that actually answers your question." Howard and Chamberlain laughed. The First People looked puzzled. Danaxe explained that in an American court, a person could refuse to testify against themselves.

John Ross asked, "So going ahead, you cannot tell us what will happen?"

"Not without a great deal of uncertainty, becoming more uncertain as time marches forward," said Peter. "However, based on the history we know, both President Lincoln and Senator Thaddeus Stevens are working to turn a couple of our ideas into reality. The first idea is the 14th Amendment. It will extend full citizenship and voting rights to all Negroes, First Peoples, and possibly women. All, if I have anything to say about it."

"The second item they are working on is the

Sanctuary States Act Amendment," said Danaxe.
"From Indian Territory we shall get Sequoyah, plus
five other territories. Nebraska, Montana Territory, and
Washington Territory for freed slaves, and The Dakota
Territories for two more First People's States. That is a
total of six states, and twelve senators. So Black Kettle,
there will be no more treaties that can be broken. There
will be laws, and you will be able to defend yourselves.
Which, General Howard, is why you are here." Howard
grunted in response to Danaxe.

"General," said Peter, "you did a lot of work
with the former freed slaves in our history. In this new
history, we think you would be greatly helpful by
agreeing to be responsible for defending and assisting
in the formation of these new states. As we speak,
enough colored troops are being assembled for ten
regiments of Mounted Rifles. When fully equipped,
they will have four horses for each man, and a similar
baggage train so they can cover land Mongolian style."
Howard and Chamberlain both whistled in
appreciation. The First Peoples looked puzzled.

Chamberlain jumped in, back in professor
mode. "Well, good cavalry units for long distances, can
average between thirty-five and fifty miles a day. Not
too many fifty-mile days. With a rider leading three
other horses, and changing between them frequently,
they can put together one hundred mile days upwards
of two thousand or more miles in some twenty days.
Say, Kansas to San Francisco in just twenty days or
less. Mongols lived north of China, and at one point
ruled a swath of land including China all the way to the
Kingdom of Hungary in Europe."

Sitting Bull chimed in, "Why do I suspect you
had a reason to suggest California at this time?"

Anton responded with a grin, "Because you know us too well." His grin faded. "There is an active campaign in California to exterminate every First Person the whites can find."

Perplexed, Stand Watie interrupted, "Are there words we can use to distinguish between your history, and what appears to now be unfolding in ours?"

"Well, in the *Ring of Fire* Series, a set of novels, they talked about uptimers, the future, and down-timers, the past. So us three would be uptimers, who know the "original" history, and are working with, you, the down-timers, to change the history the uptimers learned." Anton said.

"So in the uptime, how bad was this extermination?" asked Stand.

"Well, we believe that there were three hundred seventy thousand First Peoples in California as of 1700. By 1873, the number was thirty thousand." Anton looked away. There was silence as everyone present took in the numbers, and what they meant.

"We will be able to supply two regiments, redesignated as PIoneers, and currently waiting in Kansas," Peter said. "They will get two-thousand five hundred improved, heavier Henrys by the end of July, at which point they will head to California. They will receive two thousand per month thereafter. We'll stop the first run at ten thousand rifles total. So help is on the way. I wish it could have been sooner."

Peter turned to Chamberlain. "General, we have a very specific request for you. Later in your career, you became President of Bowdoin College. We want you to find and recruit professors and administrators for the original six Sanctuary State Colleges. There will be issues about accommodations, but we have ideas on how to deal with that."

Chamberlain responded, "I am eager to assist. I am not sure how helpful I can be."

"I suspect that as a Civil War veteran and hero, you will be more persuasive than I could ever be," said Peter. "Also, we will be giving you a letter of introduction to Mr. Theodore Roosevelt. He has agreed to help you if you accept the position."

"As for your Sanctuary States and Counties, you will need a Constitutional Amendment to do that," said Chamberlain.

Peter nodded. "Allow me to introduce our proposal for the Fifteenth Amendment: the Sanctuary State and Counties Amendment."

There followed another spate of questions and answers until, at about five o'clock, the Security Detail suggested moving back to the hotel, and mentioned they found a tavern with a room big enough to seat the group, and feed them dinner.

By the end of the evening, they had reached several understandings. Two regiments would head to California at the end of July. A third regiment would leave at the end of August with additional Henrys, with the means to cast replacement bullets and reload. A fourth regiment would be tasked with keeping them supplied with sufficient ammunition.

Chamberlain committed to meeting with Senator Thaddeus Stevens to discuss additions to the proposed Fourteenth Amendment and with President Lincoln on the Fifteenth. John Ross and Stand Watie committed to presenting Sequoyah's state Constitution as soon as Chamberlain's proposed Amendment was passed, and to finish the required elections by September 15, 1865. The men agreed to meet at the same place the next morning.

**

After breakfast the next morning. Anton, John, Peter, and Stand were disappointed when Danaxe announced she was not going along. "I am going to go check in with nurse Jenny's family and make sure they are all right.," she said. "I promised her I would do that, letters being sometimes slow, and telegrams expensive." As she walked out with her three-man security detail, with more pleas being called out, she simply sighed, "Boys and their toys."

The men, along with their security detail headed back to the stone wall, and the group of men gathered around. Peter pulled out a new Henry Rifle. "This, gentlemen, has a .45-80 bullet, with a ten round, easily interchangeable magazine. With an effective range of over 300 yards. And can accommodate an 18" bayonet. The Henrys you will be supplied with, will carry fifteen rounds, with a copper jacket, and a new style of casing, which will make these repeaters more accurate, hitting harder and farther out, say about nine hundred yards.

The next hour resulted in over three hundred rounds being fired into mostly wooden stumps, set up at fifty-yard intervals out to three hundred yards, and then two six feet tall sheets by twelve feet wide. The shooting didn't attract much attention, as one of the Security Detail had warned the local authorities of the test firing of what would become known as the Henry Pioneer Rifle. The reaction of the shooters was enthusiastic. While heavy, at about ten pounds loaded, everyone agreed the rifle would allow the proposed Pioneer regiments to take on numerically superior forces.

The last announcement of the day surprised the three First People leaders, as they were invited to ride the train to Washington. Peter explained, "Congress did not think to talk to us, and since we are using our personal train cars, we can take whomever we wish."

Everyone said their goodbyes to both Howard and Chamberlain, who had to go back to their posts.

Chapter 31

All of the women—and the four men—who filled the crowded room stood when the First Lady entered. The rustle of lace and the snapping of whalebone corsets nearly covered the startled whispers and occasional murmurs of glee.

Danaxe reached for and found the familiar stillness she always needed for moments like these. And there had been so many moments like these in the past two years.

But never one quite like this.

The crowded room stood nearly as divided as the nation had been when Danaxe had first arrived in this century. Elizabeth Cady Stanton and Susan B. Anthony stood with their supporters on one side. Lucy Stone and hers stood proudly with Frederick Douglass, Hiram Revels and John R. Lynch on the other side (while of course keeping an appropriate distance from the black men). Thaddeus Stevens stood a little apart from the other men, but not quite with either of the women's factions either.

In the uptime, the makeup had been different. Elizabeth Blackwell was in England now, instead of Washington, and Julia Ward Howe, who had accepted the invitation was nowhere to be seen. And Lucretia Mott, the peacemaker who had worked so hard to heal the rift back then, now lay dead from a carriage accident two weeks ago.

The butterflies were out in force, but at the moment, they seemed to all be in Danaxe's stomach. It was her job now, to succeed where Lucretia had failed.

But all she could think of now was the fifteen years of life her trip through time had cost a truly great woman. Of course it should not have mattered to Danaxe if the woman had been great or ordinary; her job now was to not let guilt and sorrow distract her. And to do it as the only woman of color in this room.

Danaxe had asked Lydia Hamilton Smith to be there, but the single mother and housekeeper for Senator Thaddeus Stevens had declined, citing the ammunition her presence would give to the senator's detractors, as well as the simple fact that she had never been politically active before. To start now would only provide fodder for the gossips and distract everyone involved from the work at hand.

"Please be seated," said Mary Todd Lincoln, taking the podium. "We are here on this historic day to witness —and perhaps help our learned Senator Stevens push forward —an amendment to our Constitution. I say *our* constitution because, beyond the dreams of any Founding Mother or oppressed slave, today we stand a chance of securing the right of every person in this room to participate fully in the governing of the United States. Starting today." Mrs. Lincoln paused to thunderous applause, but then began to speak again, this time staring at the young man seated beside Frederick Douglass.

"Dear me, I fear I have misspoken," the First Lady said suddenly, deviating from the speech Danaxe had secretly reviewed the night before. Danaxe's stomach threatened to drop to the floor as fear of what one of Mary's famous mood swings might do to this moment. "Mr. Lynch, are you twenty-one years of age?"

The man who would, in a different future

e, become one of Mississippi's most beloved and successful black politicians during Reconstruction smiled. "Not until next September 10, Madam First Lady. But I have no wish to ruin such an inspired speech. Should I wait outside?"

Mary Lincoln smiled back, and Danaxe's fears eased. "Certainly not. Securing these rights for our posterity is as important as for ourselves, as Mr. Morris understood when he wrote the Preamble for the document in question." She turned her gaze to the only white man in the room. "Mr. Stevens, I believe you recently proposed an amendment to Congress, which would grant full suffrage to all adult citizens of the United States, regardless of race, gender or previous condition of servitude?"

She's doing great, thought Danaxe. *Maybe I can actually sit this one out.*

"I did indeed, Madam First Lady," said the elderly radical in a powerful voice, which ended in a fit of coughing. "I was, of course, laughed off the floor."

"From where I'm sure you fled without a fight," grumbled Elizabeth Cady Stanton.

And then the shouting began. So much for sitting this one out.

"This is the Negro's hour!" cried Lucy Stone. "It's what we all fought for: an end to slavery —"

"Which is still only half-ended!" Susan Anthony's words were nearly drowned out.

"Was no one listening to Mr. Stevens?" cried Lucy Stone. "The men in Congress —yes, men —will never approve so radical a change all at once. But we have the votes to extend suffrage to Negro men. Now. This very year. I say we must take the victory that is within our grasp, and fight the battle for women's vote another day."

"Yes!" shouted the woman beside Lucy. "Surely it won't be long…"

"If we let it slip through our fingers today," Mrs. Stanton shouted, "it will be fifty years before women stand equal with men before the ballot box!"

"Fifty-five, actually," said Danaxe, but no one heard her.

"So speaks the woman whose greatest fear is that Sambo will walk into the kingdom of civil rights first." Speaking for the first time, Frederick Douglass' commanding voice momentarily silenced the room.

"I never said that," Mrs. Stanton said quietly, but in a strong voice that burned with anger. "I have many enemies in the press who have twisted my words…"

"The words you have spoken in truth are bad enough," shouted someone Danaxe couldn't see in the crowd of women. "For the good of everyone here, Mrs. Stanton, please, leave this room before you harm these good works beyond repair."

Elizabeth stood firm. "Self development is a higher duty than self sacrifice. I will not yield my principles —"

"Even at the cost of an entire race?" challenged Douglass. "White women already have access to the vote. They have it through their connections to their fathers, husbands and brothers —"

"While Negro women have endured a triple bondage that no man will even acknowledge," countered Stanton. "That of slavery, gender and race. What say you to that, Mr. Douglass?"

Douglass's reply was drowned out by a tsunami of arguments. Danaxe listened for the right moment, pitched her voice for effect and called out, "May I speak?"

There was just enough startled silence for her to wedge herself into.

"Everyone here is right!" she began. "The answer lies in finding the pieces which will give all of us what we want, and joining them together."

"Surely, you, Miss Davis, wish to see rights for all people win the day!" said Susan Anthony.

"Yet you are wise enough to know it is not yet possible," came the deep voice of Hiram Revels. "Today, you must put your race first."

"I will not be forced to choose between my brothers and my sisters!" Danaxe shouted in a voice that filled the room. "Mrs. Stanton!" Danaxe's glare met that of yet another childhood hero. "You are right to fear that suffrage for women will be dealt a terrible blow if it is not secured by this amendment. Yet your insistence that education and wealth are needed to counter ignorance and the degradation of the ballot box will only result in the corruption of those rights which you hold so dear. Your words will open the door to literacy requirements which will be nothing more than legal ways to deny voting rights to anyone those in power wish to oppress!"

As whispering filled the silence which followed her words, Danaxe turned to the men, and discovered that two tours in Afghanistan was child's play compared to publicly scolding Frederick Douglass.

But she did it anyway.

"Mr. Douglass, if you truly believe that white women have some kind of magical power over their fathers, brothers or husbands, then I find your ignorance shocking. But for a lucky few, all women in

this country remain the legal property of those fine
family members you have just named. And while many
men are reasonable, and value the opinions of the
women in their lives, many are not. And no law exists
requiring them to be so! If you think that feminine
wiles are the road to power —"

"I never said that!" Douglass seemed truly
outraged, and Danaxe was fairly certain that if his face
was of a lighter hue, it would have been red.

Danaxe smiled and paused a beat to look at both
him and Stanton. "Then you two have something in
common. You have both been accused of saying things
you did not, while some of your most brilliant words
are ignored. Can we all take a breath and perhaps
discover what else we have in common?"

Thaddeus Stevens looked at Danaxe with
admiration and rose slowly to his feet. "If it may please
the court? And truly, I have never before spoken in any
human court so wise or intimidating. But listening to all
of you today has made me see the importance of
suffrage for all! And, more importantly, a way in which
it might be accomplished." He tried to draw another
breath, but lost it in a fit of coughing. This time, the
coughing continued until he collapsed back into his
chair, and showed no sign of stopping as he collapsed
to the floor.

Danaxe drew on the last of her own strength to
run to his side. Senator Thaddeus Stevens had indeed
found a way to end the squabbling. Danaxe could only
hope he would live long enough to see it through to a
happy conclusion.

Chapter 32

Danaxe finished taking the senator's pulse, and then sat back in her chair. His smirk was nearly enough to overpower her calm. "Senator Stevens," she began evenly, "if you ever pull a stunt like that again, you will not be pretending, because I will strangle you myself."

"And I will help her," Mrs. Smith said from her place on Stevens' other side.

"Now, now, ladies," he began. At the women's combined glare, the senator stopped, took a glass of water from his bedside table and sipped thoughtfully. "The point is, it worked. Miss Davis, with the way those women were fighting, do you honestly believe anything short of medical crisis would have brought them together?"

Danaxe continued to glare, but it was no use. The man's charisma was overwhelming. And besides, he was probably right. "It was well played," she conceded. "But I am afraid it was not only their fear of losing a truly great man that caused the truce." Lydia's eyebrows rose, and Thaddeus snorted. "The last thing you said was that you had an idea of how to make everything work."

"Another good way to get yourself killed," muttered Lydia.

"My point is," Danaxe continued, "word will soon arrive at the prayer vigil that you are going to recover. When the suffragettes, the Negro leaders, and the radical Republicans all finish their hallelujahs and hosannas over your miracle recovery —"

"And everyone else in the country curses with disappointment," Lydia interjected.

" —they will be wanting to know all about this great idea of yours. Which, I fear, you do not yet have."

"I thought I would just leave that up to you, Miss Davis. You are, after all, still the hero of the hour. The woman who saved the president. The one with the crystal ball. For me, I shall just pay a visit to all those fools who are cursing with disappointment that I'm still alive —" Stevens winked at Lydia. " —and buy each of them a round of drinks."

"There's not enough liquor in all of Washington —" Danaxe began. Stevens roared with laughter, but then began coughing in earnest. He really wasn't as well as he claimed, and for the next few minutes, Danaxe was busy being a nurse.

A knock sounded on the front door, and Lydia hurried to answer it. "Young miss, you worry too much," Stevens said to Danaxe, and now there was genuine warmth in his voice. "Let them fear for my health a bit longer, and those two warring factions just might come up with my brilliant plan on their own." He finished the water, and refilled the class with brandy from a cut glass decanter.

"And if they do not?"

"I'll bluster my way through like I always do."

Lydia returned. "Senator Sumner, along with Mr. Tormey, and Mr. Pozda wish to speak with you, if you are well enough to receive visitors." She glanced at Danaxe as she spoke. Danaxe gave a slight nod, as Stevens growled, "I am fine! And I could use the company of men about now!"

Charles Sumner, another hero of all three time-travelers, entered the room carrying a copy of Charles

Dickens' latest novel, *Our Mutual Friend*, followed by Peter and Anton. Stevens hid his smile with a grimace. "Why is Grant not with you? At least *he* would have brought liquor!"

Lydia arranged more chairs in the bedroom, and Anton hurried to help her. Sumner set the richly appointed book on the bedside table. "Our good general is on another errand," he said, taking a seat. "He is with Vice President Johnson, explaining things, one drunk to another."

"Better him than me," said Stevens. "I truly despise that man."

"And he came within a heartbeat of becoming president, and thereby undoing everything we're about to accomplish." The light of a zealot shone in the New Englander's eyes, and for a moment everyone in the room went still.

Thaddeus Stevens was the first to recover. "Charles, is this your way of bringing news? Because I'm in no mood for games."

Danaxe snorted. Stevens shot her a look, but then his attention was back on his fellow senator.

"We did it! While you've been lazing about in bed, taking your ease —"

"You are about to have some very good brandy thrown in your face, Charles." Thaddeus drank from his glass, carefully ignoring Danaxe's look of reproach.

"I do apologize." Sumner held up his hands in a gesture of truce. "While your supposed near-fatal illness convinced the suffragettes and the Negroes to work together, our president pulled off a coup for the ages. All states which took up arms against the Union will be readmitted to said Union, with all property and voting rights restored —"

Thaddeus spewed brandy, alternately choking and swearing. "How is this a good thing?" he demanded when he could speak again.

" —once the existing state legislatures ratify the Fourteenth Amendment. And, I was told privately, a Fifteenth Amendment. The first as you have written it, and the second based on President Lincoln's thoughts, my friend."

At that, everyone in the room was silent.

Finally, Stevens asked, "What about the Thirteenth?"

"A done deal," replied Sumner. "It was only this last piece of legislation that had to be fought for. And at last the battle is won."

"It is not won!" Stevens barked. "Property? Lincoln's just going to hand the plantations back to the rebels?"

"The plantations," Danaxe couldn't resist jumping in. "Not the labor. Those fine ladies and gentlemen might have to pick their own cotton for a time."

Stevens smiled at that, his eyes half closed, as he imagined what Danaxe's words might look like in reality. Then he scowled. "Those slippery bastards will find a way around it! Their land should be going to their former slaves as compensation —"

"Thaddeus, the Radicals love your 'Forty Acres and a Mule Plan' — in theory. But realistically —"

"I never called it...would you please stop calling it that! But land for the former slaves is essential —"

"And they will have all the land they need," Sumner said calmly. "It was the last thing the rebs had to swallow and it was a bitter pill indeed. Three new territories. All for black Americans to settle."

"With enough assistance to make it more than a pipe dream?" Thaddeus demanded. "We surely cannot squeeze any funds from the South, and those bastards in Congress will never loosen the purse-strings enough to —"

"Charity organizations all over the North are working even as we speak to provide the essentials. And, now, with the suffragettes on board, there will be even more help available —"

"In that case, I suppose I can get out of bed." Stevens made to get up.

"Not until you recover! We're going to need you fit and healthy, Thaddeus, now more than ever —"

While the two men argued, Danaxe went to stand by her uptime friends, who were having their own quiet discussion.

"Anton, wipe that grin off your face," Peter whispered. "You look like an idiot."

"I can't help it," said Anton. "For years when I couldn't sleep, I'd imagine discussions like this. And now it's real. And I'm here."

"I know," said Peter, grinning back. "I had those same dreams."

Danaxe flashed a grin of her own, and then returned her attention to the senators.

"Three new states," Sumner was saying. "That's what the Negro territories will become. Idaho —there's talk the name will be changed to Canaan, or even Lincoln —"

"Nice neighbor for Washington," Stevens interjected.

"Another one farther east, along the Canadian border. Some territory in the midwest near Kansas will also become a Negro state," Charles continued.

"There's talk of calling that one Jubilee."

"I may have to regain enough health to travel again," said Thaddeus. "I want to see the expressions of those white settlers when they find they're about to become a minority in their own territory."

"Don't forget about the three red states who will also be joining the Union," Anton addressed the two senators for the first time.

Stevens cocked an eyebrow at his friend. "Red states? Did I miss something?"

"You were up to your neck fighting the ills of slavery and creating a future for our colored citizens," said Charles. "Someone had to look out for the interests of this country's first ones. Statehood should be easier for them, though. The Five Civilized Tribes have supposedly put together a State Constitution or are about to. We should be adding a star to the flag for Sequoyah by the end of next year. Lakota will be more troublesome, since the Lakota and the Cheyenne will each want their own state."

"That won't go far to make up for what they have lost," Stevens said moodily. "But it's something. And no one can bring back the dead."

Butterflies fluttered again in Danaxe's stomach as she heard the words that eerily echoed the child prophet Wovoka. She glanced at Peter and Anton and knew they felt it too. Then she looked to her patient and saw he was as still as she'd ever seen him, and that his face had lost color.

"Sir, are you well?" Danaxe hurried back to the senator's bed. From her nearly place in the shadows, Lydia smiled and shook her head. Clearly, she wasn't worried, so Danaxe relaxed somewhat.

The other senator was, however. "Thaddeus?"

he asked in alarm. "What is it? I thought you'd be happy!"

"I am. But…" Stevens shook his head, reached for the brandy, but discovered his hands were shaking. "I never thought I'd see the day when the world changed too fast for *me*. I was always the loudest, the wildest, the most extreme. And now… I am not sure that I can even keep up."

Danaxe took the decanter from the bedside table and poured the senator a tall drink.

Surprised back to his usual humor, Stevens raised an eyebrow. "Liquor, Nurse Danaxe? In my condition? What are you thinking?"

"That you have earned this one, sir," she replied smoothly. "And in my expert medical opinion, you need it."

Stevens smiled and raised his glass. "Come on, everybody. I hate to drink alone."

One by one, everyone in the room accepted a glass, until only Charles Sumner's hands were empty. With a mighty shrug, the famously dry senator poured himself a finger's worth, causing Stevens to nearly drop his own glass.

"To the new United States!" Sumner called.

"To equality of man before his Creator!" cried Stevens. Danaxe gasped at the words which she knew to be on his tombstone.

"To the future," Peter and Anton said together.

Danaxe thought hard, for she had never prepared for this moment. When she realized the others were waiting, she lifted her glass and said the first thing that came to her. "To miracles."

They all drank.

Chapter 33

Peter felt restless. He hoped Anton and Danaxe couldn't see it, but living as they had for the past two years, he doubted very much he could keep anything from them.

They sat in their cozy parlor, lingering over a fine breakfast, although their attention was mainly on the stack of newspapers they perused and passed back and forth.

"It's looking good," said Peter.

"Which change are you looking at?" Danaxe asked, setting down an article covering the ongoing debate on prohibition. The tide was turning against it, but the call for new laws targeting violence against women and children —both liquor related and not — was on the rise.

"The Sanctuary Bureau —known uptime as the Freedmen's Bureau." He set down one paper. "The Pioneers." He set down another. "Grant's already got half the exodus organized —including military protection for the former slaves who want to leave."

"It's the ones who don't want to leave I'm worried about," said Danaxe, picking up a different newspaper and reading aloud from the front page. "'Every effort is being made to protect our black citizens from those who would take advantage of their childlike simplicity and lead them into hellish bondage from which there will be no escape —all under the guise of bringing them to a territory of their own. While anyone with an ounce of sense can see that such a thing is impossible, the clever deceivers who hope to profit from the suffering of the black man are well aware of his vulnerability and see an opportunity.'"

"Where's that paper from?" asked Anton.

"South Carolina," replied Danaxe.

"Well, it's not like anyone who reads it will be fooled," said Anton. "And of course, the South worked hard to make sure the very people they're trying so hard to manipulate now can't read." Anton offered up his reaction-to-irony-smile.

"They don't need their former slaves to read it," Peter said angrily. "Just a few people with the the right powers of persuasion. Any pictures of the beautiful living quarters for the 'free workers' who stay?" he asked Danaxe.

"Of course," she said, spreading the paper across the breakfast table. Someone had spent a lot of money on those illustrations, thought Peter. Maybe half the fabled Confederate Treasure, since the other half had clearly gone to Oregon with Nathan Bedford Forrest. One drawing showed an elegant plantation in the background, with pretty cottages apparently replacing slave cabins in the foreground. A chart promising wages higher than the average Northern factory worker received, including old age pensions, was printed below.

On the opposite page was a cartoon. Hordes of black people were following an evilly grinning white man, very fat and dressed in the latest Northern fashion, holding aloft a sign with a picture of a mule and a large tract of tree-covered land, a smiling black man and woman holding hands next to it. In the next panel, the crowd of Negroes were falling into a flaming pit, while the man with the sign accepted a bag of money from a dirty, whip-wielding foreman. The final panel showed the former slaves, families, Peter realized, for there were children prominently displayed, chained together, in a pit, mining some kind of mineral —probably sulphur.

"They can't use violence," said Anton. "At least not like they did up-time. And they're desperate to keep their labor force." He tapped the newspaper. "If this is the best they can do, I think the former slaves will be all okay."

"There are still plenty who won't leave," Danaxe persisted. "Not the easily manipulated people who are understandably afraid of change —especially if that change involves walking hundreds of miles into the unknown." She picked up another paper. "The Liberator has been interviewing black leaders all over the South."

Anton whistled. "Dangerous job, but let's hear it for William Lloyd Garrison!"

Danaxe smiled briefly. "Yes, he's on my list of people to meet. Unfortunately, so are a few people mentioned in this article: Richard Cain, Robert DeLarge, Jefferson Long —ring any bells?"

"All black politicians who held office during Reconstruction," said Peter, not liking where this was going.

"And they're all planning to stay in the South," Danaxe said sadly. "'This is my home,' Mr. Cain told this reporter," Danaxe read from the article. "'My blessings and prayers go with all the brave souls who plan to move west, but my children were born here, and I will work to see them grow up free, working the land that is theirs by birth.'"

She added the paper to the large stack on the table. "Up-time, they were all great leaders. Now, I fear, they're going to end up swinging from trees, because the government is focusing all their resources on getting the former slaves elsewhere."

"Just as we convinced them to," sighed Anton.

"It might not be as bad as that," said Peter. "Grant seems committed to protecting the ones who are staying, as only a sizeable minority are leaving."

The others nodded. Anton read aloud from a Baltimore newspaper which covered the arrival of the first wave of Europeans immigrants, seeking opportunity —and eventually land of their own — as they filled the vacancies left by the slaves on the plantations.

Peter opened another paper, scanned the headline —and choked on his coffee.

"What?" asked Danaxe.

Peter cleared his throat and began to read. "Carthage, Mississippi. Four men were arrested on their way to Washington D.C., where they planned to kidnap President Lincoln —and force him to admit to being an imposter." Peter coughed again, read a few more lines and continued. "When questioned, one of the men went on to say that he was a loyal American who loved his president, and intended to force the current imposter to reveal the location of the real Abraham Lincoln. 'I may have called him a baboon on occasion,' the prisoner was quoted saying. 'But at least he was an American baboon! And no red-blooded American would ever lead his country to ruin the way our current so-called president has. Handing whole territories to niggers? Giving the land back to the Indians? Are my brothers and I the only men in this country who can see what's going on?"

"How did we not hear about this sooner?" asked

Anton.

"That's my question!" said Peter. "Why are we reading this in the newspaper?"

"They never made it out of Mississippi," Danaxe said patiently. "If they had gotten all the way to the White House, that would have been another story."

"Somehow, I don't think this is the last crazy story we'll be hearing," said Peter. At that, they were quiet for a time. The three continued searching the papers, but found nothing further of note.

"The biggest news for me, personally," Danaxe said when they were finished with the papers, "didn't come in a newspaper." She was holding a letter that had arrived the day before. She started to speak again, but was interrupted by a knock at the front door.

A moment later, the housekeeper entered, carrying an envelope. "Mr. Pozda, sir," she said holding it out to Anton, who took it eagerly. It was labeled Western Union Telegram.

"Frm Gen Hwrd

"To Antn Pzda

"Yu ar hrby actvtd as a mmbr of th Fdrlzd Snctrry Pnrs fr oprtns in Clfrna. Tmrrw mrnng yu wll be accmpnied to a trn twrds Knss. Upn arrvl yu wll be escrted by frmr 4th Tnnss Mnted Rfls.

Yu wll be expctd to prvde intllgnce on cndtns in Clfrnia and sltns fr said. Brng wht equpmnt yu requr to prfrm sd duts. Brng bst sddle. We ar ging Mngln. Brng Hnry. Yu wll nd to advs on tctcs. Undrstnd yu hvnt sn elphnt.

Rgrds

Gn Hwrd

Anton swallowed a few times. "Well, guessing

based on my fake discharge papers, I have just been summoned to join 4th Tennessee Mounted Rifles, under Stand Watie, to help out in saving what we can in California, per our discussion in Gettysburg." He then read the telegram that informed him that he had been activated as a member of the Sanctuary State Pioneers for operations in California, and that he would be accompanied to Kansas by members of the former 4th Tennessee Mounted Rifles. Upon arrival, Anton would be expected to provide information on the conditions in California, and solutions. And that as regards tactics, he was not a combat veteran, but that his input was considered important.

Peter cocked his head, and puzzled, asked "Why would he want you, instead of Danaxe who has seen the elephant?"

Anton looked at Peter for a moment, totally exasperated. "Seriously? Sitting Bull says upon any prolonged mention of children, my skin color will be true white. I'm a foster kid. It's what we do. Or at least what I came here to do."

Peter grimaced in acknowledgement. "Yeah, I get that. Extra points for General Howard on noticing that."

Anton snorted, "I'm betting Sitting Bull had a short conversation with the good general."

The housemaid chose that moment to speak up, "The Western Union Telegram man is standing outside, sir. I believe he is expecting a response." Anton startled for a moment, as he put together the current level of technology.

"You are correct. Give me a moment to write one." With Peter and Danaxe's assistance, he found pencil and paper, and wrote in his most legible fashion.

Gn Hwrd

Undrstd. Sddle & info wll lve tmrrw undr agrd escrt. Info wll be avlble as nded.

Undr Ordrs,

Crprl Antn Pzda.

The housekeeper took the paper to the messenger hovering at the front door. Visibly relieved, he accepted the paper, and went to mount his horse and rode off as fast as it was safe to ride on the streets of Washington.

Peter was about to say a cheery goodbye to Anton, but stopped at the troubled look on his friend's face. "What's wrong?" he asked.

"I knew we couldn't stay together forever," Anton said, trying for his usual bravado. "I just didn't think I'd be the first to go it alone."

"You're not," said Danaxe, still holding the letter. "I just didn't get to make my big announcement before the Western Union guy broke in."

"Did Harriet Tubman finally write, I mean, answer your letter?" Anton asked.

"No, this is from Grant," Danaxe said casually, making it clear that a letter from a celebrated general and future U.S. president was a distant second to a response from Harriet Tubman. "He's asking me to help with the Sanctuary Bureau."

"While I ride off with the guy who's supposed to be running it," said Anton. "I hope this doesn't turn out to be a big mistake."

"Well, in this new version of history, Grant will head it up temporarily, with Frederick Douglass set to take it over, and me as his acting second in command."

"Not bad," said Peter, and suddenly they were all laughing.

And then, as had happened so often over the past two years, their laughter cut off at the same time, and they all looked at each other.

"We knew it was going to happen," Peter said, but his voice shook. "The time's finally come when we can do more separately than together. You'll both do great."

"What about you?" asked Anton.

"The Long Range Foundation will keep me busy for the next few months, and I still believe our president might need me once or twice more. If not, Stevens and Sumner have both offered me jobs on their staff."

"Good," said Danaxe. "Because in my absence, I'm deputizing you to keep Stevens alive for at least one more year."

"I'll do my best, ma'am," Peter began, when the sound of breaking glass caused them all to duck.

Old instincts came through as they hit the floor at once without banging into each other, and the large rock that would have landed where Anton's head had been a moment before crashed into the far wall of the parlor.

Van Vorst came rushing into the room, but Peter had already scooped up the rock, doing his best to avoid fragments of shattered glass. "We're okay," he said, sliding free the paper that was wrapped around the stone. He added it to the pile of paper on the kitchen table while Van Vorst hurried outside.

A cheaply printed flyer showed a large black woman holding a scrawny white man by the neck, wringing it as she would a chicken. Despite the the classic big lips, nappy hair and angry scowl, the face was clearly intended to resemble Danaxe's. The man might have been intended to be John Wilkes Booth, but it was hard to say. The words: "You Could Be Next" ran across the top of the page, while "Join the White League and Save Our Beloved Homeland" was printed at the bottom.

"Well," said Danaxe. "It's started."

"Damn," said Anton. "I was hoping they'd go with Red Shirts again."

"They still might," said Peter. "There were so many white terrorist organizations during Reconstruction. But we'll be the only three this century to get the Star Trek humor. In the meantime," he turned to one of this two best friends. "You've scared them. What do you plan to do about it?"

"I guess I'll find out when I get to Virginia," said Danaxe.

"Uh, isn't this the part where we try to convince her not to go rushing into danger?" asked Anton.

At Peter's blank look and Danaxe's glare, Anton raised his hands in surrender. "You're right. Forget I said anything. Still, hell of an omen to go our separate ways with."

"I don't know," said Peter as the security detail returned with reports that no one had seen anything and a request to examine the paper. "I kind of like having the enemy where I can see him."

They shared a tight group hug, and everyone went to pack.

Epilogue

About thirty men were gathered around the campfire. Clouds hid the moon and vision was limited to the ring of feeble light thrown by the flames.

"How long we gonna wait?" one man grumbled.

"Until he gets here," snapped another.

"I quit taking orders when we lost the war," a middle-aged man said as he rose slowly to his feet. "I'll go when I damn well please. And I ain't waitin' on no so-called Wizard neither."

"But where will you be going, brother?" asked a voice from the shadows. There were startled exclamations from the gathered crowd as a tall man stepped into their midst. The firelight danced along his stylish beard and his piercing brown eyes, while his dove grey uniform was in far better shape than anything the men awaiting him wore. "The Yanks didn't leave you much, did they? And now the niggers and the vultures from the North are set to take the rest."

There was angry muttering around the fire, and the man who had stood sat back down.

An old man looked at the newcomer. "I know you, Bedford, though I don't reckon you remember me, bein' I was just a foot soldier, while you was the famous Wizard of the Saddle. But I ain't come here for no fancy words, or promises that are like to get me and mine killed."

"Amen!" called another. "What can we few do about any of it?"

"We are not so few," Nathan Bedford Forrest said quietly, but his voice reached every ear present.

"You brave men may be all that is left of your unit, but you are not all that remains of the Confederacy. I have spoken to many who have lost everything to this unjust War of Northern Aggression. And I have spoken to many others for whom much was spared; those with the means to start a business, or begin again with their farms —though it meant picking their own cotton —but who find the price of living so broken and humiliated too great."

"And what do you propose to do about it?" demanded a younger man.

"Strike back!" Forrest's voice was suddenly loud and angry. "Show them the war is not yet over. I, myself, was ready to give up; accept our defeat and do my best for my family with whatever crumbs our so-called president in Washington and his radical cronies saw fit to toss us.

"But then I learned something incredible." His voice dropped, and the men leaned closer to hear. "Things are not as they seem. The war. Lincoln. The land given over to the savages and niggers. There has been meddling. There has been..." Forest paused, and then shook his head as if thinking better of what he was about to say.

"The unnatural woman who prevented John Wilkes Booth from carrying out his righteous mission, and the two race-traitors who are under her spell are at the heart of it. That is all I may say for now. But if you join with me, we may yet restore —not only the South —but our entire nation to the path it was meant to follow. It will be slow and dangerous work. I will ask more from you than you have ever been asked."

From the men came a slow rumble that climbed until it grew into a ragged cheer.

"But we shall redeem our homeland!" Nathan Bedford Forrest shouted above the din. "And the South will rise again!"

END

Continue reading for an excerpt of The Uncivil War, Book 2 in the Butterflies of Gettysburg series, in early 2019.

Preview

The train came to a stop, causing Danaxe to sit up before she was fully awake. "Freedom Riders!" she cried, the cobwebs still heavy.

"What was that, dearie?" asked the older white woman who sat next to her, as she put her knitting away and gathered her things.

"I was trying to remember the name of the people who went South in the 19--" Danaxe stopped, now fully awake. "Nothing. It was just a dream."

"And a vivid one, by the sound of it," said the man across the car from her.

A porter called out their arrival in Richmond, Virginia and Danaxe looked around. They went by the name of Sanctuary Volunteers but they weren't far from the original Freedom Riders. A mixed group of black and white, men and women, most older than their twentieth century counterparts, their job was to help former slaves transition into independence and citizenship. For the most part, that would mean helping to reunite families and prepare those who wanted to travel to the new territories of Canan, Jubilee and Lincoln. Some would be starting schools for those who chose to stay. Danaxe's group would be setting up one of the many aid stations that would distribute food, information and medical care.

Plus a few plans of her own which weren't printed on any official lists.

"Oh, merciful God in Heaven!" one of the women exclaimed.

Danaxe pushed through the crowd and looked around. She had seen worse. Still, the ruined buildings, blighted landscape and rubble-filled roads were a sight she would never forget. Union soldiers directed labor crews--all white, Dani noticed--in clearing rubble. A faint odor in the breeze suggested their previous job had been burial detail.

At least that was finished.

As her eyes adjusted to the sight, Dani saw signs of improvement and healing as well. The station they were in and the tracks that had brought them were the most noteworthy. Many buildings in the distance appeared whole and sound. Dani noted several which could be turned into the Richmond district of the Sanctuary Bureau. And this time, they'd have the money and government support to make it work the way it should have up-time. Without *President* Andrew Johnson undermining it every step of the way. Without Southern terrorist organizations calling the shots…*ooh, bad pun*...

"Come along, Friends," called one of the men from her car. "This food won't unload itself!"

Danaxe snapped out of her reverie and hurried to help. Instantly, she became aware of the subtle shift in the people who stood around the train station. When the aid workers had disembarked, just moments ago, there had been perhaps fifty hungry-looking, disheveled people standing in the limited shade or sitting, heads bowed, in the hot sun. While grouped in families, or in twos or threes, they had been eerily silent, as if slowly turning into statues.

Now, they were animated, moving toward the train--more specifically, the supplies Danaxe and the others were unloading--and their numbers had doubled. They were quiet, and no one was mobbing the train--yet--but the silence was gone. Mothers urged their children forward; men hovered protectively over family members or weaker friends. Shuffling footsteps and the whisper of torn and grimy clothing created background noise which filled the void that should have been full of conversation and eager anticipation.

James, Elizabeth and their sixteen year old daughter, Susan, whom Danaxe had met at her first dinner in New York more than two years ago, had already set up a table in front of the growing pile of boxes that Dani and the others were unloading.

"There's enough for all of you, Friends," James called "so do not worry."

What he meant, Danaxe realized, as more and more people melted out of the shadows, was: keep order. Don't fight over what we've brought. As two long lines formed--one black, one white--she wasn't sure if that would be possible.

Danaxe hurried behind the large table where the people lined up, whispered to Susan to go help unload, and took her place beside James. For the next half hour, everything went fine. Dani gave out food to former slaves, while Elizabeth answered questions and took down information from those who were hoping to locate relatives. James distributed food to the hungry whites and answered the few questions that came his way, mostly reassuring people of their safety and telling them where they could get help rebuilding homes or finding new ones.

Then, the white woman with three children clinging to her skirt, who was two back in line in front of James, stepped over and snatched the bag of vegetables Danaxe was trying to give the black woman--also a mother with children--who had reached the front of Dani's line.

"We've waited long enough!" shrieked the white woman, handing the bag to her oldest child and making a grab for the canned food Dani still held. "Those nigger bastards ain't eating before my children do, and--" she broke off as Dani tightened her grip on the box. "Let go, you uppity nigger bitch! Think you can come to our home and lord it over decent, hard-working white folks--"

"The only thing I see you working hard at, gal," shouted the woman who the supplies belonged to, "is stealin' the food these folks brought to help all of us!"

The white woman, whose face was now considerably whiter, launched herself at her black neighbor, screaming words Danaxe tried not to hear as she and the other volunteers worked to keep the table from being upended.

"Adam!" Dani shouted, wondering where the team leader was, while James and the others tried to prevent a riot. In the end, it was Union soldiers who restored order, and then threatened to physically drag any further malcontents to the back of the line.

The work continued. The Northern volunteers ate and rested in shifts so the distribution of supplies and assistance could continue uninterrupted. It was nearly dark, and the end of the line finally in sight, when the next fight occurred.

A well dressed--and well fed--white man pushed his way through the diminishing crowd and grabbed the skinny, nervous-looking young black man who waited in line about three places from the front.

"Pompey! What you doin' here?" Without

waiting for an answer, the man began to drag the now terrified looking young man away. "I told you to stay away from here! Ain't you got enough work to keep you busy?"

"Where's Adam?" Dani demanded, looking around for the man whose job it was to deal with this kind of thing.

"Mr. Harvey went with some soldiers to help people who were being prevented from traveling to seek aid," said the lady who had sat knitting beside Dani during the train ride. Her face darkened. "I suggested he send someone else, as he was feeling poorly on the train."

That was the first Dani had hear of this. Her surprise must have shown in her face.

"I told him he should speak with you, Miss Davis, but...well, men can be stubborn about those things."

Dani nodded and returned her attention the drama escalating in front of her.

"I's sorry, massa, but we's hungry--" stammered the youth.

"You do realize that slavery is no more?" said a tall Negro aid worker who had appeared between Danaxe and the angry white man. He set a hand on the former's slave's bony shoulder. Danaxe saw the boy wince, and wondered about old injuries--and new ones. Richard, Danaxe's fellow aid worker, noticed as well, and shifted his grip, all the while starring the "master" firmly in the eye.

"Don't you sass me, boy!" the white Southerner began.

"That's Mr. Lawton to you, sir," Richard said quietly. "And I require you to answer my question."

The white man's jaw worked, but no sound came out. Dani wondered if he was about to have a stroke. Finally, appearing to use every ounce of self control he possessed, he said, "This here, uh, *man*, is my *em-ploy-ee.*"

"Do you have his contract with you?" Danaxe asked hopefully, since she had written the template most people were using. Danaxe had been a supporter of the idea that former slaves who were willing should stay on plantations to bring in the cotton harvest in exchange for money and whatever necessities for the journey west their former masters were willing to part with. The hope was that helping the landowners regain their wealth and giving the freed slaves a chance to acquire some for themselves before trekking into the wilderness would be good for both sides.

Dani was now rethinking the wisdom of this plan.

"Right here!" The white man drew a sheet of paper from his vest pocket and waved it like a winning lottery ticket. Then he saw Danaxe reaching for it and nearly dropped it. "You run along home, Missy--"

Danaxe caught the paper easily from his now limp fingers, read it quickly, and then passed it to Richard. One of the white male aide workers stepped forward to offer support, but stayed back until it was needed. Everyone else continued with their work, throwing occasional glances at the confrontation. Many who had received supplies paused on their journey home to watch. That could be either good or bad, Danaxe decided.

"This contract states that all former slaves in your *em-ploy,*" Dani emphasized the word the same way her opponent had, "are to work ten hours a day in exchange for three meals a day, at a level that will allow them to maintain the strength to work--and travel." She emphasized the last word as well. Dani found the next clause she was looking for and placed her right index finger beneath it. "Here is where it says no worker may be prevented from leaving the grounds during his or her free time."

"And here," Richard pointed to the final words, just above the signatures, "is where it states that the contract will be voided if any of the above agreements are violated." He turned to the wide-eyed young worker. "Which means, son, that you do not have to go back."

"Who the hell taught you niggers to read?" demanded the white man.

"My kin!" cried the youth, while his former master muttered curses about the sins of the North. "I cain't just leave 'em with *him*--"

"We can help them as well," Danaxe said. "How about we let these two fine gentlemen talk things over while you and I get a nice hot meal, and I take a look at your shoulder. I'm a healer," she added in response to his confused look. Both of the men she was backing away from looked angry. Each was clearly upset that she had declared the other a "fine gentleman". Then, they began to argue.

Long after dark, when the work of the first day was finally done and Danaxe could catch her breath, she realized that she had not seen Adam Harvey since they had left the train.

"With the way he was spewing during the train ride?" said the young man she asked. "I'd say try the nearest outhouse." Then he laughed at his own wit.

But an outhouse was exactly where they found

the Sanctuary Volunteer team leader early the next morning. He had a single gunshot wound to his head, and a note pinned to his chest with a small knife. It read, "Executed by authority of the Order of the White Rose, Protectors of the South."

Danaxe sighed and walked away from the commotion that followed the discovery. *Not camelias this time,* she thought. *But I wish they hadn't ruined my favorite flower.*

Acknowledgements

So many people made this book possible. As in all previous books written by Sandra Saidak, special thanks go to George MacDonald, for business advice, support and friendship, Donji Cullenbine for another great cover, the Whensday People Writing Group for critiquing multiple drafts, Irene Radford for professional editing and Charlotte Fisher and Robin Baylor for feedback. Additional thanks to our previously mentioned culture bearers Gregg Castro, Ann Marie Sayers and Kanyon Sayers-Roods.

Mentioned in Dispatches

For persnickety historical questions, when my Google feng shui absolutely failed, I reached out on Facebook. I would often start with the phrase "Dear Hive mind." I am thanking everyone who responded. Your efforts were collectively helpful!

For those who don't know what *Mentioned in Dispatches* means: I belong to a fan association – The Royal Manticoran Navy: The Official Honor Harrington Fan Association. If you have seen me at a sci fi con starting in 2014, I have been wearing the uniform of an allied navy of the series, The Grayson Space Navy. Most of the respondents are members of the Royal Manticoran Navy, which follows the British Royal Navy tradition of Mentioned in Dispatches, allowing the awardee to wear a white slash (at a 45 degree angle from horizontal) on their sleeve. So for those of you who stepped up to help, you are hereby awarded my personal Mentioned in Dispatches.

Dr. Christine Doyle

Marc Reeves

Heather E. Patti

Bill Lochen

H. W. Butch Clor

Cary Anne Conder

Douglas E. Berry

Jeff Israelson

Elliot Shield

Andrew Trembley

Kevin Mulkey

Drew Kitty

Darran Hirose

James Jones

Caolifhionne Mears

Dread P Stark

Donna Leaf

Steve Condrey

Peter Howdeshell
Lucas Van Enger
Lee Panache
Fred Capp
Alisa Brewster
Dan Connelly
Paul Carlson
Carl Thelen
Robert Toland
Ote MacOdo
Richard Hartman
Joseph Barrow
Joseph P Grieco
John R. Brandon III
Jim Kratzer
Charles Simpson
Lucifer Radford
Suzie Buck
Kent Brewster

Michael D. Garcia
Deborah Beatty
Cj Lowe
Kimmi Albee
Nicholas Macon Hurst
Doug Coronado
David M Sanders
Robert Demkiw
Diana Summers
Jack Warren
David P. Melsome
David Woodard
Amy-Elyse
Alana Dill
Edward Muller
Mark Bridges
Penny Horwitz
Ruggaber.

Selected Bibliography (suggested reading)

Deer, Lame, and Richard Erdoes. *Lame Deer, Seeker of Visions*. New York: Simon and Schuster, 1994.

Gulick, John. *Cherokees at the Crossroads*. Chapel Hill: Institute for Research in Social Science, University of North Carolina, 1973.

Madley, Benjamin. *An American Genocide: The United States and the California Indian Catastrophe, 1846-1873*. New Haven: Yale University Press, 2017.

Margolin, Malcolm. *The Ohlone Way: Indian Life in the San Francisco-Monterey Bay Area*. Berkeley, CA: Heyday, 2014.

Mooney, James, and James Mooney. *James Mooneys History, Myths, and Sacred Formulas of the Cherokees: Containing the Full Texts of Myths of the Cherokee (1900) and the Sacred Formulas of the Cherokees (1891) as Published by the Bureau of American Ethnology: With a New Biographical Introduction, James Mooney and the Eastern Cherokees*. Asheville, NC: Historical Images, 1992.

Author's Biographies

Sandra Saidak graduated San Francisco State University in 1985 with a B.A. in English. She is a high school English teacher by day, author by night. Her hobbies include reading, dancing, attending science fiction conventions, and maintaining an active fantasy life. Sandra lives with her husband Tom, daughters Heather and Melissa, and one cat. Her first novel, "Daughter of the Goddess Lands", an epic set in the late Neolithic Age, was published in November, 2011 by Uffington Horse Press. Learn more at http://sandrasaidak.com/

Thomas Saidak's writing career includes four years as an assistant editor for Biofuels Digest. His first professional fiction sale was a collaboration with his wife Sandra and two other friends for the Eclipse Monthly #9 cover story, *Steal, Stealth, & Magic.* His hobbies include fencing, computer games, and black powder shooting, and his neighbors are very grateful he no longer has time to keep up playing the bagpipes.